PELAGIC

A novel by
Carol Ann Ross

1

Cover design by Leslie Campbell

This novel is a work of fiction. Names, characters and incidents are a product of the author's imagination and are used fictitiously. Any resemblance to actual events or persons, living or dead, is entirely coincidental.

DEDICATION

This book is dedicated to all the people who, over the past decades, have been visiting Topsail Island. It is to the people who love the ocean and want to preserve our little sand bar. And also to Diane Batts Geary, Deborah Batts and Randy Batts, who all love Topsail as much as I do.

ACKNOWLEDGEMENTS

I never realize how little I know until I begin writing a book. It seems I grow a bit every time I begin the process. There are places I've never been, experiences I've never known and frames of mind that are beyond my reach.

For all the technical stuff, the personal knowledge, comradery and friendship, I must thank Evelyn Hobbs, Steve Midgett, Patti Blacknight, Rob Shanta, Scott Rochelle, Marlene Bottoms, Steve and Kerry Daraskavich, Mike White, Robin Lauric, Rocky Godwin, Tracey West, Lou Wilson, Terry Lippencott, Yogi Paliotti, Dee Dee Paliotti Lloyd and Steve Bailey,

A special thanks to my editor Connie Pletl for being patient, honest and good at her job.

You are all fountains of knowledge. Thank you.

"Nowadays people know the price of everything and the value of nothing." - Oscar Wilde

Chapter 1

Lissa Roseman brought the Volkswagen Jetta to a stop. She sat still for a moment, her hands resting on the steering wheel. "Make me strong today," she whispered, then inhaled a deep breath before opening the door and stepping from the vehicle. It was still dark as she walked to the rise of sand and beach grasses and stared out onto the Atlantic. A crescent moon and starlight reflected off the water like diamonds, her favorite kind, sparkling as the tide moved. She felt the familiar ache, her cheeks flushed, her eyes burned.

Willing herself to be strong, the tears subsided. Her heartbreak had turned to righteous indignation, it simply was not right. No one person, no conglomerate, should have the right to build, to destroy dunes so some rich bastard could have an ocean view a couple months out of the year. Somebody had to do something. *She* had to do something.

Still standing on the low dune, Lissa turned southward to the lights of the Scotch Bonnet fishing pier, dim in the distance. She'd surfed near there yesterday along with several of the other local kids. Turning away from the site, she watched as the dim gray light of day anticipated daybreak along the horizon.

Lissa let the cool April morning breeze play across her skin. She watched as the morning sun gradually breached the horizon and started its shimmering glow across the waters. She grinned softly, feeling the warmth on her face, the tip of her nose and cheeks. Those were the places that tended to burn easily. She thought of the cap she'd left in the Jetta. *I'll need the hat,* she thought, *it's going to be a long hot day.*

Turning her attention from the ocean to the construction site, Lissa tightened her lips, reassuring her resolve as she strode to the car where she'd placed a bag of chains and a padlock. She made her way to the vehicle, walking past the bulldozer, wishing she could ram her fist into it.

Quickly tying the chains around an arm of the raised blade of the machine, she then wrapped them around her waist tightly, slid the hook through the links and snapped shut the padlock.

The sun was up now; the workers would be arriving soon. Today their schedule called for them to cut into the dunes, destroying them for new construction. She pictured the men angry, annoyed that their work schedule had been interrupted. Lissa giggled, "Tough shit." She eased herself to the ground, sat cross-legged and, pulling the pink cap over her hair, waited for the confrontation.

Though her sight was obscured by the sand hills, Lissa could hear the breakers crashing on shore. Today would have been perfect for catching a few waves. Today would have been a good day to go to school, too. Even though it was her senior year, there was no guarantee of graduation if she missed many more days.

The last run-in with the law, another protest against development, she'd missed nearly a whole week. Her father had kept his cool then, proud, she suspected, that his daughter had the courage of her convictions. But he had warned that he would not tolerate her missing any more days. "Gal," he'd said, and he always called her Gal when he showed affection, it was one of his only ways. "Gal, I'll always be proud of you if you do the right thing. I don't give a damn what anybody says, you do what you think is right."

Lissa was doing just that. She'd even called Miss Morgan at the *Topsail Tribune* this time to give her a heads up about today's protest. She was assured that a reporter would be at the site. If she were lucky the news stations from Wilmington would also make the trek to Topsail.

Lifting her face toward the sound of tires leaving the pavement, Lissa watched as a stream of pickup trucks drove onto the site. Sand and dust fuzzed about them as they jerked simultaneously to a stop.

Exiting the vehicle, slamming the door after himself, the foreman leaned against his white Dodge Ram and slid his eyes over her, nothing lascivious there, only condemnation for interrupting his work's day. He raised a hand to silence the other men as they hooted and shouted curse words.

"Just hold your fire, boys. Cops will be here soon and they'll take care of this. Have a smoke."

She remembered him from her last sit-in experience. He'd been nonchalant then, too, shaking his head, repeating, "Just doing my job, girl. Just doing my job." Today he added, "Shouldn't you be in school?"

A few people had gathered around, were murmuring and nodding her way. She studied their faces, none were familiar. It was obvious they were not concerned about the destruction, they were just gawkers curious about the girl and the chains. They were looking for a show. She'd give them one. Lissa had memorized the spiel but she'd wait for the *Trib* before the oration.

Continuing to study the people, she noticed a few more had been added to the crowd. She smiled inwardly, *the more the merrier*, she thought. That was what she wanted, a big audience, then maybe people would pay attention.

On the perimeter of the group, standing slightly apart from them, a lean, broad shouldered young man stood. A cooler rested by his feet. He held a fishing pole in one hand, a tackle box in the other. His long brown hair, streaked golden by the sun, rested against the skin of his pink splotched shoulders. Nodding slightly, his lips lifted at the corners before he turned to make his way across the dune as the WNCT-TV van pulled into the construction site followed by Debbie Curtain from the *Tribune* and the Pender County sheriff.

Chapter 2

It never did any good. Protesting was futile. The town, the NC Department of Transportation, and anyone else with power and money placated those who might stand in their way. But so far, no one had been able to change any of the decisions handed down from the higher ups.

"Until you're in a position to wield authority," her father had said, "then someone else will make the decisions. That's just the way it is."

He was right, she knew he was right and she hated his being right. There wasn't a thing she could do to stop all the progress. *Cancer progresses, too, not all progress is good.* "Why can't people understand that?" Lissa said aloud.

Her brow furrowed in disgust, her head lowered as she walked to her father's car.

He'd driven all the way to Burgaw to pick her up. Luckily, he was good friends with the local police chief. A quick phone call had kept her waiting on a lobby bench instead of in a jail cell.

Lissa raised her eyes quickly to meet her father's. "Sorry Daddy."

He grunted and rolled his cigar to the other side of his mouth.

They drove in silence for several miles, until John Roseman reached to his lips to extract the El Producto from them. "Had a talk with the principal. No more days. You can't miss any more days, Gal. Understand?"

"Yes sir."

"I mean it young lady. This ain't some game you're playing. And it might be fine and dandy to get your name in the paper and be on TV but if all you want is attention, you can stand in front of the shop stark naked." He paused, his face and ears reddening as he spoke, "Get your ass in school, keep your ass in school. Go to college, make your difference that way."

"Yes sir," Lissa muttered again. She'd heard the lecture before. She waited for the rest of it.

"But I don't care how much college you have, you're not going to put a dent in the agenda they have planned for this island. You may as well learn to roll with the flow, Gal. You'll be a lot happier. Take a look at Myrtle Beach. By the time you're my age, that's what this place will look like."

"Yes sir." She rolled her eyes.

****

Her toes grabbing the sand as she made her way up the dune, Lissa mumbled to herself, "I'm tired of these old farts around here letting shit happen. They'd don't give a damn about Topsail." She reached the top of the dune and looked toward Surf City Fishing Pier, nearly half a mile south of where she stood. Few people came to the island this time of year, except to fish. She liked it this way before tourist season. Facing the ocean, she hollered, "What are you going to do about it - all the construction?" She blew a long breath from her lips. "We need a damn good hurricane to wipe these damn condos off the face of the earth." She scowled as she trudged down the dune toward the water, surf board under her arm.

The wetsuit she wore was uncomfortable but the early April water temperature called for something to keep her warm. She tugged at the neckline of the suit and glimpsed a lone fisherman on the shore as he cast out a line.

Her eyes studied him for a moment as she walked into the water and past a breaker. *He's the kid I saw the other day at the construction site.* She noticed his long hair, now pulled back in a ponytail - he turned to nod to her.

Lissa grinned; he must have recognized her, too.

Her knees bent, holding her feet in the air, Lissa paddled farther then maneuvered the board across the swells to where she determined a good one might be. Holding steady, she bobbed with the low swells, her eyes sliding now and then to study the young fisherman.

It seemed like forever, nothing was moving - Lissa continued to bob in the water. It was almost a dead calm day,

13

surely as the morning progressed the wind would pick up and the waves would be worth surfing. Sighing, a bored breath exited her lips as she relaxed on the board to feel the tidal movement beneath her. Now and then her gaze drifted to the young fisherman. He stood in the water swaying with the tides as well.

His lean body stood thigh deep, his broad shoulders dipped and reached as he cast and reeled in the fishing pole he wielded. "Probably a jock," she smirked.

Lissa wasn't too sure about how she felt about jocks. Most of the ones she knew at school had girls flitting around them all the time and were so full of themselves, so arrogant. It made her sick.

The few she'd dated had been polite but never asked her out for the second date. "Probably because I don't put out," she mumbled. She always had liked the quieter guys, the ones who liked to read and talk politics.

Her friend, Marsha, had told her to never talk politics with boys. *They hate it; they don't like their women being smarter than they are - so if you want to date, don't talk politics.*

Lissa rolled her eyes at the thought; she'd be just fine if she never went out on another date again.

Turning her head, she maneuvered her board to what she thought might be a good wave. It rolled beneath her, flattening out and into another wave near the shore.

She glanced again toward the fisherman. He was cute. She liked the long hair. One thing was for sure - he was not forward. Often, young men approached her, curious about the girl on the board. But this fellow didn't even seem interested. Other than the few glances he threw her way, he'd hardly acknowledged her at all.

She studied him as he reeled in a line then waded to shore to attach more bait and cast the line again.

He turned to her, this time she didn't turn away and neither did he. They scrutinized each other as they both moved to the rhythm of the ocean; her body rising and falling with the swells as she lay on the board, his resisting the waves as they pushed against his body. Oblivious to the tasks at hand, Lissa and the fisherman were more into the eye contact and studying each other than either surfing or fishing.

Suddenly his fishing pole jerked and his attention turned to reeling, he smiled quickly to Lissa as he slowly backed toward the shore. She watched, anticipating his catch, hoping it was a big one, and it was - a pretty good sized Spanish mackerel. He held it up for her to see.

She nodded and waved, then maneuvered her board a few strokes farther out and waited for a wave, still watching the fisherman as he threw the mackerel into the cooler and cast out a newly baited line.

By now at least forty-five minutes had passed and no decent waves had come about so Lissa paddled to shore. She

15

tugged at the uncomfortable wetsuit and unzipped it to reveal a bright yellow bikini top. She walked toward the fisherman.

"Hi," she spoke, flipping her wet hair away from her face.

Unconsciously, the young man's eyes drifted to the yellow top peeking from her wet suit. Walking toward her, he held a newly caught fish in his hand. "Not much action on the water today, huh?"

Lissa fought the urge to smile broadly. She didn't want to seem too pleased that he was noticing her. "No, too calm out there today for any good waves. I see that you're doing pretty good though."

"Yeah," he nodded. "So far, this is my second Spanish of the day, I caught a couple last week, too." He seemed proud, his face glowed. "I've never caught many Spanish until this summer."

"Really? I go out on my dad's boat pretty often and we catch quite a few, they're fun to catch - put up a good fight."

The boy nodded and grinned. "Yeah, they do put up a good fight but they poop out pretty fast, too."

Lissa settled the surf board in the sand and walked with him to where he had stacked his fishing paraphernalia.

"I saw you the other day chained to that bulldozer. What was that all about?"

"They're putting up condos and tearing down the dunes to do it. I hate condominiums."

"They're ugly as hell, now if they built something that doesn't look like a box —"

"They shouldn't be building them at all - not in the dunes. Why don't they build on the sound or on the mainland?" She shook her head angrily. "Every time I think about them building one I get so mad. They're tearing up the dunes. What do you think is going to happen when they start tearing up the dunes?" Hands on hips, Lissa waited for the young man to answer.

He shrugged, "It's just sand."

Her eyes widened, glared. Her lips tightened into a straight line. "Sand, is that all you think it is - sand? That's what this place is, a giant sand bar. God - Mother Nature - whatever you want to call it, made it this way and those damn corporations feed people..."

"Wait a minute, I'm with you. I like the dunes, I like the way it all looks, I like the quiet when I come to fish. Really - I'm with you on that. And you're right, before long there won't be any dunes."

She held his eyes for a moment longer, then closed hers and took a deep breath, "Sorry, I get on my soap box and I, well, I just hate to see Topsail chipped away at."

"Don't want it looking like Coney Island.'

"Never been there, but I've heard." She smiled at the young man, warming to the thought of a like-minded friend. Not many of her friends gave a damn. They were excited about the new buildings, the new shops that were popping up everywhere.

The young fisherman settled himself in the sand, his legs bent at the knees, his bare feet digging into the sand nervously.

Lissa joined him to sit at the shore. "So you're really into fishing, huh?"

He nodded, "Kinda my thing, calms me." He studied her face, scanning across her high cheek bones and the sprinkle of freckles there.

"That's what surfing does for me. I'm in another world." Her hand touched her heart. "It's like —" Lissa looked into his eyes. "It's better than church, or maybe it is my church."

He eyed her curiously. "I don't go much - to church, used to. But since I moved out of my parents' place, I don't go anymore."

"You need to learn how to surf."

"Never even tried, looks too dangerous for me and then there's the sharks."

"Sharks? You wade out to your hips when you fish, that's deep enough for a shark, one could get you that close in." She raised a brow playfully. "Now, I'm out on the board, most of the time I keep my feet up." Her eyes steeled for a moment. "But it's never a guarantee that you won't get bitten by something. We are intruding into their world, the world of the fishes - sometimes I don't think they like it very much."

"Are you trying to scare me?" he teased.

"You should be afraid - very afraid," Lissa joked in return. "No, really, I'll show you sometime - that is if you want to."

He nodded, "I'd like that, sounds cool." His eyes found her feet, hidden in the sand and moved up to study her form. She looked good, athletic. Her lips, as she spoke, crinkled in places, occasionally her tongue glided over them. He liked the way her windblown hair licked at her face.

He nodded as she spoke, he would agree with just about anything as he sat next to her feeling the warmth of her body. They talked politics, mostly local - about who was running the town and allowing all the changes. They talked religion; he agreed he could talk to God just as well in the sand as in a building.

Lissa surmised that the young man was someone who gave a damn and he surmised that this surfer girl was someone he wanted to spend time with.

As he leaned in, Lissa could feel his eyes studying her. She felt her face blush and she pulled her shoulders in and her eyes away from his.

"My name's Murdoch, Murdoch Soucek, but everyone calls me Doc."

"Doc? What's up, Doc?" she teased.

"Like I haven't heard that a million times."

"Sorry, I guess it's more like doctor - right?"

Doc shrugged, "I guess, who knows."

"Maybe you'll be a doctor someday."

He shrugged again, "Who knows."

Had she touched a chord? Had she said something wrong? Maybe he didn't like the name. Lissa changed the subject, moving on to more relevant topics like music and movies.

He'd seen Jurassic Park and loved it. He'd seen it with some friends one wild weekend at Davidson College. He and a friend had skipped a class and gone to Charlotte, fielding a day of fun for the pent up teens.

"It was crazy. Some friends and I skipped two whole days, camped out in the woods - went fishing - had a great time." He laughed, nodded his head. "Man, it was so cool. I imagine we didn't smell very good when we went to the movies, the couple sitting next to me and my friend Bill moved a few minutes after we sat down." He laughed again. "My old man would have ripped me a new one if he'd ever found out."

"And he didn't, I assume."

"Hell no, I wouldn't be sitting here if he had. He'd have shipped me up north somewhere."

Doc talked about the trip to Europe with his parents after his high school graduation; he delivered a litany of places he'd visited as if they had been interesting but not as exciting as he'd anticipated. The Parthenon in Greece, the Vatican in Rome, the Eiffel Tower in Paris, Big Ben in London. "We stayed in hotels, took the local tours. I want to go back some day and *really* see those places."

Lissa's curiosity peeked as she listened to him recount the experiences, she had always dreamed of visiting Europe.

20

"I'd like to visit Russia and Japan someday, maybe Australia." His eyes slid to hers.

"Wow. I'd love to go anywhere. It sounds so wonderful."

"It's pretty neat. I guess."

"My, you've done so much, been so many places." Her eyes rested on her knees. "The farthest I've been is Myrtle Beach." She looked at the sky, at the position of the sun, she thought of how they must have been sitting there, talking for hours. "I have to go. I've got to run some errands for my father." Rising from the sand, she waited for him to stand.

He rose, kicked the sand from his feet and looked into her face. Lissa studied his features - the seconds creeping by as they held each other's gaze. The air seemed sparked with intensity before he finally spoke. "I'm going to the arcade around seven, if you can come, I'll see you there."

She'd be there. There was no way on earth that she would miss seeing Doc again.

Her pulse quickened at the thought of him, her heart rose in her throat. Imaged in her mind were his hands, how their ecru color looked so pale next to her own, and how she had longed to just touch them as she sat next to him in the sand. She wondered if he liked her as much. *He must have,* she thought. *He wants me to meet him.*

Chapter 3

He was waiting outside on the walkway feeding the Koi when she drove up. Opening his hand he let the remainder of the food pellets drop into the water below as he watched her exit the car and move toward him.

Anticipating the smile, the beaming smile he's seen on her face, Doc's own reddened. The girl glowed when she smiled and he liked it.

"It always amazes me the way they stir the water and frenzy about for food. I know darn well they are fed a lot and often - they eat like pigs."

"Pig fish," Doc joked.

"Ha, that's funny." Lissa gazed into the fish pond. He walked to her side and leaned gently against her shoulder.

"Did you know," he began, "that Koi are carp?"

"Yes, I did," she retorted.

"And that they can live for over thirty years?"

"If someone doesn't eat them."

"Ha, I don't think these have any problem being eaten."

"Yeah, I know that." She faced him, her eyes twinkling, her mouth puckered into a sassy grin. "You forget, I'm from here, I know a lot about fish and fishing."

"Humph." He jostled his shoulder against hers, "Well, did you know that in Japan Koi are symbols of love?"

Her eyes turning quickly from his, she released a tiny gasp, "Oh, look at that one, it's chasing the other one around the pond."

"See, what did I tell you? They're in love."

"You're a laugh a minute, Murdoch - Doc. What's up, Doc?" She teased.

Shaking his head, he slid his gaze to her. "Will I never hear the end of that?"

"Sorry."

Reaching for her hand, he pulled her toward the entrance and held the door open for her.

"Thank you, kind sir."

"My pleasure, my lady."

Lissa curtsied as she walked though a broad room filled with young people playing video games, skee ball and gator bash, just to name a few.

After a couple of hours, the couple dug into their pocket to retrieve tickets they'd won.

"What do you want?" Doc unrolled his and handed them to the clerk at the counter.

"Three-hundred-and-eighty-seven. You can get a sand fiddler aquarium or the stuffed turtle," the clerk rattled off. "Or you can combine prizes and get several things." He pointed to the selection of rubber toys, candy and assorted trinkets.

"I have three-hundred-and-seventy-one." She turned to Doc.

"With his that makes seven-hundred-and-fifty-eight."

"What do you want?" Doc asked.

"You can get the visor or I can give you a voucher for anything in the store." The clerk looked at the couple.

"Pick out what you want."

Doc eased his fingers to thread through Lissa's as they perused the selection of touristy gifts lining the walls.

They strode past the stuffed animals, puzzles, hats and costume jewelry into the book section. Lissa selected a book identifying different types of shells along the eastern seaboard. Doc selected a book of poetry. His eyes scanned pages as his fingers slowly turned them.

"Hmm." He browsed her profile then lowered his eyes to re-read a passage, this time aloud -

> In the broad and silky morn
> The sun is warm upon my heart
> And I know it won't be long
> Before fated love holds my hand
> And guides me to your side
>
> I long to know your lips again
> And taste the salt upon your skin
> And know your thoughts as you do mine

And drink the sweet joy of us
As we swim in our pelagic love.

"Poetry? You like poetry?" Lissa asked

"Good poetry," Doc replied.

"Pelagic?"

"Deep water. You see I do know something about the ocean that you don't." He read the poem again, this time more slowly.

She caught her breath as they stood facing one another. It was as if time had stopped. She felt her face numb. "It's nice." Her heart beat wildly as she turned away. Nobody had ever read poetry to her before and it felt awkward coming from someone she had just met.

"I had a really good time today on the beach," he said, breaking the silence.

"Me too."

More silence.

"Hey! Want to go skating?" Doc blurted as he moved toward the checkout counter.

Lissa nodded.

The evening was lighter, the mood jovial as they skated around and around the rink, laughing as one fell down or chased the other. After an hour of that they strode hand in hand across the road to the putt-putt and played a round of miniature golf.

Then it was off to the Beach Grill where they chatted about music and movies and sipped soft drinks.

"Ever go swimming at night?" Doc asked.

"It's not a good idea to swim at night."

He raised a brow. "Really, sea monsters?"

"Sharks feed at night - well, they feed in the day, too, but especially at night."

"Trying to scare me again with the sharks?"

"No, it's true."

"Okay - how about walking on the beach at night, is that safe?"

"With you?" Lissa teased.

"I'm safe. I won't bite." Clasping his hand over his head to mimic a fin, he made the infamous sound of the movie Jaws. "Doo dunt, doo dunt, doo dunt."

She slapped at his shoulder gently. "You're nuts."

"I know, *doo dunt, doo dunt,*" his voice rasped. "Come on, let's go walk on the beach."

Walking hand in hand Murdoch led the way from the restaurant. He held her hand tightly as they walked slowly toward the dunes and pulled her up as they trudged upward through the loose sand.

On the beach they both kicked off their shoes, settling them at the base of a sand dune.

He grabbed at a sea oats stalk, snapping it off and proceeded to tickle Lissa with the almond shaped flakes.

27

She tossed her head, turned and sprinted toward the shore, he followed as they splashed ankle deep into the cool water.

She turned, grabbed the stalk from his hand and chased him.

Playing like children, splashing through the water, they raced toward the dunes, their laughter echoing in the salty night air, until the wilted stalk fell from her hands.

Murdoch reached an arm around Lissa's waist and pulled her to him, leaned into her and pressed his lips on hers. Her arms circled his neck as he inched closer.

It was a deep kiss, one like Lissa had never experienced before. She felt his tongue against hers, and the wet exchange of saliva - its warmth.

Standing inches from her face, he stared into it as he stroked her arm. "I have to go back to Pittsburg tomorrow. I'll try to get back down here to Grammy's next week. I'll miss you." He kissed her again, just as deeply, just as long. "I'll call you."

Chapter 4

Her father had warned her - one more brush with the law and there would be consequences. Lissa imagined punishment could have been worse but having no car to drive was bad enough. She blew a sigh and rolled her eyes as she stepped on to the school bus.

Most of the seniors drove to school and now here she was relegated to riding the big yellow monster with freshmen. She scanned the seats looking for something empty. There was nothing.

Her eyes resting upon Marsha, a sometimes friend, she stepped toward the back of the bus and sat down.

"Sorry I wasn't at the sit-in," Marsha whined. "My parents wouldn't let me go."

"Umph," Lissa shrugged.

"Hey, why do you think I'm doing riding the bus today? My mother heard me talking to Mike on the phone about it and not only did she ground me for the weekend, but she made me ride this damn thing."

"Sorry - sorry to cause so much trouble." Lissa turned to look out the window, a smile slowly coming to her lips.

"What's the smiling all about?"

Lissa shrugged.

"Are you going to do something else? What harebrained scheme have you cooked up now? Look, I don't want to get kicked out of school and I would like to get my car back at least by summer."

Lissa shook her head; the anger over development seemed trivial now. Her mind was on something else, someone else.

"No, nothing like that. They're going to do whatever developers do."

"Then what are you so happy about? You look like the cat that swallowed the canary."

Lissa shook her head and continued gazing out the window rapt in the intense new feelings for Murdoch. Today she was less angry at the world, at least the Topsail Island world and the encroaching development. Right now she was recounting his arms around her, him kissing her and his promise to see her soon.

****

"So when are you going to teach me to surf?" Doc watched Lissa trudge down the dune toward him, her surf board tucked beneath her arm.

"You want to learn to surf. Hmm." she settled the board in the sand, holding it upright with one hand. "City boy like you

30

wants to learn to surf." she scrunched her nose and shook her head. "I don't know. I don't know if you have what it takes. It's more than just standing on a board in the water."

"Oh please, it can't be that hard." Settling the fishing pole in a holder, he shifted his eyes playfully and raised a brow. "If you can do it, I'm sure it's got to be a piece of cake."

"Ha, I've got *stoke* - I'm good - you've seen me."

"Yeah." His eyes studied her body. "I have." He grinned. "You look good."

"Ha, get over it, Mr. Soucek." Blushing, Lissa turned from the ocean back to Doc. "If you want to learn, you'll need a surfboard - I'll be prepared to point and laugh.

"Not hardly."

"You know," she said, then began speaking like a pirate, "arrr, there be sharks in them there waters, Mr. Soucek."

"Arrr," he mimicked, "I know that, missy - sand sharks, they are. I'm not one to be worryin' 'bout such creatures, arrr."

"You get the board, I'll teach you, Mr. Know-It-All."

"What kind - short or long? And what's the difference?"

"Depends on what you're looking for."

"What do you mean? You have a longboard, but I've noticed that most of the guys do short."

"Not all of them. Like I said, it depends on what you want. A short board will get you there, you get the thrill - I guess that's what you'd call it. A longboard is more of a dance. You can do more." She crossed her legs at the ankle. "Cross stepping." She

31

moved forward on a make believe board. "Riding the nose -
hang ten - hang five - drop knee turns." Her expressions
intense, her body animated, he listened to the passion with
which she spoke and was mesmerized.

She looked up at him. "There's just more to the dance - for
me anyway. It's like I become more of the wave when I surf
long. But it's a preference. Get whatever you like."

It was quiet, except for the crashing of the waves. Doc
didn't know what to say as he stared at her, lost in the
discovery of this fascinating young woman so unlike anyone
else he'd met before.

"I'll—" Lissa swallowed. "I'll teach you how to ride the curl."

He nodded. "Um hum."

Stepping into him, she jostled the fishing pole in its holder.
"Earth to Murdoch, come in."

A blush, a guffaw and he shook his head. "Damn,
daydreaming again."

"Yeah, if that's what you want to call it. You just don't know
what to do with this gal, do you?" Lissa laughed, her head
tilting back. "This is just a whole different world for you, isn't
it?"

"Yep."

Tossing her hair away from her face, she grabbed her board
and tramped through the small breakers at shore. Wading
farther out, she pulled her body atop the surfboard and
paddled out beyond the breakers.

His eyes following her, he cast his line just at the break of the waves; he felt a slight tug as the tide pulled the sinker back and forth and as his body swayed with the tidal movement.

As he reeled, just a bit to take the slack out of the line, he leaned into the breakers crashing against his body. His feet sought stability in the sandy bottom as he waited. His eyes never leaving Lissa, he watched as she bobbed in the water, her legs straddling the board as she waited, her body gyrating with the slow dip and rise of the tide.

They watched one another, the physical movements of each other, as they swayed and dipped with the sea.

Then, three small jerks on the line indicated that Doc had a strike, instinctively he jerked back then slowly began reeling - then a bit faster. He felt the play of the fish as it strained against the hook and line and adjusted the force of his reeling. He didn't want to lose this one.

"Got one?" Lissa called out.

Grinning broadly, he nodded, still reeling as the line tensed and pole bent.

She watched intently, her body still aware of the movements below her; she felt the swell of a wave and laid herself prone on the board, waiting for the momentum to catch her. Standing, she balanced herself, positioning her feet just so, moving along the board, crossing her legs, moving back - maneuvering her actions with the subtly of the ocean's, her

33

eyes all the time on him, watching as he reeled, as he moved backward and grasping the line that held the fish at the end.

"Whoo hoo!" They both hollered.

Doc held the fish high; Lissa rode the wave to near where he stood.

"Damn, that was cool."

"What a rush."

Chapter 5

A week later, she saw him on the beach where they had met before. He'd been waiting it seemed, his fishing pole standing staunchly in a holder, him pacing about until he saw her crest a dune.

Walking toward her, the smile broadened across his face as she descended toward the shore.

This time, even before they spoke, Murdoch gathered Lissa in his arms and kissed her. It was a deep kiss, long and slow. He felt her breasts against his chest as their bodies meshed together. His hands caressed her back, pulling her even closer.

A sigh escaped her lips as she inched from him to gaze into his hazel eyes. They were such sad eyes, she had thought before, such desirous eyes.

He held her face in his hand. "I was hoping I had the right place."

Lissa nodded.

"I missed you." He touched her lips lightly with his own.

She nodded again, moving her fingertips to the sides of his face and near his lips. She kissed him softly again and smiled. "So, how have you been?"

"Absolutely great." Reaching his hand around her waist he guided her as they walked along the shore, their footprints fading into the soft sand at the shore as they walked toward Barnacle Bill's Fishing Pier.

"Want a Coke?" he asked.

She nodded and the couple walked in through the beach access and chose a booth by the plate glass window.

Doc's hand reached across the table, his long slim fingers grasping hers. His eyes seemed to bore into Lissa's as she waited for him to speak, but no words came.

"What? What is it?" she asked.

He tilted his head to the side. "I thought about you a lot."

Lissa felt her heart beating, and wanted to speak, but what could she say back to such a statement? She'd always thought she was rather boring. She shrugged and said, "Thank you."

"I've just never had so much fun. You - you're a lot of fun to be with."

"You too." She lowered her eyes.

"Look, we're having a cookout this evening, want to come?"

Lissa nodded. "I'd love to."

"I want to show you off to my family."

Curling her upper lip, she chortled. "I'm nobody special, just little ol' me - you sure you want them to see the podunk girl you're hanging around with?"

"Podunk? Not hardly. You're gorgeous – smart – funny - I bet every guy around her has a bead on you."

"Only ten or twelve," she teased. "I think it will be fun and I'll finally get to see where you live."

"It's not really where I live; I stay with my Grammy when I visit. But my parents have a house here, too."

"Is the cookout there?"

He shook his head. "It's at Grammy's house; it's pretty cool, kind of old, but feels really homey. I like it better than the new place."

"And you like homey, city boy that you are."

He rolled his eyes. "I'm not all that citified, I lived in Brownsville. It's a small town - used to be big, kind of died out in the last few decades - so my dad says. We left there when I was about seven and moved to Pittsburg, Dad got into business then, he does pretty good."

Lissa listened intently, she found him so interesting. He'd done so many things, been so many places. Her life had only been on the island. She watched as he spoke, how his lips formed the words, the expressions through his eyes, the turn of his head and movement of his hands as he explained his life thus far - what living in a small town was like, how different the city was, and how many more things there were to do.

"I see the Steelers every chance I get - Lorelei used to drag me to Benedum Center for shows and concerts," he said rolling his eyes.

"You don't like that kind of thing?"

"It's okay. Depends on what's on, whose playing. It's her way of making amends when she drags me there. Usually after a week of the silent treatment."

"Silent treatment?"

"Oh yeah, my mother is a real piece of work. She doles out the guilt every chance she gets. When she doesn't get her way or - hell, I don't know - when she's in a snit over who knows what, she gives me this look like she just stepped in something and then she refuses to talk to me, ignores me, for days sometimes."

Lissa shook her head. "Sounds like she's got a problem."

"That's who she is." He moved his head to avoid Lissa's gaze.

"Well, at least you get to go places and see exciting things. I've never been anywhere - I'd like to see what a big city looks like. I'd love to go to a play or big concert." She paused. "But I don't think anything could top living here. "

He nodded.

"Am I going to get to meet your grandmother?" Lissa broke the silence; she tilted in to him, pushing him playfully.

"Yeah, she'll be there. She's pretty cool for an old lady. She's not really what you call a local, but she and grandpa vacationed here for decades - he passed away about five years ago."

"Sorry - where were they from originally?"

"He was from PA, she was from South Carolina. They met at a dance in Wrightsville Beach - the Lumina - it was real popular back in the day."

"I've heard my dad talk about it. Sounds cool."

"Grammy always talks about it - about how she and Grandpa met. He was stationed in Paris Island, South Carolina and he and some buddies went to a dance there. It was supposed to be this great big love story between them. I remember how he doted one her. Grandpa used to say it was love at first sight; he loved her southern accent."

"My, my, I do *declah*," Lissa giggled, batted her lashes and fanned herself with a hand.

Doc grinned broadly. "They moved up to Pittsburg, after Grandpa got out of the Marines and then started vacationing here in the '50s. He built her the little house she lives in now. My dad remembers coming here as a boy."

"What's the name? Maybe I know her."

"Same as mine, Soucek - Emilia Soucek**.**"

Lissa shook her head. "I can't say the name is familiar. But then if she was not a resident, I probably wouldn't."

"Well, you know, only a few times a year."

Nodding, Lissa felt Doc's fingers rub against hers; she nervously accepted his touch. "I don't remember seeing you here on the island before either."

"I don't come often but when I do I usually stay with Grammy and fish on Jolly Roger Pier. Somebody said the fishing was good at the north end and then I heard about all the construction going on - wanted to check it out." He held his breath briefly and turned away. "That's when I saw you. You didn't look very happy about the bulldozers."

"I wish I knew who was doing this." She scowled. "I know the construction company but it's all hush hush about who the developer is. At least no one will tell me."

Doc exhaled audibly. "I know who it is."

"You? How do you know?"

"It's my father. It's his company."

"What? Why didn't you tell me?"

"I wanted to, but I thought you wouldn't like me very much."

Lissa's eyes blinked an apology.

"I can't help what my father does. He and I don't get along very well. He hates my long hair, says I look like a '60s hippie."

"I like your hair."

"Says I look like a girl - calls me Nancy. I don't think there's much about me that he likes at all."

"He can't be very smart then, if he feels that way." Lissa reached to touch his hand.

"If I ever try to talk with him about anything, man, he just shoots me down, says I don't know anything - always giving me some bullshit answer that is supposed to end any discussion I want to have."

"Yeah, Daddy sort of does that to me sometimes - tells me I don't understand the world but mostly he just walks away if we disagree. We don't do a lot of talking."

"Hell, I wish my dad did that, give me some peace, but he's always giving me the big lecture." Murdoch rolled eyes. "What in the hell am I supposed to do?"

"I'd like to talk with your father. Maybe he needs to get a local's point of view. Is he going to be at the cookout? Maybe he doesn't understand what he's doing."

"He understands exactly what he is doing. He justifies everything to fit his own agenda."

"Just wait until I meet him," the heated words hissed from Lissa's lips.

"He'll laugh at you, Lissa. He'll say things to placate you - I know my father. Whatever you say won't mean anything to him."

Her mouth tensed and she stared sternly into his face.

"Whoa, that's one deadly look you have."

"Sorry, I just don't like the idea of bullies. Your father sounds like a bully."

"You'll meet him at the cookout. I'll introduce you."

"Will your mother be there, too?"

"Oh yes, Mother will be there. She spent the day primping and preening her feathers for tonight's *casual* event. She always overdresses. I don't think she could stand it if someone wore something that cost more than what she wore. Lorelei should be at Grammy's now doing her best to insult her."

"What a piece of work."

"Oh, Grammy can hold her own. One, she doesn't care what my mother thinks of her and two, she can make Mother feel very inadequate."

"I'd love to see that," Lissa teased.

"You will, but first I want you to see the big house, my parent's house. You're really going to love this." He sneered. "I mean, you're *really* going to love this behemoth my father built for my mother."

Murdoch opened the door of his Jeep for Lissa. "It's at the north end of the island. It stands all by itself but Dad says in a couple of years there will be houses everywhere."

"Do they rent it out?"

"Nope, it's empty except when his and her majesty come and that's about twice a year."

Her mouth dropping open, Lissa's eyes hooded as she released a curse word. "Sorry. I try not to cuss - but sometimes—"

"You couldn't have said it better."

"What a waste."

"Mother hates it here."

"So why build the house?"

"When they first came, Mother loved it - said it reminded her of the beaches in South Carolina when she was a child. But once Dad had it built, she decided she didn't like it at all."

"Your mother is from South Carolina, too?"

"Yep."

"Did she know your grandmother?"

"No - different side of the tracks."

"Ahh." Lissa's eyes lit up.

"Grammy would never have wanted something so big and ostentatious."

"And that's what your mother wanted?"

"Um hum. But she hates it now."

"What?"

"It's this little game Mother and Dad play. She's tries to see what hoops she can make him jump through. He gives her what she wants then he finds another mistress."

"What a horrible way to live."

"Tell me about it."

"Can't wait to meet your parents," Lissa smirked.

Driving slowly Murdoch reached to find a station on the radio, his fingers punching a tab playing Pink Floyd's *The Wall*, he smiled. "I sure do hate having to go back to Davidson this September."

Lissa rocked gently to the beat of the music. It captured her sentiment toward development exactly.

Driving the long lonesome road past Salty's Fishing Pier to the north end of Topsail Island, the couple listened to the radio. Lissa counted the number of houses. A few more had been built on the north end in the last few years but it was still a pretty deserted place - good for fishermen and time away from crowds.

The small dunes there washed across the black top road and this afternoon, since the wind had picked up a bit, the sand stood like a gossamer curtain as it blew from the north. It was warmer than last month's breeze, the sun shone from a different angle and the ocean had taken on a more restful look. Even now on weekends, tourists were beginning their treks to the quaint island of Topsail.

Doc turned the volume up as a recognizable tune began.

"I like this station," Lissa commented, still rocking to a bluesy beat.

Murdoch nodded to her as he drove slowly toward his parent's house. "The Stones are the best." he nodded his head rhythmically as he pulled into the gravel driveway.

"I remember when they built this. I couldn't believe the amount of scrub oaks they destroyed. They planted those damn palm trees and Pampas grass."

Murdoch teased a haughty grin.

"I hated it then. I hate it now. They tore down the dunes for it."

"We have an elevator." Doc's eye brows raised and pressed down on the remote control, the garage doors raised noisily.

"I'm impressed," Lissa sneered in return. "But the stairs are fine for me." Not waiting for Doc to open her door, Lissa headed toward the steps leading to the first floor of the three-story home. She passed by a dark green Jaguar and eyed the plush dark tan leather interior as she walked by. "Nice car, is it your father's?"

"It's mine." Doc shrugged and slid a smug grin her way.

"Must be nice."

"Yep." Doc nodded as he walked with her toward the stairway.

"Gee whiz, this place is big. Do you ever stay here?"

"Once in a while, but not very often. If my parents are here, but I explained that situation to you, nope, I guess I don't stay here very often. I parked the Jag here because there isn't room at Grammy's."

Striding to reach the top of the stairwell first, Doc reached for the knob and inserted a key. "There you are, ma'am." He smiled and pushed open the door.

Lissa stepped onto the polished hard wood floors of the living room. She had to admit the place was beautiful. The blond oak furniture was obviously expensive and it matched the frames of the art hanging on the walls.

"It's certainly spacious and it is very nice but couldn't they have settled for a nice view of the sound instead?" she asked sarcastically.

"Let me show you the rest of the place." He cast a snide glance to Lissa and threaded his arm through hers, proceeding to lead her from one glorious room to another. All were impeccably neat and clean, all were adorned with fine furniture and elaborate decorations. Lissa was impressed and maybe even a little jealous. Ambivalent feelings of the finery money could buy and how its power was changing her island home swirled inside her.

She had never been in such a fine home. Part of her was attracted to the comfort, another part of her saw the waste in it standing unused for so long.

"It's all so clean, so organized, so unlived in. Geez, we've always got a pair of shoes sitting around or a stray glass or a magazine. And Charlie is always jumping up on the furniture. "

"Charlie?"

"My dog, Charlie - big furry mutt. Love him to death."

"Dogs, my parents would never let me have one."

"Figures. Your parents have everything planned out for you - your whole life - what you're supposed to love, who—"

"My father worked very hard to have a nice place at the beach. He deserves to have nice things, don't you think?"

"I'm sorry, guess I'm being too judgmental."

"Growing up in Brownsville he rarely got to the ocean and when he met my mother, well, he'd always promised her an oceanfront home like she had in Charleston."

Smiling, Lissa touched his shoulder, "it is a nice place, it really is, but—"

"I know - could have built it on the mainland or at least not have destroyed a dune to do it. Mother wanted an ocean view, even though she rarely comes, even though she says she hates it now. That's what she said she wanted, so that's what Dad gave her."

"What a waste," Lissa mumbled. She wondered if he approved of his father's business, if he really did hate all the building. *But he'd said he did, hadn't he? Hadn't he expressed dislike for the development, the over development of the island?*

She wasn't sure. She felt so much for Murdoch. She couldn't dismiss him for what his father was. He had no control over his father's business. He'd said that. And Lissa liked Murdoch so very much. She loved him, yes, that is what it was - love. She'd never loved anybody before. This was it. This is what she read about in the Bronte sister's books, seen in movies. But those media didn't even touch the depths to which she felt.

Lissa loved when Doc touched her, when he spoke, when he laughed. She loved everything about him. The way he walked, the way he held himself, the way he straightened his shoulders when he felt threatened.

He must have felt the same way about her or he wouldn't hold her like he did, kiss her like he did and want to be with her so much. Would he?

"I like my Grammy's house better," Doc interrupted her thoughts. "It feels more like a home than this place." He groaned. "IT still has the original knotty pine paneling inside, window air conditioners in all the rooms and an old kitchen table, it's yellow and red. Grammy has had it since the '50s. It's like walking back in time."

"Sounds like the place where me and my daddy live. It's old like that - a pretty simple place, nothing fancy. Nothing like this at all."

Suddenly she felt the difference between her and Doc. He was born to money, she was not. He was used to finer things in life, he would go to one of the better colleges in the country. He had traveled, seen so much of the world. All Lissa knew was the island. And if she went to college at all, it would probably be Cape Fear Community College.

He must have read her thoughts and he leaned even closer to her, wrapping an arm around her shoulders and pulling her to kiss him.

She felt the wetness of the tip of his tongue and the pulse of his lips as they pressed against hers. She reciprocated, reaching her arms around his neck and stepping into him. Her hands smoothly traced his shoulders and she felt the muscles of them respond as he tightened his grip.

She'd never felt so dizzy, so out of control, and control was one of the things she liked having at all times. Lissa pulled herself from his grasp. "Whew." She smiled briefly. "I think we better go on over to your grandmother's place. Do I need to change into something a little dressier?"

Murdoch shook his head. "You look great."

Chapter 6

There were several cars parked in front of the little block cottage where the cookout was taking place. All were newer models, mostly Audis and Mercedes. Instantly Lissa wished she had changed into something a little more dressy.

"That's my father." Murdoch nodded toward a group of men by the grill. "He's the one in a suit. I'm sure Mother had something to do with that," he whispered as his father approached.

"Dad, this is Lissa Roseman. Lissa, this is my father Grayson." Doc released his arm from around Lissa's waist as she and his father shook hands.

Grayson pressed both of his hands around Lissa's. "My, you are a beautiful young woman. I can see why Doc is so smitten with you."

The comment disarmed Lissa. She was not used to men in expensive suits complimenting her. She blushed lightly, then fought for her composure before saying what she'd been practicing as she and Doc drove to the little sound side house.

"Mr. Soucek—"

"Call me Grayson, please."

"Grayson, I understand that you are responsible for much of the development—"

"You know," he interrupted, "I knew you were going to question me about that. A smart young lady like you doesn't miss a thing. But let me assure you that you don't understand everything."

"I understand that the dunes are being destroyed."

"Young lady, come have a seat with me. You've been so misinformed." He turned to his son. "Doc, why don't you get a drink for your mother? I see her alone; her glass is empty and you know how Lorelei loves her Bloody Marys."

Doc's eyes questioned Lissa's.

She nodded. "Take care of your mother, I'll be just fine." Her eyes slid from Doc's to Grayson's. "Mr. Soucek, please explain things to me. I'm just a poor little southern girl and I'm sure you know so much more than I do."

Grayson smiled at her sarcasm. "Oh, I'm sure you're an intelligent young woman but you are young and maybe you haven't gotten all the facts yet."

Guiding her to a nearby table Grayson pulled out a chair for her.

"Thank you." Lissa sat, her legs crossed at the ankles, her hands resting in her lap. "Please explain to me how it is just fine to tear down sand dunes to build houses."

The conversation was rather short - Grayson explained how unaware of the problem he was when he built his home and how he had very little to do with the development of the island.

He was actually heading a committee that was writing a bill to preserve the dunes.

What to believe? Lissa thought as she listened to the man. His words were polished, much of what he said was in legalize - words she really did not understand. All she knew was that she did not like Grayson Soucek and trusted him only as far as she could throw him. She was so glad Doc was not like his father.

"You see dear," Grayson said as he patted her hand. "It's all for the best. You people down here are going to benefit greatly from all the development. You won't have to rely on some fisherman to take care of you." He patted her hand again. "You don't want to grow up and marry some fisherman, now do you?"

What's wrong with that? Her eyes glared.

"People are going to come here and they need a place to stay so my buildings are in compliance with the laws and regulations of North Carolina."

Lissa nodded. It was futile to argue with the man. He had all the answers; she sounded like a rube talking with him. Maybe, like her father had told before, she needed to go to college, learn a few things, then have the power and knowledge to fight bastards like Grayson Soucek.

Rising from the table, Lissa extended her hand, "I understand you and things that are happening well, very well, Mr. Soucek. Thank you."

Searching the room for Doc, she found him making his way to her.

"Well?" He pulled her close and kissed her lips lightly.

"Are you sure he's your father?" she asked sardonically.

"Yep, that's my father," he chuckled.

"You don't seem to be anything like him. You don't believe that do you? That the condos are good for the island?"

"No," he answered quickly. "We're different but Dad isn't so bad. It's just who he is and believe me, you'll never change his mind."

Her eyes followed Grayson as he walked to the grill. One of the men there handed him a mixed drink, he laughed and flicked a lighter to light a cigarette.

Her eyes left him to scan the backyard and study the people who had come to the cookout. Only a few looked familiar, the rest she'd never seen before. But they looked like fine people, dressed much more casually than Grayson Soucek. They stood chatting, laughing, enjoying the music and comradery. Many had milled about to schmooze with the new elite - the new developer.

Lissa sighed then noticed a tall woman, dressed to the nines, her hair pulled back into a bun. Holding a drink in her hands she stood statuesquely eyeing Lissa and Doc cautiously. The woman did not look pleased but she smiled anyway when her eye's reached Lissa's.

"That's mother," Murdoch said as he watched the woman make her way toward him and Lissa.

Nearing, she purred in a thick Charleston accent, "Doc, are you goin' to introduce me to this sweet lovely girl or am I goin' to have to do it myself?"

Murdoch blushed and lifted his eyes to his mother's. "Mother, this is Lissa Roseman, and Lissa, this is my beautiful mother."

Lissa nodded. "Pleased to meet you, Mrs. Soucek."

"Now, she's a pretty thing, Doc." Lorelei patted her son's shoulder. "You know, sweetie, I think your daddy has somethin' he wants to talk to you about. Why don't you get on over to him and I'll keep little miss Lissa company?"

He squeezed Lissa's hand before releasing it and moving toward the grill and his father.

"How old are you dear?" Lorelei asked softly.

"Eighteen."

"Eighteen? My, I could have sworn you were just a baby - not even sixteen."

"I turned eighteen in November."

"And you're just graduating? Did you fail a grade in school, sugar?"

The tone, the words laced with condescension, did not surprise Lissa. Doc had warned her of his mother's arrogance.

Smiling to herself, she answered, stressing her own accent. "Well, my momma, God rest her soul, died when I was only seven. I missed lots of school and my daddy just thought it best I repeat the second grade."

"You know, Murdoch – Doc - we call him Doc 'cause he's going to be a doctor, we decided that even before he was born," Lorelei tittered. "Well, Doc was so smart he skipped a grade and graduated when he was seventeen and barely seventeen at that. That sweet boy had just turned seventeen two weeks prior, otherwise he'd been sixteen when he graduated - too bad you couldn't have done something like that and been able to graduate when you were supposed to."

She'd been taught to be polite, to not strike back when someone insulted her. *Walk away, don't worry about the small stuff or the small people,* her daddy had taught her. Lissa reminded herself of that and grinned. "Excuse me, I think I need to go to the lady's room but it's been lovely talking to you, Mrs. Soucek."

Chapter 7

"That's my mother, Queen Lorelei. She sits in the judgement seat of all mankind." Murdoch stretched his legs into the sand, and looking toward the setting sun resting in an indigo sky, raised his shoulders. "She's what my daddy calls southern stealth, you don't know you've been hit until it's all over."

"Your family is going to give southerners a bad name," Lissa joked.

"Yeah, I know." He breathed in heavily and thrust a book toward her.

"What's this?"

"The other day, when we were shopping in the stores - the book with the poem you and I both liked. I wanted you to have it."

Lissa rubbed the cover, held the book to her chest.

"Open it. Read the first page."

"You have opened the world for me. You will always be my world. Yours forever, Doc."

Lissa thumbed through the pages to find the poem - the one they'd read together that day. She read it silently, then pulled him to her lips and kissed him slowly, gently. "I love you, Murdoch Soucek."

"I know." He smiled. "I wish I'd met you years ago and we could have been kids together."

"Me too." She rested her head on his shoulder. "That would have been cool. I guess meeting southern women and taking them back north is tradition in your family," she giggled.

"Yes, seems to be. I'd love to take you to Pittsburg, you'd like it. The winters are cold but there is so much to do. We go to the theater - I'd take you to New York City, we could go to Europe—"

"I'd love it." Lissa threw her head back and laughed. She studied his face. "You know I'm not worldly at all - I might feel out of place in all those hoity-toity places."

"They're not hoity-toity. You'd be fine."

"I bet Lorelei—"

"Don't let her fool you. My mother grew up dirt poor, she puts on this façade."

"She pretentious."

"I guess you might call her that but I suppose it is her way of putting her past behind her."

"How did she and your father meet? Was your daddy in the military - Camp Lejeune - is that how he met your mother?"

Doc shook his head. "Dad met my mother on a trip to Charleston with his parents. She was at some party - I don't know. Guess the men in my family have something for southern women."

"We're not all that bad, you know." She smiled and winked.

56

"Grandmother can be stealthy, like my father says, but she's never been mean spirited - not like Mother. She's all love and honey child and loves to bake me cookies. I guess Dad was hoping he'd marry someone like her." Doc shrugged and turned away.

Lissa shook her head. "That's got to be tough to take some times, huh?"

"Yeah, I try to avoid her at all costs and when there's no way of doing that, I simply ask her how high she wants me to jump. But she's got this, I don't know, she gives me this look - she's always done it - like there's something wrong and it's my fault that it is." He blew a breath from his lips. "I'm so glad she's not around very much."

"Really?"

"Mother stays mostly in Charleston at our house there. I'm pretty sure she came up this weekend to check you out. Dad told her I was seeing someone - sorry."

"Don't be sorry, it's not your fault." Lissa scooted closer to him in the sand. "Your parents don't live together?" Lissa asked shyly.

"We have a house in Charleston and a townhouse in Pittsburg. Dad has a condo in Chicago and another somewhere else, hell, I quit counting what all he has. He does most of his business up north and Mother says she can't stand the cold weather, so most of the year she stays in Charleston."

Lissa's brow furrowed. "Oh."

"Yeah, I know what you mean, it sounds odd. My parents rarely spend time with one another. I'm sure Dad has a girl or two stashed away in each of the company offices. And Mother sees the pool boy or the golf pro." He rolled his eyes. "I try to keep out of her way. She's always picking on me about my hair. Either it's too long and needs cut or needs changed in some way. Last month she told me I should bleach it - says the sun has screwed it up and it needs to be one color." He rolled his eyes.

"No pleasing her, huh?"

"Humph, no way to please that woman. Dad keeps her in jewelry and a few times a year ships her off on a cruise or to Europe for a few weeks. My brother and sister hardly ever speak to her or is it she doesn't speak to them? When she's pissed or doesn't get her way she quits talking to you or if she does talk to you it's to cut you down."

Lissa's brow furrowed, the twisted expression on his face belied the pain he felt. Reaching her hand to his, she pressed it softly. "Sorry."

"No big deal." He shrugged. "I don't see her that much anymore."

"You said you have a brother and sister?"

"Older, they're way older than me." He snickered, "Yeah, I'm the baby. I think I came along to make sure Dad didn't leave. Cal's in California and Suzy lives in England with her husband and kids. They're in their thirties. I hardly know them at all."

Lifting his head, Doc looked to the ocean. His mouth held tightly, he drew his legs closer to his chest.

Raising her hand to Doc's face, Lissa gently drew a finger along the line of his jaw. She traced his eyebrow then leaned her head into the hollow of his shoulder.

His arm reached around her as he pulled her to him. "I've never told anybody this stuff before."

She snuggled closer. "I'm sorry about your mother - your dad, wish it was different for you. I never really got to know my mom."

"The queen said you told her she died but that's all she said. I bet she didn't even ask you anything about her. Did she?"

Lissa shook her head and shrugged. "It doesn't matter." She paused for a moment. "Momma had a weak heart; she died giving birth to my brother."

"I didn't know you had a brother."

"I don't. He died, too - they both did."

His arm wrapped around her waist he turned to kiss her.

Her trembling breath escaping, Lissa felt Doc's hands on her skin, caressing her back and then her hips.

Her hands slid from his shoulders to his chest, she leaned into him more as his hands explored her neck and breasts, he gently pushed her to lie in the sand, his hands stroking her thighs and between them.

"Not here," she whispered.

The boat house was dank and damp. Oars lay scattered against one wall, a couple of worn out motors stood on saw horses, an old Naugahyde sofa accented another corner.

But it was quiet, it was private and with a view of the setting sun on the marshes of Topsail Island.

Lissa pulled the t-shirt over her head, her hair tumbled about her face. Doc reached for her, pulling her to him by the hips. "I love you," he murmured.

His fingers found the clasp to Lissa's bra, she fumbled with the buttons of his shorts, but slowly. Their eyes held by the hunger to feel wanted - to touch each other as no one had touched either one of them before.

"I love you, too," Lissa whispered as they lay close, holding one another.

Murdoch pressed his lips against hers, then her neck, her cheeks, her eyes.

She held his face in her hands, stroking it gently, small gasps escaping her lips as he touched the most private parts of her body, making small circles on her skin, arousing her to a reality she'd never imagined.

Clinging to him tightly, Lissa held his eyes, her lips trembling against his.

Their bodies drenched in sweat, Lissa and Doc sighed as a cooling breeze swept through the open shutters of the boat house. Their lips brushed against one another's lazily.

Doc repeated the three words, Lissa's head fell back against the sofa, small sounds of pleasure falling from her lips. They both smiled broadly, kissed each other deeply again, then, with just a bit more knowledge, repeated their act of trust and love.

Chapter 8

Lissa graduated on time; there had been no further episodes with developers and construction workers. She kept her distance, stayed away and if she noticed a bulldozer or truck passing on the road, she made sure to turn her head, look the other way. She was convinced, after meeting Grayson Soucek, that opposition was futile.

Even after making calls to environmental groups, she realized that they could be bought. Laws prohibiting building on wetlands did nothing to deter the builder with the most money. It seemed all things could be justified, everything was for sale.

Quelling her anger and disappointment with city planning and other powers that be, she resigned herself to the fact that nothing could be done until she had a degree under her belt - some sense of the real world and how it worked.

As she made her way across the stage to accept her diploma, Lissa saw her father's face beaming from ear to ear. Murdoch sat next him and they both cheered and clapped wildly as she received her diploma.

Afterward they all dined a celebratory dinner at the Breezeway Restaurant, located on the Intracoastal Waterway, and devoured Mahi Mahi, clams and butterfly shrimp.

"What are you doing this summer besides fishing?" John Roseman asked. His attention focusing on Doc while he sipped from a glass of iced tea.

"Your daughter is going to teach me how to surf."

"She's good - you'll have a fine teacher."

"She going to help me pick out a board but I like the water warmer, so I guess we'll start the lessons this week - now that she's out of school and has more time."

John studied the young man, he wasn't sure if he liked him or not. He wondered if he was taking advantage of his daughter. "She still has to work at the shop four days a week."

"Maybe I could help her there some. I don't know much about boats and motors but I'm willing to learn."

That was a good comment, he liked that. If the boy was willing to learn and be in a setting where the father was around, maybe the kid was okay. "Maybe, we'll see. You can drop by sometime if you like."

Doc nodded and reached for Lissa's hand. "Thank you, sir."

"I guess you'll be going back to college in the fall - huh?"

"Yes sir, I'll be doing that."

"Lissa says you're going to Davidson. Why not one of the universities up north?"

"Davidson has the best pre-med program - at least that's what my mother says."

"It's very prestigious. I know you have to have a good GPA and high SAT scores to get in."

"Alumni doesn't hurt. My grandfather, my mother's father, went there."

John relaxed a bit more into his chair. He nodded, studying Doc. "So you plan on becoming a doctor?"

Doc shrugged. "I don't know. I've been thinking about that. I'm not sure."

"Not sure? You're not sure if you want to be a doctor?"

"No sir, I'm not. I sort of got into pre-med because my mother wanted me to."

"Ahh, and now you're questioning it."

Doc nodded.

"What else have you been considering?"

Doc shrugged again. "Different things. I've been thinking of transferring to Wilmington, UNCW."

"Pre-med? Do they even have that there?"

"I was thinking physical education but I don't know. I'd really like to stay here and go to Wilmington."

"What does your father have to say about that?" John slid his eyes to Lissa and raised a brow.

"I haven't told him yet, still thinking about it. I never really wanted to become a surgeon or medical doctor."

John watched Doc's eyes lower. It was obvious the boy was struggling.

"I think the poop is going to hit the propeller when I tell my parents I'm thinking of transferring and that I've decided to change my major."

65

"The queen isn't going to like that. I mean, your parents named you Murdoch, Doc, for a reason," Lissa interjected.

Doc shook his head. "Not much I can do about that. They'll see after I explain things to them."

Lissa's father adjusted himself in the chair, "Are you sure?" He asked, raising a brow.

Doc rolled his eyes, "I just don't see myself being a doctor. All that blood. I never wanted it. I was a jock in school, loved sports - phys-ed just seems the right place for me to be - and then I might just take a year off and figure everything out."

"Stay in school, son. Whatever you do, don't drop out. You won't ever go back again. Believe me, I know that. I felt the same way you do at your age, well, maybe a little older. I was going into law, had three years, hated it, then decided I'd start my own business. Thought I'd get rich quick with my own boat business." John laughed and patted Murdoch on the back. "Well, I'm not rich but I'm happy for the most part. Just stay in school, think about it. A doctor makes lots of money."

Murdoch grinned. "I'm still thinking about it. There are so many things I could do, it doesn't have to be medicine."

"I like physical ed. My scholarships were in sports. I excelled in track and basketball. I've even thought of being a coach." He stabbed a scallop with his fork. "I don't know yet. But I don't think it's medicine."

Chapter 9

Lissa dangled her legs from the dock of Emilia Soucek's sound side home. She watched as Murdoch baited his hook and cast it out into the water. "Tomorrow morning I'll meet you at the Scotch Bonnet fishing pier."

Doc nodded. "I'll be there."

Lissa watched him, he was so pensive, so quiet since the conversation with her father the night before.

"You're not going back to Davidson? Why? I know what you told my dad but that's a big decision."

"I've never wanted to go into medicine, not that kind of medicine anyway. But when I mentioned it to my parents when I was in high school, hell, you would have thought I started a war."

"But you've got a year under your belt now. Wouldn't you lose the credits?"

"I don't care. I just know that since I've met you, things look differently to me."

"I bet your parents are really going to hate me because of this."

"You shouldn't care about that either."

A slight tug on the line indicated a fish was on the hook. Doc jerked slightly and reeled in. A mullet danced wildly; he grasped the fish, pulled out the hook and tossed it in a cooler. "That makes four." He smiled to Lissa as he settled next to her on the wooden bench.

"You've opened my eyes to things. I have to follow my own rules, do what I want, live my life - it is not my father's life to live."

"What about Lorelei?"

"Mother? Humph, she'll just quit talking to me for a while. She's big with doling out the guilt. "I'm sure she'll say something about being disappointed in me, how I've ruined her life."

"Ruined her life?"

"That's my mother. It's always all about her."

Sitting silently, stunned by the sudden turn of events, Lissa felt herself becoming even more enthralled. Here was this beautiful young man, one whom she thought had it all together, had it all, money, style, opportunity - and he was discovering new things, altering his path and it seemed because of her. She felt flattered, vulnerable and wanted to give so much of herself to him.

"This is a big deal, Doc. Are you sure that is what you want to do? Are you sure you're making this decision for yourself and not for me?"

He shook his head. "Being with you, talking with you and your father, has encouraged me to look at what I really want. I don't want to cut on people, I don't want to hand out pills." His eyes sparkled for a moment. "For the first time in my life, I know what I don't want."

"And you don't want to be a doctor?'

"Mother wants me to be a plastic surgeon."

Lissa sniggered.

"Father wants me to be a cardiologist."

"And what do you want?"

"I'm not sure, I know I want you, I know I want you to teach me to surf." He grabbed the hat on her head and placed it on his own.

"Pink isn't your color, sweetie."

"Too bad." Doc opened the lid of the cooler. "Four fish, that's enough for dinner. I thought we'd go to the north end, build a little fire and cook out. How about it?"

"I'll make some slaw."

"Sounds good." Settling the pole against the railing, Doc reached for Lissa.

"You stink, you smell like fish."

"Not for long." Scooping Lissa in his arms, he carried her to the boat lift and jumped into the water.

Wrapping her arms around his neck, she pulled herself to him and kissed his salty mouth. "What am I going to do with you, Murdoch Soucek? You make me so happy."

＊＊＊＊＊＊＊＊＊＊＊

"I bought the one you suggested and then went back and got the shorter board, too."

"Mr. Moneybags," Lissa tittered.

"The guy at surf shop said it was best for me to start out with a long board but I could graduate to a short." Doc settled the two boards against his Jeep.

"Must be nice." Lissa walked toward the Jeep studying the surfboards. "You think you're going to learn that fast. You think you'll graduate from the long board to the short in just one day."

"Sure," he winked.

"And you got the most expensive ones, I see."

"Only the best." Doc winked again.

"Well, I know what's floating around in your head, and it's not brains."

"Look, I'm not stupid, I know it's going to take time but this is so cool. I like both boards and well, the guy at the shop talked me into it."

"You're easy."

"Yeah, I know."

"For learning, you could have gotten an inexpensive Wavestorm. Just because a board costs a lot of money doesn't mean you'll surf any better or learn quicker."

"I know, Miss Smarty-Pants, I just wanted to get the best."

"Okay. Put the short board back in the Jeep and grab the Bing." She shook her head. "Bing's a nice board. Wish I could afford one."

"When I get good enough to do the short one, I'll give it to you."

"I'll be too old by then," she laughed.

"Always the jokester. You just wait. I'm good at everything I try."

"Have you ever tried being humble?"

Doc grinned, "Nope."

"You're so full of it."

"I know." He grinned again, turned to shove the short board in the Jeep and grabbed a towel. "Let's do it, babe. I'm putty in your hands."

"I hope the guy at the surf shop sold you some base coat and wax."

"Sure did and he told me how to apply it. See, I'm on top of things today." Doc knelt on the sand and prepared the board.

Lissa splashed into the water, striding to waist deep and then pulled herself atop the board, paddled out a few feet and watched Murdoch at the shore.

In minutes he followed and they both paddled out far beyond the breakers.

"I know you've body surfed before," she began.

"Who hasn't?"

"Then you know the feel of when a wave is coming, you know to wait until you feel the momentum build before trying to take it."

Doc nodded.

"That's it. You feel that, then you stand up, get your balance and go."

"You make it sound so easy."

Lissa giggled, paused and nodded her head, "You feel that?" She flipped on her belly as a wave rose beneath her.

"Yeah." Murdock did the same.

"Now wait...wait...wait...GO!" Her arms paddling with the wave, Lissa rose to her feet. "Middle of the board, balance yourself—"

She watched him crouch, bent over, his hands still holding on to the board. "Let go, balance yourself, move to find your bal— Crap!" Reaching the shore, Lissa searched the water to find Doc breeching , his board tethered to his foot.

"Wipeout!" Lissa laughed loudly. "Point and laugh, point and laugh." She arched her finger as she jumped from her board.

Doc waded to shore, tossed the board on the sand and flopped down. "It's not as easy as it looks."

"You'll get it. Like you say, you're good at everything you try."

"Smartass."

72

Sidling next to him, Lissa threaded her arm through his. "You ready to go again?" She pressed her wet salty lips against his.

"Hell yes." Standing, Doc gathered his board and raced toward the waves. "I'll get this down, you give me a few days."

"Few years," Lissa chided.

"Few days - and I'll be as good as you."

"Never."

The board before him, Doc pulled his body on and paddled. "I can do this – you - it's you. *You* know how to motivate me."

"I like your attitude." Lissa splashed him and maneuvered her board away. "Wish you could be as adamant about dealing with your father and his damn development."

Murdoch shrugged. "Let's not talk about that right now."

Chapter 10

"Herring's, this place has been here forever. I used to get fish heads here all the time when I was a kid."

"Fish heads?"

"For crabbing, excellent bait."

"You never cease to amaze me, Lissa. I mean, you're such a sophisticated lady."

"Hardy, har har. You're so funny."

Doc wrapped an arm around her as they entered the store

"I hope this place never changes."

"I usually get my bait at Thomas Tackle." He reached for her and turned her face to his. "Thanks for teaching me to surf."

"Amend that statement," she teased.

"*Trying* to teach me?"

Moving into the hollow of his shoulder, she nested her head against his chest. "I think you're right or maybe it's just that you are determined. But you really did good today. I'm proud of you."

"I think I rode for thirty seconds at the most," he chuckled.

"Yeah, but you have it right, you know when to catch it. It's just going to be balance for you. You simply have to find your balance and then the sky's the limit.'

Lissa perused the flip flop display and swimsuits, Doc moved directly to the fishing poles and lures.

"Can I help you?" The young clerk asked.

"Just looking but we're thinking of renting a kayak."

"I'll set you up, no problem. Have you kayaked before?"

"I've done a little - Aspinwall on the Allegheny River—"

"Um," the clerk nodded.

"And Ten Mile Creek on the Monongahela, it's pretty scenic."

"Yeah, that's pretty nice. It's a calm ride, like it is here. No white water," the clerk chuckled. "Do you need a guide?"

"No, we're fine. I've done it a thousand times."

"Oh yeah, I recognize you. You're the Roseman girl - Lissa. How you doing?"

Lissa stepped into the kayak. Sliding low into the seat, she grasped the paddle and pushed away from the dock.

Doc briskly paddled to reach her as she maneuvered through the water. "Any alligators?"

"Only a few."

"Shit. It only takes one."

"Wussy-man."

He tapped her kayak with his paddle.

"Hey, are you trying to tip me over?" She tapped her paddle against his kayak. "The gators won't bother you. And besides they're small. Locals keep them culled."

They paddled silently along the marsh and into the sound past oyster beds and the occasional private dock.

"Shh," Doc whispered. "A snowy egret." He pointed to a tiny jut of land with a bird standing staunchly. Suddenly it thrust its head into the shallow water retrieving a wriggling fish at the end of its beak. "Wow, man, that was cool."

"*Wow, man,*" Lissa mimicked. "Is that how doctors talk?"

"If they're impressed, if they find something awesome." He paddled ahead, hugging the shoreline.

Lissa followed, occasionally pointing out a bird, other aquatic animal or landmark. They passed a small alligator resting in the marsh and listened to the trill of the red winged blackbirds clustered in the snug, small water oaks on the shore.

A few more minutes of silence passed as they paddled silently in the sound. Doc raised his arm and pointed.

"Dolphins, wow. I don't think I've ever seen dolphins in the sound before."

"Good feeding grounds, lots of shrimp and little fish."

Bringing the paddle inside the boat, Doc drifted with the tide, watching the dolphins as they dipped and rose.

"I think—"

"Shh." Lissa pressed a finger to her lips and nodded as two of the dolphins neared Doc's kayak.

Slowly he reached a hand to touch the dorsal fin of the nearest. His fingers, feeling the touch slick skin, slid down to the body. Doc rubbed his hand along the dolphin; it raised its head and caught his eyes. He gasped. Slowly the dolphin moved to Lissa, she petted it, too. For nearly five minutes they caressed them till finally they dove and swam away.

"My God, that was fantastic. I can't believe it." Doc's face shone brightly, his eyes wide with wonder.

"Even I've never been able to do that. Sometimes they'll swim next to me but they've never let me pet them before."

They still tingled with excitement as they continued paddling along through the sound waters. Smiling at each other every time they caught the other's eye.

"What a day!" Doc exclaimed. "So cool."

"Yeah."

"You brought the sandwiches, didn't you?" Doc called as the sun rose in the sky.

"Yes, you have the Pepsis?"

"Sure do." Doc turned the kayak toward a small island in the sound and stepped out to pull it onto the sand.

Flapping the blanket against the breeze, Lissa waited for it to settle on to sand. "This is going to be fun."

Doc opened the tiny cooler and pulled out two cans of cola. "It sure is." He popped a top.

"Chicken or bologna?" Kneeling on the blanket, Lissa reached for a canned drink and sipped. "Now this is nice, this is heaven."

"Yep." Doc laid his head in her lap. "Sure is."

Lissa threaded her fingers through his long hair, drew her fingers along the curves of his cheekbones. "So you really are thinking of transferring to UNC Wilmington?"

"Yeah, I think it's time I started doing what I want instead of what my parents do."

"It will be interesting to see how that goes."

"Yeah, I'm sure the shit will hit the fan, but what can they do - disown me?" He pondered his last statement. "Yeah, it is going to be interesting to see how Dad takes it. And then, Mother - hell, no telling what she'll do."

"Let's change the subject. It's too pretty a day to spend talking about them." Lissa bent to kiss his forehead then lifted her head to the sound of barge making its way through the Intracoastal.

Doc turned too and watched as it plowed through the waters just beyond the sound. It carried several bulldozers and large trucks.

"Damn," Lissa hissed.

"I know you hate all the development. I don't like it either. I've been coming here since I was a little kid - it's changing.

"I know."

"But look, you've finally got a big grocery store here, Food Lion came in, there's a pharmacy on the island. Now, that's not a bad thing is it?

"No. Not yet. I've seen what they've done to Myrtle Beach - it's bumper to bumper. As long as the bigger businesses are kept on the other side of the bridge, it's okay. I just don't want the dunes messed with or the houses bunched up. It's getting too crowded. Building into the dunes is just wrong, Doc. It destroys them. Try building a sand castle and see what happens when you move the sand around for a section, it does affect the entire thing. You just can't build on the dunes and expect them to stay."

"But progress—"

"Screw progress. I'm so tired of hearing about progress. This has nothing to do with that. This has everything to do with somebody lining their pockets. That's what progress is about." Lissa could feel her face flushing, her voice rising.

Murdoch leaned back a bit.

"Sorry. I get upset when I think about it. But I love Topsail and I just don't like seeing it destroyed." She inhaled deeply then smiled. "It makes me feel so insignificant, that I have no power to do anything - no one is going to listen to me."

Murdoch wrapped an arm around her shoulder. "Sorry, sweetie. Just lean on me. I'll make it all better." He kissed her head. "Look what you've done for me."

"What?"

"Taught me to surf," he grinned. "Sorta, but I'm getting better. And you've helped me see what I truly want."

"Want?"

"At least what I don't want. I feel that for the first time, I'm seeing that I have some control in my life."

"Wish I did."

"You're such a good teacher - I think I like surfing better than fishing. It's so—" He looked into her eyes. "Cleans my head. Being with you, clears my head."

Every day, even rainy days, Lissa and Murdoch took to the waves, and if there were none they fished or spent the time floating on their boards, talking about their lives - the possibilities, hopes and dreams. They were inseparable that summer. Doc helped out at the boat shop and learned about motors and anything else that pertained to the nautical way of life.

John Roseman liked him. Found him to be diligent, reliable and eager to learn. He took the boy out fishing several times with Lissa to the Gulf Stream and even to fifteen mile rock. It felt like a family to him, one he'd never known before. Lissa felt that way, too. For as long as she could remember it had always been just her and her father. Doc felt right, he felt right to John, too.

On the water it was as if the holiness of the sea manifested as something beyond words. It was the tie that bound them together.

Chapter 11

It was August, Grayson Soucek considered how it was time to have the all-important talk with his son about returning to college. Certainly Murdoch was ready to move on.

Having spent much of his time in Europe that summer, Grayson had barely seen the boy. But no news was good news and he suspected that his son was doing what all young men his age were doing, getting laid. The little surfer girl was cute, Grayson grinned as he thought of his son's youth and his own days of sowing wild oats.

It prompted him to think of his wife, Lorelei, and what she was up to. Her call to London had prompted him to return early. Other than that, he hadn't heard from her in weeks.

He imagined that she and Emanuel were enjoying the pool and house he'd built in Charleston. He'd noticed a somewhat large withdrawal from their joint bank account for a little over ten thousand. He assumed it was some sort of gift for her lover. He shrugged, thinking how ten thousand was so much less than the millions he'd amassed over the years since he and Lorelei had married. It was a small price to pay for either of their infidelities.

Their lifestyles where never spoken of but, of course, he expected she knew of his dalliances, as he did hers.

He grinned and recalled the last few hours in London with Denise. He'd been keeping her in a flat for the last three years.

It's all a compromise, he thought to himself. A little here a little there - no one got hurt. And he did love Lorelei. She was still beautiful, even in her fifties. She had kept her figure and, of course, there had been a little nip and tuck here and there.

A few new on the market procedures had flattened her tummy and done away with that little bag of skin forming under her chin. Lorelei looked good and he was proud to have her on his arm whenever they attended a function. What was wrong with either one of them playing around, just as long as they came together in the end? He smiled to himself then recalled the conversation he'd had with her only a few days before.

What was it Lorelei had said? "Your mother mentioned that the Doc and that girl look like they are in love - or something. Maybe you need to drop whatever it is - or *whoever* it is — you're doing, and get back here."

Grayson smirked, surely his son wasn't involved in any serious manner with the girl. More than likely Murdoch was just having fun.

But he had learned that when Lorelei expressed disapproval, the best thing was to comply with her wishes. He would make the effort to check in on his son, maybe they could go see a game together or something. Weren't the Pirates playing the Reds in a couple of days?

Chuckling, Grayson reassured himself that there was nothing wrong with a little fun, he certainly wouldn't have thrown the girl out of his bed if he'd been younger. Hell, he wouldn't throw her out now. But it was time for his son to move on, time to get serious about life and go back to Davidson.

They would meet at the beach house at noon for lunch. He'd have it catered from the Riverview Cafe in Sneads Ferry. Settled in the center of Murdoch's plate would be a new platinum VISA with a twenty thousand dollar limit.

Pulling the Mercedes into the drive of the North Topsail house, Grayson powered the garage door open then cursed under his breath as he noticed the jade green Jaguar. It was dusty and a line of cobwebs led from one of the beams of wood to a side mirror. It didn't appear as if his son had been using the Jag at all that summer. As he backed up to pull into the adjoining bay he noticed the van from the Riverview rolling slowly down the road. Lunch was on its way.

Grayson glanced at his Rolex, already Doc was twenty minutes late. He shook his head, assuming his son was busy boning the surfer girl. He chuckled at the idea as he stood before the window overlooking the driveway of his house.

There he is, he thought, watching his son pull the cherry red Jeep into the drive. The boy's hair was tied back in a ponytail.

He hated that. But he knew it was the style and that when his son finally grew up, he'd laugh about the "do" he wore as a teen.

"Hi son," Grayson said extending a hand as Doc exited the elevator. "Long time no see."

Murdoch nodded, shook his father's hand and seated himself at the table. "Well, we might as well get this over with."

Stunned by the unexpected response, Grayson gritted his teeth. He was not used to belligerence from his son. "Alright, I can see you've developed an attitude this summer. What's up?"

"I'm not going back to Davidson."

"Like hell you're not. The tuition is paid for, you're established there—"

"Dad, you need to listen to me. I don't want to go back. You knew before I ever started there, I told you. I didn't and I don't want to be a doctor."

"I don't give a flying fuck what you want. You're going back." He paused for a moment, edging near his son. "I've fed and clothed you for nearly twenty years. I built you a fine home, you have everything you could ever want. And you're going to tell me you aren't going to go to college. Bullshit."

"I didn't say I don't want to go to college. I don't want to go to Davidson, I don't want pre-med."

"Then what is it you want?"

"I was thinking Phys Ed. I can get that at UNC Wilmington."

"Ah, I get it. You want to stay around here."

Murdoch nodded.

"Why do you want to stay here? Does it have something to do with that girl you saw this summer?"

"I'm still seeing her."

"Your mother was right."

Doc rolled his eyes. "I should have known she'd stick her nose in my business."

"She's your mother. She's supposed to stick her nose in your business."

"Then why didn't she call me - have *the talk* with me? Oh, that's right. When mother is mad at me she cuts me out, denies my existence."

Grayson slid his eyes to his son, they exchanged a glance of shared but guarded understanding.

"I know how she is, but that's not the point." Grayson drummed the table with his fingers. "Look, you idiot, you need to fall in line and return to Davidson. This little fling is just that. You need to get over it. You need to forget about this little sandbar and this surfer girl you've been spending time with. *This,"* he spread his arms wide, "is only a small part of what lay ahead in your future."

"But I don't want pre-med. I don't want Davidson. I have no desire to be a doctor. I like it here."

"It's nice. I remember having a nice time here when I was your age. But I moved on to better things, more important things. It's time for you to do the same."

"I don't want the same things you want—"

"Don't kid yourself, Murdoch. You do want the same things. If it wasn't for all my hard work, investments, business savvy, you wouldn't live such a comfortable life. The world is bigger than Topsail Island, if you'd traveled like I have—"

"You and mother prance around like royalty when you travel. You have no idea what the real people are like."

"You don't know shit. You're too young to understand. I talk to people, I've had a drink with the common man."

"Listen to yourself, 'the common man,' just who the hell is that supposed to be?"

"I talk—" Grayson growled through his teeth. "Why in the hell am I explaining things to you? What is there to talk about? People are people. We all want the same things."

"Are you sure people aren't telling you what you want to hear?"

Grayson's face reddened. "Smart ass brat, rules change when you grow up. You don't get to do whatever you want. You'll find out when you're a *man*."

"I hope I never turn out to be the kind of *man* you are - the kind that rather than stand up to his wife, cheats on her - you've got whores all over Europe." Murdoch's chest rose, he stepped closer to his father. "If you like it so much over there why don't you just move?"

Lighting a cigarette, Grayson crossed his legs, leaned back in the chair and calmed himself. "Son, plain and simple, I don't give a damn what you think of me. But I'm the one footing the bills. And you need to understand that this island is nothing except what we can make out of it. This place is good for nothing except investing.

"But I can see that little daydreamer has turned your head a bit. She's turning you into a damn tree hugger."

"You don't know crap. You think just because I care for the island, for something besides what I can get out of it, that I'm ignorant of what life is about. I've watched you, I know what you are about and I don't want it."

Grayson inhaled, shifted in his seat and continued, this time in a softer tone of voice. "Why don't you look at the development of this over rated sandbar as a gift? A gift to the people who get to come here and enjoy the ocean - we're giving them places to stay, to eat, to shop - look at it that way." He pulled another cigarette from the case in his jacket and rolled it gently between his fingers, lighting it he exhaled a plume of smoke as he pulled it from his lips. "If you can't go along with and understand what I'm telling you to do then maybe you need a little incentive."

Doc scowled, it angered him to hear his father speak so poorly of a place he'd grown so fond of. All he'd spoken was the antitheses of what Lissa espoused. Couldn't he see that so much development was destroying the natural beauty of this little sand bar?

"You're going back to Davidson and that's final. Playtime is over. This entire summer you've been with that little beach bum, she's not for you Murdoch. Your mother is appalled, she's beside herself with hurt because you have lowered your standards. Doc, this girl will not fit into our family. Now get rid of her. Tell her that it's been fun but it's time to move on. She's not our kind of people."

Doc eyed his father suspiciously, hadn't he always bragged about his willingness to accept anyone? Hadn't he advocated the claim that we are all equal? "Lissa's great, she's—"

"She's from the wrong side of the tracks, son. My God, Murdoch, her father runs a boat repair shop. She'll probably end up with some fisherman and squirt out three or four little fishermen."

"So," Murdoch shook his head, "You're such a big dog in the Kiwanis club, so altruistic. All that stuff about being the same is just a bunch of bullshit, isn't it? It gets you into the best clubs where you meet the right people. It gets you invited to the Whitehouse. You get to hobnob with the Clintons."

"It's nice meeting the president." Grayson grinned. "This girl..."

"Lissa."

"Whatever her name is, is not for you. She's only eighteen. This will pass."

"UNC Wilmington is a good school. I'll be near the beach, I can stay at Grammy's beach house, that will save you money and I know how you like to save money."

"Damn it all, Murdoch, this isn't about money. It's about your future and you're not wasting it on some piece of ass that you'll forget about next month. If you still want to drive the Jag, if you like living rent free you'll do what I say."

"You wouldn't."

"You watch me. You try to make it out there in the real world without a pot to piss in. I'll not give you a freaking damn dime - see how you like working for minimum wage. Lorelei is right, she's with me on this one, she saw right through that little girl. She's looking for a sugar daddy.

"I assume you two have been screwing," He looked snidely at his son. "Well, it's just sex - so what. You can screw anybody you want. This island trash, this Lissa, will never be anything but a baby machine. Now do what I say and dump that little bitch."

"You can't live my life. You can't tell me what to do."

Grayson rose from the chair. "You're not twenty-one, I *can* tell you what to do. I can make decisions for you and if you don't like them. I can make it hard on you. You better believe I will. Now get the hell out of my house and tell the little bitch good-bye."

****

It was early morning, the sun had been up for only half an hour or so. Lissa watched Doc descend from the dunes, surfboard beneath his arm.

Bounding up to him she tiptoed to kiss his lips. "Looks like it's going to be a good day, nice swells this morning."

Doc nodded, avoiding her eyes and took a deep breath.

"What's up, Doc?" Lissa teased.

"It's nothing."

"Nope, it's something. You look like somebody just licked the red off your candy."

He grinned. "No, nothing like that. It's just my father. He's such an asshole. I hate his guts."

"No, don't say that. I know he can be a jerk and he's self-absorbed and greedy and cruel and a philanderer and—"

Doc laughed, "And an S.O.B. and all kinds of things. You definitely have him pegged right."

"Yeah, but he is your father, Murdoch, and you shouldn't hate him." Lissa stretched to run her fingers through his hair, sliding the long strands to behind his ear. "There's not a thing you can do to change him. Just don't be like him."

His eyes were sorrowful, pain etched in tiny lines of his face. As he released the surfboard to the sand, he shook his head, "My father is a giant dick, he doesn't really give a damn about me or what I want."

"So you had an argument about going to med school?"

Nodding, Doc heaved another sigh. "He just doesn't get it. I don't want to be a doctor. I never wanted to be one. He and mother—"

"Did you talk with your mother, too?"

"Believe me, she's around in *spirit* whenever I talk with Dad. She pulls his chain. I know she put him up to—" He stopped mid-sentence.

"Put him up to what?"

"Oh, they both want me to go back to Davidson. They're both being assholes."

Lissa pulled Doc toward the water. "Get your board, let's do what we came for. It will make you feel better."

Gathering her into his arms, Doc hugged Lissa, held her tightly against his body. "I love you so much."

"I love you, too."

He kissed her lips lightly and hugged her for a long time. "I really love you, Lissa. You mean the world to me."

Looking into his eyes, Lissa held his face in her hands. "I'm so sorry he's such a butthead. I'm sorry he hurts you like he does - that they both do." Her frown disappearing into a broad smile Lissa grabbed Doc's arm. "Come on now, it's time to go to church."

It was a good morning for surfing. The water was just warm enough. It felt good to have something other than his parents on his mind. The water always did that for Doc and for Lissa. Conversation was lost in the physical experience as they both caught three good waves in a row.

Doc was laughing as they walked to shore after the last ride. He pulled open a cooler, extracting a couple of Gatorades. "Let's go to Wilmington tonight. There's a concert at Greenfield Park."

Lissa scooted closer to him, and threading a handful of sand through her closed fist, poured it on Murdoch.

"What are you doing?" He grinned.

"Trying to annoy you." Lissa giggled.

"Annoy, you want to know what annoying is, huh?" He grabbed her by the waist, rushed to the water and tossed her in. They both body surfed for a few more minutes then headed to their homes to dress for the evening.

A few hours in the ocean always refreshed his mind, made him think more clearly, stripped the stress from his thoughts. Now, Murdoch reasoned that his father wouldn't dare kick him out of the house, the threat was just another one of his tactics to get his way, or really Lorelei's way because he was sure his father was doing her biding.

He wanted to be near Lissa. She made him laugh, made him happy. Made him feel a way about life that he'd never felt before, made him feel like there were opportunities in life other than the ones his parents had set before him.

He chuckled, recalling how enraged he had been when talking with his father and how liberating it had felt to stand up to him.

There was no need to tell Lissa of the threats his father had made. He wasn't about to whine to the woman he loved or complain about a problem that he had resolved.

Chapter 12

"I invited you here to make you an offer." Grayson unfolded the napkin and placed it in his lap and reached for a hush puppy from the basket set in the center of the table. "This podunk little town doesn't have much but the restaurants around here sure do know how to make hush puppies." He bit in to one and closed his eyes for a moment. "Umm, damn good."

"So what's the offer, *Dad*?"

Grayson cocked his head to the side. "I'm not used to you being so confrontational with me son, so blatant in disregarding my wishes. You've developed an attitude I just don't like."

Murdoch sat quietly and waited for his father to continue.

"Like I said, I have an offer I want to make to you." He waited for a few seconds for his son to respond. "Don't you want to know what it is?"

Doc shook his head slowly.

"So that's the way it's going to be. You're still pissed off about our last conversation."

Again Murdoch sat quietly waiting for his father to continue.

"Have it your way." He reached for another hush puppy. "I know you won't mind, I ordered you a filet, same as mine - medium rare."

"I'm not hungry."

As he shrugged, a grin played upon his lips. Grayson shifted his eyes to bear down on his son's. "The offer, well - Ferrari. Metallic green. It's yours if you like. I noticed you haven't been driving the Jag."

"The Jeep's fine." Doc focused on his father's eyes. "Is that the proposition? You'll give me a Ferrari if I go back to Davidson?"

"Ferrari, a trip to Europe on your own or with one of your friends. Your mother says—"

"Mother. I know she's the one behind all of this."

"She's not going to give in Doc. Your mother would cut off her nose to spite her face, and you know that. She's not about to give in until she gets her way."

"Giving you the silent treatment too, Dad?"

"When it gets too quiet, I find something else to do." Grayson grinned, lifting his eyes in an all knowing glare.

"You have that luxury. But this time I'm not letting you or Mother bully me."

"This isn't bullying, son. We know what is best for you. I know you're still seeing the girl."

"Lissa's her name."

"I know you're still seeing Lissa. And I can see where you could care for her. She's pretty and she's smart. But son, she can't afford to go to the kind of schools you do. And what you are doing is depriving yourself of a better life simply to please her."

"You make me sick. It's not like that at all. I never wanted to do pre-med. You bribed me into it. I've told you so many times, Dad—"

"What? What is it you want?"

"I just know it's not medicine and transferring to UNC-W will give me the time to figure out just what it is I want. It's a good school, too."

Flipping open the silver case, Grayson fingered a thin brown cigarette.

"You can't smoke in here," Doc muttered.

Grayson nodded as he pulled a cigarette from the case and rolled it between his fingers.

"Why are you doing this, Dad?" Doc felt his muscles tighten. "Why won't you let me live my own life?"

"Because you are a boy and you don't know what you want. You need time away from this fairytale land you've been living in for the past three and a half months." He tapped the un-lit cigarette on the table. "It's best."

"No! You won't do this to me."

"Why don't you talk with your big brother, Cal and find out just what I will and won't do?"

Doc pushed away from the table. "You're a bastard."

Grayson's face reddened, he balled his fists, placing them on the table. "Damnit, you'll do what I tell you to do."

"I'm out of here." Doc threw the napkin on the table and walked briskly toward the restaurant exit. His heart raced and he felt tears rising in his eyes.

Oh how he wanted to see Lissa, to have her comfort him. Walking toward the Jeep, he heard the ding of the key control, the lights flicked on. As he approached the vehicle, he watched the tow truck pull into place ahead of it. He stood speechless.

"Murdoch." Grayson lifted a hand to rest on Doc's shoulder.

"This isn't fair! This isn't right!"

"Everything is a compromise, son. Nobody gets what they want. Life is not fair. Now, you do what I tell you to do. Just go back this semester. If after that you want to transfer to another college, you'll have my blessing."

Murdock stared at his father.

"You think the Jeep is the only thing you'll find missing? Check the garage, your bank account. Son." He rubbed the boy's shoulder. "This is all for the best. Oh, I have this for you." Grayson reached into the breast pocket of his suit. "Your mother gave me this."

Murdock took the envelope from his father's hand.

"Read it. It's from your mother."

Lifting the tab, Doc pulled out the pages and unfolded them. He studied the first. "What is this?" He held the blank page, then the second page, blank also. Four words were typed at the bottom of the third page – "I have no son."

"What the hell is this?" Doc shook his head. "Oh, I get it. She has nothing to say to me, she hates me."

"Your mother refuses to speak to either you or me until you go back to Davidson."

Chapter 13

He had made the call to Cal. His brother confirmed their father's ruthlessness when following Lorelei's orders. "It doesn't matter what Dad wants, I'm sure he wouldn't give a damn where you went. It's Mother's way or the highway or rather the bank way. And basically I don't think she cares either, she just likes the control and one way or another she'll have it. She's been busting his balls for as long as I can remember."

"Does she talk to you?"

"Ha, if that's what you want to call it. She'll call to ask about something financial every once in a while. She never asks about me or my family. But you should know, Doc. That's how she is."

"Dad?"

"I see him when he comes to California on business. We usually have dinner somewhere."

"What did you do to them?"

"I didn't marry the right girl, Doc. Much like your situation - I simply didn't follow orders or pick the proper mate. Your sister hasn't talked to Mother in years."

"What did she do?"

"I don't know. I don't ask and Suzy won't tell, all I know is that she was in therapy for years."

"I can understand that."

"When Dad flies to London he usually checks in with her."

"You mean when he not with *what's her name*."

"Denise. I've met her. I like her. She puts up with Dad."

"So it's true, he'll really kick me out?"

"He'll cut you off and Mother will undermine you every chance she gets."

"I don't care. I'm not going to let them run my life."

"Look, do what the old man says, for a while anyway. Go back to Davidson."

"No."

"Take the credit card he gave you, play the game, and after a few months you can do what you want with your life. Give them a little time."

****

"You're going back?"

Doc nodded; his feet dangling into the sound waters. "I've got to do what the old man says, at least for a semester. Davidson. I hate it there."

Lissa stroked his slumped shoulders.

"I talked with my brother, he says things will cool down if I just go back for a while."

"But you'll come on the weekends, right?" Lissa wrapped her arms around his neck and reached to kiss him.

Murdoch pulled her close. "Every weekend that I can." Burying his face in her hair, he sighed heavily.

His warm breath filtering through her hair, Lissa felt herself rouse. "I can't believe you're going back to Davidson."

"It's bad, I've been disowned - no car, took the jeep - hell, Mother won't talk to me at all. She hasn't said a word to me and Dad acts like I robbed a bank or something."

"Is that a bad thing, I mean, them not talking to you?" Lissa teased.

His lips drawing into a smirk, Doc released a *humph* and shook his head. "Well, not really, but it drives me crazy. I'll ask her to pass the peas at dinner and all she does is lift her head and give me this hateful stare, and I don't even get the peas." He chuckled lightly.

"Sounds like you're her whipping boy."

"Something like that." Caressing Lissa's check with his lips, Doc cupped her face. "It's bad, I've been disowned."

"Because of me?"

"Lissa, if it wasn't you, it would be someone or something else. Cal says they did the same thing to him when he got married."

"Married?"

Nodding, Doc looked longingly into her eyes. "Someday we're going to do that."

Her eyes burned, she hurt for Doc and wanted to ease that pain. "I love you."

"I'm not following their plan. You just happen to not be on their agenda, no woman is, it's just not in the plans they've made for my life."

"Geez, Doc. I'm sorry you have to go through this."

"Just something I've got to do."

"I'm here for you when you need me."

"I know." He turned to study his grandmother's house. "She's been watching us.'

"Pro or con?"

"No, Grammy's never liked Lorelei. She's tolerated her to keep the peace. When I woke up this morning Grammy had a big breakfast with waffles and eggs - could have fed an army. She told me she loved me, kissed me on the head. And then she told me that if I ever needed someone to talk to that she was here for me."

"Sounds like she knows."

"Yeah, she knows how Lorelei is. I must have been a kid, really young, but I remember Grammy and Dad arguing about Mother and something about Lorelei holding the purse strings. I knew what that meant, even then. We didn't come down here for a couple of years after that."

"Your mother sounds scary."

"You have no idea. Hmm." Closing his eyes, Doc kicked at the water. "There won't be any problem when I come down to visit. Grammy will be fine with us meeting here." Murdoch rose from the dock and stretched out his hand.

Lissa grasped it and stood beside him. "I like her."

"I promise I'll be back every couple of weeks, I'll call every couple of days." He pressed his lips on hers. "I'm going to miss the hell out of you."

"It'll work out."

"I'm not going to let them win. They're not going to run my life for me. That's for sure. I might even have to get a job at the new Food Lion."

"Bagboy?"

"May I carry your groceries out for you, ma'am?" He teased back.

"Oh geez Doc, what are you going to do?"

"I'm giving them what they want for now but I *will* be dropping out of med school. I've made my mind up about that."

"Still physical education?"

Doc nodded. "I love it. I love the idea of working with other people...kids." His eyes searching hers, he grinned broadly. "Our kids."

****

It was Tuesday and he would be calling. In fact, Lissa was surprised that Doc had not called the day before.

But she knew he was missing her, loving her and wanting her because that was what she was feeling, too.

Today Doc would call.

Curling her legs beside her in the oversized chair, Lissa glanced at the phone. She sighed, feeling the wave of emotion in her breast. The anticipation of his voice - telling her how he loved her - filled her with peace and all-consuming elation.

The day passed with no call.

Wednesday passed with no call, as did Thursday, Friday and the weekend.

There was no air to breath, no sight but his face, no feel or sound that did not remind her of Doc and she longed for the call, a word.

Every step, every noise, every move was made in expectation that he would be waiting to find her eyes and all they held in her heart. It hurt so much as she envisioned Murdoch unable to call her because surely he would if he could.

Lissa called Emile Soucek - no answer. She called again.

She drove to Grammy's cottage; there was no car in the driveway. Lissa drove by the little home again and again and again. On Sunday she stopped and walked out on the pier and gazed into the same water that Doc had, sat where they had sat nearly two weeks before. Had it been only two weeks? It seemed forever.

The tears would not stop as she envisioned him hurt or worse and unable to reach her.

By mid-September Lissa resigned herself to calling Davidson.

"I'm trying to reach Murdoch Soucek. He's a sophomore in pre-med."

"Hold please."

Several long minutes elapsed before the speaker returned.

"May I take a message?"

"Is he there?" Lissa asked.

"He's enrolled. Would you like to leave a message?"

"Tell him—" Her head was swimming, angry that he had not called her, anxious to her his voice. "Tell him that Lissa Roseman called."

"Is that all?"

"Yes."

"Miss Roseman, I will leave a message. Thank you for calling." The speaker hung up.

So he's there and he hasn't called me. Why hasn't he?

"Is he sick?" She spoke aloud. Anger rose in her. *How dare he do this? How dare he not call me? How dare he make me wait? How dare he play this game? Son of a bitch.*

Another day passed, she drove again by his grandmother's home, the car was there this time.

"Hello," Grammy Soucek answered the door, a slight smile across her lips, her eyes filled with regret.

"Have you heard from Murdoch?"

"Sweetie, I haven't heard from him since he left for college."

"Is he still at Davidson?"

The older woman was silent for a few moments. "As far as I know. I'm sorry, sweetie. You haven't heard from him?"

Lissa shook her head. "No." she bit her lip to quash the pain she felt rising in her chest.

"I'm sorry sweetie, but the last I heard he was at school. Grayson called though."

Her interest piqued, Lissa lifted her head to face the older woman.

"Grayson said they were going to England to visit Suzy and her family but I haven't heard from him since."

"Oh." *He's in England, that's why he hasn't called - but why?* Her head swam again with questions.

"Are you okay, Lissa, sweetie?"

"Yes ma'am. I'm okay. Thank you for telling me."

The older woman nodded her head. "You're welcome."

"If you see or hear from him, tell him I came by."

Grammy pressed her hand into Lissa's. "I will, sweetie. Again, I'm so sorry. If I knew how to get in touch with Murdoch, I would."

A brief smile crossed her lips as she turned toward her Jetta. *Why?*

It was all *whys.* Why had he not called? Why had he not told her he was going to England? Why hadn't he at least left word? A sense of overwhelming loss consumed Lissa as she reached for the car door and slid inside. She wanted to curl into a ball and weep away the pain.

The next day she knew he'd call. Maybe Grammy really did know where he was at and had called him. Maybe now that he knew she was so worried, he'd call. Maybe, maybe, maybe. At dusk she drove by Grammy's house again. She drove to his parent's house. If his car with there, it was in the garage but the place looked empty and as callus and forbidding as it had from its construction.

Two months passed, then three and still there was no call, no message, no letter, nothing from Doc.

How she longed, cried, believing he could not have wanted to hurt her, that there was some mysterious reason forcing him to stay away. No one abandons another, treats them as if they never existed, no one could be that cruel, certainly not Doc.

Always looking for a different outcome, Lissa continued to drive by his grandmother's cottage and by Doc's house. December came and the lights in Emily Soucek's home ceased to shine. Lissa wondered what had happened there. But how could she ever know. Nobody was talking with her, no one was communicating with her at all. She walked out onto the sound side dock where only a few months before Doc and she had fished and played in the water. Now it was so cold, so bare and lonely, like her. She ached and could not conceive of feeling otherwise.

Certainly the Doc she was in love with would have never treated her so heartlessly.

The Doc she knew - who was he? Why had he told her he loved her? Why had he opened himself to her? Now, all trace of him was gone; it was as if *they* had never existed.

"If he wanted to see you he would, Lissa." Her father leaned against the Jetta, his arms folded across his chest, a cigar protruding from the corner of his mouth. "If he wanted to talk to you, he would." Scowling, John Roseman, bit into the stogie. "Life's hard. This isn't the first time you're going to get hurt. You better get tough."

The words hurt. He could have hugged her, comforted her in some way. But her father had never been demonstrative with his feeling. He'd been stoic and proud.

"I'm sorry, Gal. I liked the fella. He seemed like a good sort. But you know where he comes from and people raised that way don't see things like the rest of us."

She hated him being right. Lissa nodded her head.

****

Lorelei scanned the letter she'd typed –

It's over. I've met someone else. Please do not bother
my grandmother again or try to call me.
It was fun.

Lorelei picked up the pen, studied her son's signature on a
recent form and signed it as near to his own as she could.

"White trash," she groaned. Lorelei licked the tab and sealed
the envelope.

Chapter 14

"I don't get the Jeep or the Jag, right?"

"Nope." Grayson held the steering wheel with one hand, the other rested on the console.

"So how am I supposed to get around while I'm at Davidson?"

"You're not."

"I get it. You think I'll sneak back to Topsail."

"You got it."

"You smug bastard."

"Call me what you want. I don't give a damn. I'm the one who holds these strings, smartass."

"Humph. You're not going to stop me, old man."

"I might not be able to stop you but I can *delay* the hell out of you."

His eyes scanning the scenery, Murdoch shook his head. "This isn't the way to Davidson."

"I thought we might take a little trip to see your sister in England." Grayson pulled a cigarette from his case and lit it.

Doc turned away.

"Banbury, such a quaint little town. Lots of peace and quiet there." Blowing a ring into the air, Grayson chuckled. "I thought it would be nice to visit Suzy."

"You mean Denise," Doc's voice cut sharply though the building tension.

"Wiseass, yes, I'm sure by now you understand your mother's and my *marriage*."

"So, why the urgency to get me back to Davidson, when we aren't even going there?"

"We have a few days before classes start. I'm just keeping an eye you, *son*."

Murdoch turned to watch the houses and yards pass by on the way to the airport. He imaged Lissa smiling in his head; the smile turning downward as she waited for the call that would not come. "Shit," he muttered.

****

"I'll be damned if you're going to keep me from calling Lissa." Doc jerked away from his father's grasp to walk briskly from disembarking.

Heathrow was not crowded, few people stood in his way as he scanned the airport for a phone booth. Reaching into his pocket for change he stepped into the nearest one and lifted the receiver.

"Damn." He counted the American coins. Quickly he calculated the rate of exchange. "Shit." Murdock slipped the coins back in his pocket and reached for his wallet to count the bills there.

"Forgot about the good old English pound, didn't you?" Grayson stood casually by the booth. "Son, if you can wait I'm sure your sister will let you use her phone when we get to her house."

His nostril flaring, Doc wanted to reach out and punch his father. He wanted to slap the shit eating grin off his face. "You've got me here now. As soon as I—"

"What? As soon as you get some money you'll be on the plane back? Is that what you think?"

Murdock strode beside his father, determined to find a way to contact Lissa.

"Okay, okay. You want to go back. I get it. Cool down. There's nothing you can do right now."

"You manipulative bastard, all you're doing is solidifying my determination to *not* do what you want. You've pulled the last string, old man."

His stride just as determined as his son's, Grayson led the way to the Aston Martin, turned the key and fastened his seat belt.

"You and Mother are real pieces of work, you know that? I've had it." Murdoch slammed the door.

"Hold on to your knickers boy, we'll be at Suzy's house in a little over an hour. Enjoy the ride." Grayson pressed the accelerator, and slid the gear shift into third, then fourth as he edged onto Motorway 25.

"It's nice here this time of year. Thought you—"

"Give me a break, you don't think of me or what I want. Save it. You've been dictating my life to me ever since I can remember. But that's ending."

"That's what I want to talk with you about."

Doc turned, studied the lines of his father's profile. "I don't trust you."

"You don't have much choice right now. You're under twenty-one."

"I don't have to be twenty-one. I'm over eighteen. And you don't get it. You're saddled with Herr Mother and you'll jump through hoops to keep her from getting her fair share of the assets even if it means screwing up my life."

Grayson pressed harder on the accelerator. "You don't understand."

"Yes I do. The dough, the cash cow—"

Chuckling, Grayson interjected, "Is that what you're calling your mother now?"

"You think it's funny. It's not, it's my life. But nothing has ever meant anything to you except money."

"It's nice to have around, son."

"Quit calling me that. I don't want to be your son."

His foot pressing harder on the accelerator, Grayson grinded his teeth, and holding the steering wheel firmly sped past the car in front of him, quickly turning onto the access to M-40.

"I've been trying to tell you, I'm going to talk with her. You finish this semester at Davidson, I promise I'll work with her, you can then transfer to Wilmington or wherever you want."

"Why are you telling me this now? Damn Dad, do you have any idea what kind of hell you are putting me through?"

He watched his father reach for the silver cigarette case. "Those damn things are going to kill you."

"We all have to die sometime," Grayson chuckled. "And I guess you're letting your pecker dictate where you go to school. I understand that. Why do you think I come to London so often?"

Rolling his eyes, Murdoch tensed as he watched his father speed past cars on the motorway.

"What's the matter, boy? You don't think your old man has it in him?" Grayson stepped harder on the accelerator as he reached for the lighter, he flicked his thumb across the spark wheel. "Shit, doesn't work." He flicked his thumb against it again and again.

"Damn lighter, cost a mint and it still doesn't work." Grayson tossed the lighter into the rear seat. "Where's my matches?" He patted his breast pocket and cursed as he took his eyes from the road.

****

Grayson, mangled in the twisted steel of the Aston Martin, was DOA. Doc, who'd forgotten to buckle up, was thrown from the car and landed against a railing. A deep gash ran from his forehead to the left cheekbone.

His eyes focused on the blurred face before him; Lissa's smile imaged. It was her, she was here now. Opening his mouth to speak, Doc felt the scratch and pain in his throat, only garbled words exited.

"Mr. Soucek?"

He blinked, focusing again on the image. Nodding, Doc released a sound, "Li—Li."

"Mr. Soucek? Murdoch?"

The face now was becoming clearer. It was not Lissa. Doc swallowed.

"Mr. Soucek. I am Doctor Jones. I'm glad to see you are with us now." The woman smiled and rested her hand on his shoulder.

Murdoch nodded again.

"It's been six days since you arrived. Are you aware of why you are here?"

Murdoch shook his head slowly, moved a hand to his face and winced. His fingers felt the bandage covering most of the left side of his face and the eye.

"That's right. You've been hurt. You were in a car accident."

"My father?"

"I'm sorry, Mr. Soucek. He died in the wreck."

Turning his face away, Murdoch's lips trembled.

"I'm sorry. We've contacted the rest of your family. Your sister and brother have both been in to see you, they should be back this afternoon. We are expecting your mother soon."

Yeah right. Murdoch closed his eyes to the thought of his mother appearing. It was the last thing he wanted. He didn't care how she felt, if she felt at all. He wanted Lissa. "I need to make a phone call," he whispered against the pain in his throat.

"We'll talk about that later. Right now you have to get your rest." The woman slid her hands into the pockets of the jacket she wore. "I can tell you more about your injuries if you like."

Murdoch's hand once again rose to the side of his face, his fingers tapped lightly the thick padding over his eye.

"Sorry. More than likely the sight in your left eye will be limited."

Chapter 15

Christmas was unbearable, every tinkle reminded her of his laughter, every twinkle his eyes. The chill in the air reminded her only of how warm he could have made her. The ocean, where God had always existed, didn't have the answers anymore. All she saw when she looked upon that expanse was the empty spot where Doc had been, where they had laughed and loved and were no more.

She was glad to see the tree thrown to the road, the street decorations taken down and the empty streets of the island return. They again were a reminder of how vacant was her life.

It had all been a lie, he was a lie, a liar, someone who used her and discarded her as if she were nothing. Didn't she even deserve one kind word, an explanation? To be abandoned so abruptly without explanation was harrowing. The realization oozed through her like molasses, covering her with the dim, dull pain of acceptance.

Doc was gone, gone away from her. The air was different now. Any peace, shards of it, had to be found at the shore. She walked alone, Charlie by her side against the cooling evening air. Tears had dried to her cheeks and the sound, the pounding of the waves shouted *he's gone, he's gone.*

Not far away Scotch Bonnet Fishing Pier stood; it was closed for the winter but today she heard laughter and music coming from the restaurant there. *Ah, New Year's,* she thought. *They must be having the New Year's party tonight.* She looked to the small crowd of people gathered at the Bonnet and she walked toward them.

The warmness cocooned her as she entered from the beach access and moved to a window side table. Now days she could not keep her eyes off the ocean, its rhythmic pull quelled her doubts and pain. It was always telling her something, *he's gone, move on, you love him, he loves you.* It seemed the reflection of her heart as it told the truth and made it palpable, letting the love she had known settle in her bones, and reassuring her that everything, though beyond her power; it was what gave her strength.

"Hi."

Lissa looked into the young man's face, she recognized it. "Hi Tom."

Settling a mixed drink before her, Tom grinned broadly. "Haven't seen you in a while, not since graduation. You doing okay?"

Lissa nodded, "Yep, fine as frog's fur." She slid her eyes away from him and wrapped her fingers around the drink.

She'd never been a drinker, never enjoyed the taste of alcohol but it seemed the polite thing to do since the drink had been brought to her and it was New Year's Eve. The party hats and decorations declared it, as did the loud music, laughter and couples dancing.

Tom asked her to dance, she said yes. He asked her to walk on the beach, Lissa leaned into him. His arms were strong and warm, his breath was warm too on her neck, his kisses soft as Doc's.

****

The mirror didn't lie, he was hideous. Stitches jutted from his face from above his left eyebrow to his jawline. What was left was bruised and swollen.

The doctor had told him he was lucky to have not lost his eye. There was however, a partial loss of vision.

His right arm had been broken in two places, along with a large gash in his right thigh. No muscle had been destroyed though. Yes, he had been lucky.

"I wish I was dead," Doc muttered. "How can this be?" Doc felt lost, like the last several months of his life had been a dream - a good dream with Lissa, a nightmare with his father and mother.

Lorelei had no sympathy. She'd entered his room in London and remarked on the tragedy of having to cart him away from

125

Topsail and how that had caused the series of events ending in her husband's death and his own disfigurement.

She noted the comparison with Frankenstein's monster. "I can't bear to look at you now, it's just too revolting." Lorelei left the room, her hands waving wildly, bellowing about making arrangements for a flight to Charleston and the best hospital there, how expensive it was and what a pity her son had not been more responsible in his life choices.

At this point, Murdoch would have rather stayed with his sister in Banbury and, to his surprise, Suzy convinced Lorelei to let her take care of him.

"You need to call her."

"It's been too long."

"It's never too long when you love someone."

"I'm hideous."

"You do look a fright, baby brother, but if she loves you it won't matter."

Variations of this conversation continued throughout the fall and into winter. Doc ached for the loss of Lissa, convincing himself that she would see him as the monster his mother described, that she would not want him, she would not be able to look at his disgusting features.

Thanksgiving passed, Christmas passed. His scars were healing, he was getting used to the limited vision in his eye and by January, with the help of his sister and her family, Murdoch had been persuaded to return to the states.

"She'll hate me for not calling or coming to her."

"That wasn't your fault."

"Not according to Mother."

"I'm sure by now, little brother, you understand that I did not even want to be on the same continent as that woman. The narcissistic bitch made my life a living hell."

"You have it nice here."

"Forget her, forget her money and make your own life Murdoch. She will make you feel guilty for breathing. Why she ever had children is beyond me."

****

Afraid, ashamed, fearful of rejection, Doc did not call Lissa before arriving at the airport in Wilmington. His heart racing, his brow beaded with sweat from anxiety and the mild sixty degree weather, Doc buckled the seatbelt inside the Avis rental. A flash of having not buckled the one in his father's car imaged in his head. It had probably saved his life. Over five months had passed since he'd driven, he felt nervous but determined as he slid into drive and motored northward on Highway 17 toward Topsail Island.

It was late in the day, the sky just turning pink from the afternoon sun as he crossed the swing bridge at Surf City.

Turning left at the light, Doc slowly drove in the direction of Lissa and John Roseman's home. No cars sat in the drive and the house looked lifeless.

He rounded to check out the parking lot at Barnacle Bill's fishing pier. It too stood empty but then it was February and the piers were closed for the winter season.

He drove past all the piers, Salty's, Scotch Bonnet, Ocean City, Jolly Roger and the others. Their lots were vacant as well. *Where could she be*? he thought.

Parking at the road next to the high rise bridge on the north end of the island Doc sat thinking, his car idling as he pictured Lissa. The apprehension he'd felt before was gone. Now, he did want to find her and frantically he searched his head for places she could be. He pulled out onto the highway and headed south.

He drove by Roseman's Boat Repair Shop. It was closed. Past Ward Realty and the IGA grocery store and the gift shop, he saw no familiar vehicles. Across the way a few cars were parked at Batts Grill; he and Lissa had been there a few times to get shrimp platters, they were always stacked high and tasty with fries and hushpuppies. *Lissa loved the hell out of those things.* Smiling to himself, Doc pulled into the lot and walked in. A couple of recognizable faces lifted theirs to peruse him. He felt self-conscious as he remembered the scar across his face.

"Tea," he nodded as the waitress asked for an order.

"Anything else?"

"Shrimp platter."

The waitress wrote down the order and turned to leave.

"Hey, have you seen the Rosemans around? John and Lissa?"

"I'm pretty sure she's still on her honeymoon. John - if he ain't home you might find him at the Mermaid Bar."

"Honeymoon?" his voice trembled.

"Yeah, Lissa married some kid she knew in high school. Surprised us all. But I guess when you're in love, you're in love."

Stunned, Doc sat quietly, the words replaying in his head. The pain washing across him.

"Here you go, honey. Ice tea. Would you like a straw?"

Shaking his head, Doc reached into his back pocket to withdraw the wallet. He flipped a twenty onto the table. "Keep the change." He walked out and drove away.

Chapter 16

She was half way through the latest Mark Helprin book, *Paris in the Present Tense*. She loved his writing, it was like baklava, so sweet and rich, Lissa savored every word.

Sighing heavily she closed the cover and wiggled her feet propped high on the railing of her back porch. Gazing out into the marsh she watched a lone red-winged black bird as it flew to the branch of a scrub oak and settled itself there.

His neck lifting, his throat pulsing, the bird released the delicate trill it was famous for. Oh, how she loved the sound it made and how she never tired of it.

The sun was hanging low in the blue sky, reddening the horizon into shades of mauve, indigo and orange.

Every evening, hell, every day, her view was a portrait. The sight filled her with optimism, always reminding her how good life was.

It had become especially good in the last few months - a man, a good man, had entered her life and for the first time in many years she found herself welcoming this new romance. Even if it did not work out, she was happy she had opened herself up to feeling once again.

Stretching as she rose, Lissa felt the cool nip of the mid-March afternoon play across her skin. She loved this time of year. She wanted to linger, to read a few more chapters, enjoy the day. But if she was going to be ready for Rick, she better shower and dress. By the location of the sun she was sure it was past six by now. Stepping from the porch into the kitchen, she glanced at the clock above the table. "Yep, six-twenty, better get busy."

He'd said seven-thirty but he was normally a few minutes early. She giggled as she thought of the tall good looking man in her life. Every day, every time he came around she wanted to pinch herself to make sure it was not a dream. *Why would such a hunk want me?* she'd thought numerous times.

Lissa striped the tank top and shorts from her body, unclasped her bra and threw the items on the bed as she passed on her way to the bathroom.

Shimmying out of her underwear, she tossed them across the room to the bed and stepped into the shower stall.

Lathering her hair, she ran her fingers through the strands, scrunching them, feeling the shampoo as it escaped her hair under the shower head. She opened her eyes, reached for the bar of soap and ran the wash cloth across her body. She wanted to be clean, to smell good for this man. She liked him. She liked him a lot.

How many dates had it been since her marriage - her failed fourteen year marriage - the one she leapt for after the young fisherman had dumped her that summer?

Oh, nineteen was way too young to be getting married and twenty certainly was too young to be having a child. But she'd done it and she'd tried to make it work.

After that it took years to even consider a serious relationship, she spent most of that time wondering why she had been such a failure at love and then too, trying to find the better parts of herself. Raising a child and having a full time job left little time for serious relationships. She'd discovered how strong she really was; she guarded herself and was not looking for someone else to save her or make her whole.

But with Rick she thought she was ready, this seemed right. Rick felt right. He was comfortable, real - there was certainly no pretense about him and he loved the ocean as she did. That was a prerequisite for any relationship.

She liked his old fashioned ways, opening doors for her, helping her carry heavy things. He kind of reminded her of her father in that sense.

Daddy, she grinned, he'd mellowed a bit through the years. He hugged her freely, told her he loved her. He learned, like most people, changed with experience and time, much of his stoicism replaced with compassion.

At sixty-five he was still handsome and tall. Women still flashed their eyes coquettishly at him. They had always flirted, made fools of themselves, all to get the charming John Roseman to give them an ounce of attention.

Years ago, when she lived at home, Lissa had heard him sneak in late nights not to wake her. She had wondered why he never slept over with any of his women friends. He'd never brought one home either.

But it changed when she married Tom. After that her father dated frequently and attained a reputation for being a ladies' man , that is until Linda. She'd played hard to get just enough to snare him.

Lissa was glad she had. She couldn't have picked out a better woman for her father. Linda and John complimented one another. He gritty and indifferent in ways and Linda pretty, strong and self-sufficient.

A glance in the steamed mirror and Lissa recalled the call from her father earlier in the day; he and Linda were going dancing at the Moose Lodge.

She liked seeing him happy. She liked the fact that this sassy woman, three years older than her father, had kept the roguish player following her around like a puppy. Linda had captured and cultivated a part of her father that exposed the kinder and softer parts of himself.

He and Linda were always doing something - taking in a movie in Wilmington, going to a concert somewhere, flying to Linda's home in New York. Once, she'd accompanied the couple there. She saw *Les Miserables*, visited Times Square and the Statue of Liberty and the 911 Memorial. It was enough for her and satisfied her curiosity enough to say that at least she had been to the big city. But she was glad to get home to Topsail Island and her little house in Surf City.

As for her father, Lissa had never seen him so alive and happy.

She glanced once again at the clock, she had thirty minutes to dry her hair and to dress.

Tossing her locks, Lissa giggled, she was glad she'd cut her hair. It now bobbed just beneath her ears. She liked the new cut, it felt young and free. Besides it sure was easier to tend to and would be cooler for the summer, the light curls blow- dried quickly.

She applied a touch of liner and mascara, slipped on the linen dress she'd bought at Surf City Gifts, the little shop next to the IGA, and studied the line of sandals against the closet wall. That was what would eat away at the minutes. She had to admit, she was a shoe-aholic. Her eyes slid from the pair of white sandals with the silver anchors, to the high spikey, strappy ones that tied at the ankle.

She and Rick had planned on driving to Wilmington to Thailian Hall for a concert and then to the Pilot House for a late dinner.

The straps, she thought. *If we were staying around the island we'd walk on the beach after dinner then the slip-ons would be fine.*

Sliding her feet into the shoes, Lissa rested on the bed and bent to buckle the straps around her ankles. She knew Rick liked the shoes and the sexy look. His eyes had told her so.

All the poster boys in the world couldn't hold a candle to him. He wasn't all jock, as she had first assumed, and he wasn't stuck on himself either. There wasn't a hint of arrogance about him, no swagger or pretense. He was the real thing. She thought of the first day they'd met. He strode into the boat shop and explained to her how the diesel engines in the sport fisherman he captained had blown fifty miles out in the Gulf Stream. Lissa was impressed with his demeanor - not condescending as some would be to a woman working in a man's field, or flirtatious, assuming because of his good looks he could influence her. He was technical, all business, accepted her knowledge, appreciated her help.

He came several times in the next two weeks, each time a little more at ease, a little more friendly. Finally he asked her to dinner.

Rising to check her image in the mirror, Lissa warmed to the thought of their first meeting. She smoothed the dress she wore and studied her legs. Rick loved them, and often spouted the ZZ Top tune, when she dressed up. *She's got legs*, he warbled.

Lissa smiled at the way Rick's compliments always made her feel. *Now if I just had a smaller ass and slimmer tummy,* Lissa thought patting herself as her eyes drifted to the photograph of her daughter Abigale, on the chest of drawers.

Abby was in her dress whites, the little hat on her head cocked slightly to the side. The epaulets of her uniform indicating she was a Lieutenant. Lissa was proud. At least someone was traveling the world, seeing all the places she wished she could have gone.

The knock at the door startled her, and she glanced quickly to the clock once again. It was seven twenty. She rolled her eyes. "He's always early," she sighed and giggled. "I guess it's better than being late."

"Hey beautiful, Rick greeted her, her pale green eyes looking upward to meet his.

"Hey shorty," Lissa teased as he bent to kiss her cheek. The height difference was nearly a foot, it could have been intimidating if she hadn't of come to learn that Rick was one of the kindest, gentlest and shyest men she'd ever met. What he lacked in self-confidence though, he made up for in height.

Gorgeous, she thought. Obviously he liked her look, that made Lissa feel good, sexy, wanted. But Rick could have had any woman he wanted. It baffled her that she was who he had chosen.

His broad shoulders tugged against his shirt, strands of his blond hair falling across his brow accented the bluest eyes she'd ever seen. Lissa looked into them and couldn't help but smile.

He bent to kiss her, his arm around her waist.

Holding her stance, Lissa returned the kiss. "You're always early." She smiled broadly.

"Can't wait to see you." He slid his eyes along her frame, they rested at her feet. "Love those shoes." Rick's eyes twinkled, he kissed Lissa's cheek. "You look stunning."

Threading her arm through his, Lissa thought of how few men complimented her. Her ex had never, and of the few men she'd been on dates with in the past several years only one had offered a compliment, if that was what you wanted to call it.

He'd invited her over for Thanksgiving dinner. *You clean up good*, he had commented as he proceeded to pour himself a drink.

That didn't last long. As she recalled, that Thanksgiving was the last time she had seen old what's his name.

"I was thinking," Rick started as he held the car door for Lissa.

"Be careful of that, thinking can get you in trouble," she chided.

"Ha. Funny already, huh?"

Lissa crinkled her nose and grinned.

"Anyway, I was thinking of taking a trip to Alaska." He slid into the driver's seat.

"Oh," Lissa paused. "You going fishing up there? How long will you be gone?"

"I'm not going fishing. I was thinking of us, you and me going together, staying a week in Seward at my parent's home. It's right on the ocean, cool little fishing town and it's absolutely beautiful this time of year."

She sat quietly for a few moments as they drove along. *So now it's getting a little more serious.* She felt her pulse quicken. One part of her feared the path she was being led down, another wanted it desperately.

"I've told Mom and Dad about you, sent them a picture."

She could tell Rick was a little nervous, it was in his voice and in the way he gripped the steering wheel. She smiled at him and scooted closer. She warmed at the thought of him wanting her to meet his family. It had been a long, long time since she had felt wanted, this wanted.

Reaching her hand to his face, Lissa stoked his cheek. "That sounds so nice. I've never been to Alaska. Daddy and Linda went a couple of years ago - said they loved it - went dog sledding and watched the whales. It sounds like such a beautiful place."

"It is. And as of now it has not been inundated with developers, at least not around Seward."

"Sounds great." She wriggled in the seat. "When we going?"

****

Chapter 17

"Throw the line, Honey." Rick stepped from the boat onto the dock and reached his hand to catch the line from Lissa. He loved that look on her face, the one of concentration where she pulled her lips in, furrowed her brow just a bit and squinted her eyes - then the release of all those tense muscles and her face relaxing into the slightest expression of satisfaction. That was the moment, the one that blew him away, caught him, the moment he'd seen that look, he knew he was a goner.

Lissa was indeed a sensuous and intense woman, Rick loved that about her. It seemed the most simple of exercises or activities brought her the most pleasure. Take bathing, just on a lark, one day he'd slid into the bathtub with her, grabbed her foot and began massaging. The pressure and stroking of her instep and pads of her feet was hypnotic for Lissa, she moaned as he pulled on her toes. Relaxing, trusting, it lulled her into consummate submission. She would have hung from the chandelier for Rick at that point. Maybe he had a foot fetish or maybe it was the last step before consummating their passion, regardless, she was happy for it all, from beginning in the tub to the final throws in bed. Their lovemaking had become an art.

It was comforting to Rick to know he could bring such pleasure to someone he loved, someone with whom he shared so much. And he had his doubts, as almost everyone does in new relationships, that it would last.

He was always walking that fine line, should he or shouldn't he - reach for the hand, give the compliment, hold the door - he just wasn't sure what women wanted anymore.

As a widower, he always garnered sympathy from women, even though, truth be told, he and Gloria had filed for divorce a week before the car accident that took her life.

He could have used the widower line to bed untold numbers. But he never felt comfortable about that. Unlike so many he shied away from getting too involved, wanting to at least be friends before he got intimate.

Some women were looking for a sugar daddy or someone to save them or just simply a man in their lives. He'd been through the screaming banshees and possessive types that showed themselves after a few weeks of dating. No, he didn't want that anymore. So he'd taken it slow with Lissa, studying her, feeling her out in situations. She was cool when some would have been stressed, she angered slowly, but when she did, it was over quickly, an apology for the few curse words that exited her lips summed it up.

Now and then she *was* compulsive, he liked that. And she was most definitely passionate about many of the things he was – reading, they traded books all the time, quoted passages to one another, read to one another. They both loved chocolate covered cherries. Pink Floyd was a religious experience between the two. They both loved fishing, it was a panacea for anything and everything.

Having been born and raised near the ocean, Rick had grown up fishing with his father. Sometimes they even ventured into the wilder country and fly fished Bear Lake. That type of fishing was an art and he relished it every time he got the chance.

On their trip to Alaska he'd taught Lissa to fly fish. She liked it, fell into it naturally as if she'd been doing it her whole life. As he watched her, studying the pensive look of purpose and exhilaration on her face, he fell even farther.

But it was the ocean, their shared love and respect for that surreptitious and sacred entity, that sealed their bond.

Some people visit the seaside and go back to their lives, dream about being near it again. But Lissa and Rick had become like the fish they caught, suffocated by the absence of water whenever they were not near the life source.

When Lissa had first mentioned that there was a philosophy of the ocean, Rick knew exactly what she was talking about. He'd held back his wonder and delight in finding someone so prolifically in tune with his own passions. He dare not let her know he could be putty in her hands.

Rick was in love and he knew it. He thought about her from the time he woke up until the time he laid his head on the pillow. Images of the way she crinkled her lips when she was pleased and the way she slid her eyes to him, the way her shoulder dipped when she laughed, played in his head constantly.

It was a wonderful week in Alaska. They did all the things a tourist does except without a tour guide. Lissa's experience there was a bit more off the beaten trail.

They watched the Grays and Humpbacks from the family fishing boat while Rick's brothers and father hauled in their catch. They hiked Exit Glacier on a trek by dogsled to his Uncle Sam's home near Bear Lake where they fished.

After dinner with his family they played monopoly or canasta. It all felt so good, so natural. It was obvious that his family adored her; he knew they would.

As the week progressed the nervousness between the couple, the dynamic between them and the Moran family, diminished and it seemed the relationship had moved to a new depth.

****

In a few days it would be Rick's birthday, Lissa wondered what would be suitable for her new boyfriend. Clothing? A nice leather wallet? A Shimano fishing reel? He had all those things. She wanted to give him something unusual, something unique, something he could keep forever.

Rick kept a penknife in his pocket, given to him by his old friend, Ortum. The knife obviously meant a lot to him, the friendship even more. That's what Lissa wanted to be to Rick, his best friend. She wanted to give him a gift that would mean as much, conjure as many memories as the scrimshaw penknife did for him.

She'd felt the tinge of pensiveness - the feeling that she could never be all, everything to a lover, a mate. It made her feel incomplete and at the same time ashamed because Lissa was well aware that no one could be everything to anybody.

That first love, with the boy from Pennsylvania, had left scars that were still healing along with the scars from her marriage. She'd held on to them, now it was time to let go and trust - release the urge to protect herself and the feeling that she was too vulnerable to do so.

The boy's image had faded with time, his image blurred to only reminiscences of windblown, sun bleached hair, and a smile that still brought one to her own lips. It was always a good memory until the pain of his departure slipped into her thoughts. Years had definitely diminished the hurt, time had left her with the knowledge that there are no definites in life.

It had made her hesitant to enter into relationships, but Rick, he had wiped away so much of what had been holding her back. She would take the chance, dare to love again, throw everything into the ring. She wanted to make him happy. This obsession with the past belonged in the past and she had to force those battle worn images away, live life for now and she needed to get over jealousies and things she had no control over.

Imaging Rick in her thoughts, she saw the crinkles of his smiling eyes, the upturn of his lips as he recalled one of the stories of he and his friend - the one about Ortum ready and waiting at the end of some race there had been between two teams of runners. Ortum had been waiting at the finish line with what looked like a big jug of iced tea. Rick reached for it, chugged it down only to spew it back - it was a mixture of cayenne pepper, Pepsi, and garlic juice.

If it had been her as the butt of that prank she would have slugged the guy but she understood the jokes, the closeness of friendship, she longed for that type of relationship.

"What to do, what to do?" Lissa spoke aloud. "A party, a birthday party?"

She walked against the breeze. Still thinking of a gift, a party, something to knock his socks off.

He was out fishing now, he and one of his regular crew were in the Gulf Stream trolling for big fish. She asked for grouper or mahi if he had the chance to drop a line. That would be nice for dinner. The freezer was getting low.

Her eyes studied the horizon as she looked toward where the Cloud Nine might be. The cool breeze felt nice on her face, not too cold, but with just enough chill to remind her that it was still early spring.

Ahead a few hundred yards was a small group of young people paddling out to past the breakers. She remembered well when she had been one of them. How many times had she been in the water in the past year? She could count them on one hand.

Maybe it's time to get back out there, she thought.

That had been a good time, when she surfed all summer, nearly all year - back when she was so free and came and went as she pleased. The water was God, the beach her church.

That feeling had never changed. She still felt the spiritual pull of the sea. She knew the power it afforded to her life, its honesty, its demand for self-awareness.

But raising a kid, going to college and working at the boat shop left little time for extracurricular activities. Her life had become purposeful, she'd become a responsible businesswoman. There was little time for surfing and after a few of years, Lissa had put her surfboard away.

"You're the boss now. Me, I'm a part-time employee." Three days after Abby left for the Navy, John Roseman placed the keys to Roseman Boat Works in her hand. "I'm retiring—at least semi-retiring. I've earned it. Linda and I want to travel.

Lissa wasn't surprised. In fact, she'd hinted that it was time for her father to let her take over. She understood the computer better, he was always getting confused and impatient. Now, her father worked two or three days a week and helped out when things got busy during the summer.

Lissa was both excited and overwhelmed, but mostly proud. She was running a business, it was rewarding to be in charge of something that made her the bottom line. Life was good, she knew she had a slice of paradise living on Topsail Island. And long ago she'd accepted the fact that perhaps she had been idealistic in her youth. And now there was Rick.

He had conjured an awakening in her, a part of her she thought would never be again. Rick had erased the feelings of loss and it felt so good. She was rolling with it. No, she couldn't complain about a thing.

Lissa turned toward the surfers, she could hear their banter, joking and laughing. Man, how she wished she was one of them. She wanted to feel the water, feel the rush and today the waves looked just perfect for surfing. She thought for a moment about scurrying back to her house and digging the surfboard out of the garage. *No,* she thought.

She was in the moment, the water on her feet felt cool and so welcoming as she walked along the shore. She wanted the rush of water now. The thought made her smile, she felt light and happy.

Lissa inched a few feet farther to where the water came over her ankles. "Ah, damn. I wish I could jump in right now. It feels so good, so great!" She almost skipped in delight as the water pulled her.

Beneath her snug t-shirt Lissa wore a pink jogging bra. She'd worn a pair of jogging capris as well. "Could pass for a wet suit," she whispered to herself.

Part of her said no, that she should simply enjoy the walk, the cool water on her feet, and the spring sun beating down on her. The other part wanted to dive into the water, catch a wave and body surf to shore.

Studying the water and the way the sun glistened off the waves, the low tide and the white and frothy edges of the water compelled her even more to succumb to her urges and become part of what owned her.

It had been a long time since Lissa had body surfed, ages it seemed. But today it all felt right; she was drawn to feeling the water encompassing her. Closing her eyes, Lissa drank in the sun beating on her skin, smoothed the t-shirt, took a deep breath and raced into the waves.

The coolness was somewhat shocking but it felt good. God, it felt so good! She laughed aloud, "This is what I need, just to feel good!" She dove into an oncoming wave and stroked to past the breakers, then leaned back into the water.

Tilting her head back, Lissa relaxed into the lazy swells and closed her eyes against the thin wash of sea water covering her face. She grinned, lying still, buoyant in the ever moving sea, the warmth of the sun resting on her tanned skin, giggling as the ocean water tickled her ears. Her cradled body waited to rise higher with a swell suitable for surfing.

Relinquishing herself to the tidal movement, she concentrated on keeping afloat, resisting the urge to tread water and watch the sea, encouraging herself to be patient. It was a game, one to bide the seconds or minutes until she felt the rise of the perfect swell.

And there it was. Quickly she flipped, stretching her arms forward, swimming, hoping to catch the crest of the oncoming wave. She felt the rush, pushing her forward, the sting of salt water against her face. Eyes closed, maneuvering her body to tautness and fluidity with what carried her forward.

Adrenaline pumping, Lissa flew with the water, then from nowhere came the bump and instantaneous exploding pain, whatever it was shook her hard before letting go.

The pain was beyond belief, her mind raced around it, fought against it. Had she slammed into something under the water, perhaps a piling from one of the old fishing piers? The shock of it all left her confused, disoriented and she struggled to swim.

Lissa knew she was in shock as she glimpsed toward her leg and the cloud of red sea water around her. Her eyes stinging from the salt water, all she could think of was getting to shore.

She heard the voices, watched them reach to pull her from the water. She remembered looking into the faces of two young surfers and hearing them mumble words. That was the last thing before she awoke in the hospital.

Chapter 18

"Miss Roseman, can you hear me?" the doctor asked as he leaned a bit closer. "Look this way, to me."

Lissa tried to focus on the man standing next to her. He smiled gently.

"You're a lucky woman. If those two boys hadn't of been there to pull you from the water, if they hadn't of applied a tourniquet, I wouldn't be here talking to you."

Clearing her mind, trying to clear her mind, Lissa watched the doctor's lips move. She acknowledged his words, letting them and the events seep into her. Yes, she'd been bit by a shark, a bull shark, so the doctor explained. *But she'd seen no fin, there was no warning,* she thought as he continued.

"Your lower leg, the calf, was shredded nearly - a large portion of muscle was taken," the doctor explained. "Your Achilles tendon was torn on both ends."

The words bit into her, she could only imagine the damage. Everything the doctor said sounded so unreal, Lissa felt herself breathing rapidly, the doctor settled a hand on her shoulder.

"We gave you a plasma transfusion. You're lucky to be here." He reached for her hand, "Young lady, you are very lucky you did not bleed to death."

She closed her eyes, picturing how inviting the water had been that morning. Lissa shook her head. *It was just so damn pretty. Everything was as I wished it would be. I was thinking of Rick, his birthday,* the thought pained her. *What a shitty birthday present this is.* She bit her lip, "If I'd had my board, maybe…"

"Don't start with what ifs. There's nothing you can do about that. Fortunately, the shark let you go."

Her eyes filling with tears, Lissa swallowed, "My leg is all there?"

The doctor lifted a shoulder. "Your leg, Lissa, is fine from the knee up. It's the calf area, your ankle."

Lissa could hear the regret in Dr. Morrison's voice. She knew it wasn't good news he was trying to tell her.

"You have a decision to make. And you don't have very long, maybe a couple of days to decide whether or not you want to keep your leg or—"

Her eyes widened, she felt the lump in her throat and the tears streaming down her face. "Amputate?" She felt the downward pull of her lips as she struggled to retain her composure.

"Yes. Below the knee. You've had significant soft tissue and arterial damage. There has been severe nerve damage. Right now the blood flow to the remainder of your leg is questionable. If you keep the leg there will more than likely be ongoing problems."

Lissa's face scrunched into a scowl, her brow furrowed deeply. "What do you mean?"

"Without the muscles and an Achilles tendon you can't achieve movement." Dr. Morrison demonstrated with his wrist and hand, flipping it up and down, pushing against the bed. "You have no joint to speak of, no muscles or tendons to move the foot forward or adjust as you walk. So much has been torn away, damaged. The leg simply won't heal well, it will be relatively useless and at some point in time you may have to amputate it anyway."

"And if—"

"If we take the lower leg, leaving the knee, we can fit you with prosthesis. After therapy there will be a quicker return to functional activities."

Imagining a hard plastic apparatus, Lissa bit into her bottom lip, she imaged the blades of the young Olympian from South Africa—she saw herself, a long thin running blade attached to her leg. She tensed her jaw, reinforcing her resolve to keep calm and shook her head. "No." Her eyes blazed into Dr. Morrison's.

"I—I can't do it. I can't lose my leg."

"I want you to think about it, Lissa. Talk with your family about it."

Her family, they must be devastated. They would be so disappointed, ashamed, she thought. "Rick," her lips mouthed the word almost silently. She couldn't bear the thought of his disappointment, of his hurt.

Doctor Morrison nodded. "Your family is in the waiting room. They'll be in shortly. Talk with them. I know they will support you and be there to help you, Lissa."

She watched the doctor leave the room, it felt so empty, so unforgiving. In moments, she knew her family would enter - and Rick. She dreaded the look in his eyes.

Chapter 19

Her father fought to keep his stoic equanimity, though Lissa noticed the quiver of his lips and the redness of his eyes as he, Linda, Rick and Abby entered the room. Her father's words, "Fucking shark, I'll kill the bastard," brought a smile to her face. She pictured her father, momentarily, striking out into the ocean, like Ahab hunting his white whale.

"Momma," Abby, still in her uniform, cradled her mother's head next to her own. "Momma, I'm so sorry this happened to you."

It had been nearly a year since she'd seen her daughter and though they spoke often on the phone, the sight of Abby and how she held herself, exuding the feeling of control and self-confidence filled Lissa with pride.

Abby stepped back from the bed. "I've got two weeks leave. I'm here."

"I know, baby." She smiled at her daughter then looked to her father.

When John bent to kiss her forehead Lissa felt the damp stubble of his day old beard. He rubbed his face with his large hands, "Sorry Gal, I should have shaved."

Linda reached for his hand when his voice first cracked, she squeezed it hard as she spoke to Lissa, "Sweetie, anything you need, anything at all. We've decided we're taking care of you. Your place or ours, it doesn't matter which."

Rick had been standing near the foot of Lissa's bed, his head bent low. Raising it, she saw the look. Was it remorse, disgust? She wasn't sure but he stood alone, perhaps being respectful of the precedence of immediate family.

Lissa looked to him, she saw the pain in his eyes and tracks of tears on his cheeks. It was obvious he'd come directly from his fishing boat to the hospital. He had a full two days growth on his face, his cheeks and nose were sunburned, his blond hair was wild and stuck up as if he'd run fingers through it instead of a comb. Lissa breathed in the faint aroma of sea and fish, she chuckled lightly as her eyes met his.

John and Linda moved aside to let the man stand near her.

"Happy Birthday," the words stumbled from her lips.

Puzzled, Rick looked toward her leg then back to Lissa.

"I was going to have such a great birthday party for you." She shook her head. "Sorry. I'm so sorry." She looked to her father and Linda. "The doctor says I should have my leg amputated."

His lips parted in disbelief, "No." He shook his head and backed away. Gathering his composure, Rick reached for her hand.

John nodded, "We talked with him. We agree. But Gal, this is ultimately your decision."

The somber discussion with her family was short, all recognizing that this wound was not going to heal on its own. Her leg was destroyed. She was maimed, she would have to live with that and in time accept it.

The process of acceptance was sickening, then demoralizing. The discussion seemed so clinical so unfeeling, so surreal.

Lissa sobbed as Rick and her family left the room. She would never be whole, she would never be like the others. It occurred to Lissa that though she had often felt as if she were different, the thing making her truly that way now was not a frame of mind but a physical flaw.

At that thought Lissa shook her head as images of herself running, surfing, jumping into waves or onto the boat raced through her head. The comprehension was overwhelming. She would never do those things again.

Things as simple as tiptoeing, pushing off on a surfboard, dancing, kicking the wall when she got mad. She would never do those things again either.

Feeling the tightness again in her throat, the well of tears at her eyes, Lissa willed herself to stop. Her lips drawn tightly, she cursed beneath her breath, her fists beat the bed. *Have your fit,* she heard her father's words — the ones he'd spoken to her as a little girl when she couldn't have her way.

Have your fit. Get it over with. Then do what you have to do.

The decision to amputate her lower leg was certainly not an easy one. Lissa would have preferred to have never needed to consider it at all. It took a while for all the events, the changes and loss to sink in and as dreamlike as the truth was, it was the truth - her lower leg would have to be amputated. She would be handicapped for the rest of her life. There would be things she would never again be able to do.

****

Three days after the operation, Lissa was home, her home. She'd chosen to stay there rather than her father's house. Abby was there, donning a pair of Bermuda shorts and a tank top. She reminded Lissa of the daughter who once lived at home with her. Only this one was all grown up.

Until her flight back to Spain, Abby stayed with Lissa, cooked her meals, bathed her, washed her hair. As they had before, they talked politics and religion. Albeit this time, Lissa recognized that her daughter was more restrained, more knowledgeable and less filled with righteous indignation.

"I've seen the world, Momma. It gave me a different perspective."

"Any boyfriends?"

"There's more to life than men." Abby rolled her eyes. "But yes, there is one. When you feel better I'll bring him by. You'll like him."

"Name?"

"Jack."

"Jack?"

"Jackson Ian Stewart Smythe." Abby blushed. "He's from England."

Lissa smiled, she nodded, "You're happy. I can tell it. You've got the twinkle in your eye - you're in love."

Abby's smile broadened. "Oh gosh, Momma. He is such a good man. I met him at Cadiz, that's a small city in between Rota, where I'm stationed, and Gibraltar where his base is. We both were at the beach."

Watching her daughter's eyes light up, hearing the enthusiasm in her voice, she felt giddy, too. "My little girl's in love." She held her arms out for a hug. "Don't let anything or anyone keep you from being happy."

Abby stayed through the first week of the home health physical therapy visits and then was on her way back to Spain. Lissa felt good knowing her daughter had found herself and along the way found someone who loved her. It warmed Lissa to know her daughter was doing well in life.

Rick spent several nights after Abby left, sleeping on the daybed in the sunroom. She was confused about him now, wondering if the look in his eyes was pity or something else. She hadn't spoken to him much with all the family around so often. But she could feel herself pulling away from him, wondering what he must truly think of her now.

Linda stayed for a few days, spending nights. John came over during those days. Lissa could see the pain in her father's eyes and she suspected that her injury was even more devastating to him than to herself.

"Girl, that man waits on you hand and foot. Rick has taken such a load off your father. He helps out at the shop. He's been taking your father out on his boat. Rick's been a gem, Lissa," Linda said.

"Your daddy was so worried about you, honey. But after the way Rick has stepped up to the plate, he's calmed down - it's eased his mind." She settled a glass of iced tea on the end table and sat next to Lissa on the couch. "Rick's a good man, a keeper."

"I know, I want for nothing," Lissa smiled. "But sometimes he seems a little squeamish around my stump, he always turns away when I have to tend to it."

"It will take him some time. But he'll get used to how things are."

"I hope you're right."

"He's there for you all the time though, isn't he?"

"Yes, *all* the time. Sometimes I wish he would give me a few minutes to myself. He needs to get back out there, back in the ocean, back to work."

"He's concerned."

"Feels sorry, there's a difference and I can't stand someone feeling sorry for me."

"Especially yourself?" Linda slid her eyes knowingly to Lissa.

"Look, I'm not as helpless as you think." Pulling herself up to rest against the pillows, Lissa pulled the sheet back to expose the stump of her leg. "It's healing well. It won't be much longer and they'll fit me for prosthesis. I'll be able to get around just fine then."

Linda nodded, "It looks good - you look good. Especially after all you've been through."

"Um." Lissa's eyes shifted away from Linda's.

"Rick dotes on you. Enjoy it. It doesn't last forever. And by the way, when are you two going to tie the knot?"

Shrugging, Lissa pulled the sheet back over her leg. "I don't know, maybe Rick doesn't want—"

"Don't think that way. He's in love with you - *you.* Not the lower half of your leg. I doubt that it matters to him at all."

"I don't want anyone feeling sorry for me, Linda. And I see the pity in his eyes."

"That's not pity, that's concern. He's worried about you, how this is going to affect you. Now, quit fiddle-farting around and feeling sorry for yourself. Let the man love you. I know he wants to marry you." Linda leaned in closer. "I can tell."

A faint smile returning to her face, Lissa responded, "I've thought about marrying him. He's asked me before - before I lost my leg. But my last marriage was a flop. Maybe we both just need some time now, to think about things, to make sure. I'm not the same person anymore." Lissa lifted her chin in defiance. "I just don't know anymore."

"Scared?"

"Yep,"

"I know what you mean. With your father—"

"Do I want to hear this?" Lissa tittered.

"Nothing graphic, sweetie. I promise."

"Okay."

"With your father I felt the same way. I wasn't sure if I ever wanted to get married again - ever. And then it seems that marriage is old fashioned, passé, people are simply living together these days."

"I know - nothing wrong with that is there?"

"I guess not. But marriage asks for a commitment, a real one with consequences. I argued with your daddy for months about how if we loved each other we didn't need that piece of paper."

162

"Arguing with Daddy is futile. If he wants something he usually gets it."

"Well, John was very persuasive and I guess we married more for him than for me. He wanted to make the commitment and so many men do not, Lissa. Men are different, they know they're roamers, I guess the word fits them. Anyway, they know they can be persuaded to roam, so when they want a commitment, it's because they want that extra incentive - and Rick wants you."

Lissa nodded her head. "When you put it that way, it makes sense."

"The big question is do you love him?"

Her eyes meeting Linda's, Lissa quickly answered, "Oh yes, I do love Rick. Who wouldn't? He's one of the nicest people I know. He's giving, compassionate, patient, and thoughtful."

"Are you *in* love with him?"

Lissa raised a shoulder. "I thought I was. For so long I wanted to feel that tingle, the excitement, the yearning. I thought it was the real thing with Rick. But now? I'm not sure. She sighed, "Sometimes - sometimes I feel that tug, he makes me happy, makes me want to be happy and I know I miss him when he comes in late from fishing or if he has to go out of town. But then sometimes I don't."

"I see."

"What do you mean, you see?"

"You don't feel the fire?"

"I don't know anymore." She searched Linda's face. "Rick is safe, he loves me. I love him. He's a good man and would never hurt me. What more could I ask for? Right? "

"You need to be sure. Right now I think you have more doubts about yourself than Rick. I think he will be there for you through thick and thin as long as you don't push him away."

Lissa nodded. "I know."

"Don't do that, Lissa. It would be a mistake."

Lissa nodded. Linda was right but now everything seemed askew, uncertain. It would take time. "It's weird, Linda, everything has been jerked from beneath me. It's going to take time for me to get back to the way things were - if they can ever be the same. I'm just not sure, maybe the old me is gone. I wish you could crawl inside my head and see what I'm going through."

Linda leaned into Lissa and squeezed her arm. "Sugar, that's what you need to tell Rick, the man wants to be there for you."

Chapter 20

"I think we're ready for a prosthetic limb, Lissa." Doctor Morrison smiled over his glasses. "You realize this will only be a temporary one. The residual is still swelled quite a bit, it may take a while for that to happen, so expect several adjustments along the way.

"I'm going to refer you to an Orthoptist, Dr. Steinman. He's very good and I think you will like him. He'll be able to help you more. You know, there are so many new apparatus out there, new things happening all the time. And then your home health nurse will help a lot, too." He leaned closer to Lissa. "Listen to her. Do what she says. Okay, young lady?"

Lissa nodded and smiled, anxious to move forward, eager to get her life back to as normal as possible. "Thank you, Doctor."

Linda pulled the wheel chair to the examination table and helped Lissa transfer.

"Thanks," Lissa glanced a grateful thank you to her step-mother. She had been such a help, but it was tiresome thanking everyone so often and Lissa longed to be able to be self-sufficient.

Home health physical therapy was helping with the adjustment to wearing a prosthetic but sometimes it was nerve racking trying to get things just so. It wasn't as easy as the videos showed.

"Apply the ointment." Nancy motioned toward a tube on the nightstand next to Lissa's bed. She stood, arms folded across her chest.

"I did that last time."

"You have to get it on their good, honey - now roll the liner onto the residual." She nodded watching Lissa follow instruction. "Now, roll on the prosthetic sock, now place your stump in the socket, um hum, that's right."

"It feels loose."

Nancy nodded. "Okay, but go ahead and roll the sleeve up - that will create a seal."

Lissa's eyes lit up, "Oh, now I get it."

"The light bulb went on?" Nancy laughed.

"It's not as easy as it looks."

"It will be second nature to you before long." Bending to bring the vacuum pump closer to Lissa, she continued. "Now all you have to do is remove the air from the socket and it should be snug."

"What if it's not?"

"Then you add another sock, or if it doesn't fit at all then you'll have to get fitted for another one."

"Thanks," Lissa said the word again. She was thankful. Thankful for people who were there for her, thankful that these people didn't mind that she was clumsy and impatient.

"Every day or so you're going to notice a bit less swelling so you'll have to add another sock - and it will be sensitive at first, but you'll get the hang of it."

"Thanks," Lissa was so tired of saying thanks.

"I get paid to do this, sweetie."

"Not enough."

She had assumed the balancing would come easily once she started wearing the prosthetic, after all, she'd been a surfer most of her life and that's what surfing was all about. She thought she'd have an edge but boy was she mistaken - the weight distribution was different. Her body weight shifted differently, it felt odd and unfamiliar as she practiced walking with the first of her prosthetic limbs.

It was maddening.

"Remember, the doctor said it would take time to find the right one and the right fit. Things are always going to be changing, get used to it," Nancy admonished.

Getting in and out of bed, out of the tub or shower and learning to navigate from room to room were tasks in themselves. Then there was the matter of reinforcing safety around the home - like removing scatter rugs and the positioning of furniture.

Nancy was patient and caring and for the life of her Lissa could not fathom how someone could put up with her outbursts of frustration, the cursing and yelling. Once she threw a cola bottle across the room.

Nancy took it all in stride, moved aside when necessary and sighed as Lissa worked through the failures. "I've seen it all before," she uttered once when Lissa apologized. "It's normal, try to channel your frustration into other areas."

Yeah, sure, Lissa thought. *Easy for someone with both legs to say.* The frustration of being unable to maneuver the most simple of functions, trying to balance her body in a new way without tumbling over was exasperating but there was never a time when Lissa wanted to give up. She worked hard, feeling her body again, getting used to a different sense of self and reminding herself that though there may be the sensation of a leg below her left knee, there was none at all.

"Proprioception."

"Speak English, Nancy."

"I am, butthead. Proprioception is where you feel the sensation, the reaction to things in the knee, in your case, rather than a foot or ankle, which you don't have anymore."

"Proprioception," Lissa said the word slowly.

"That's right, put your head there. Get used to the sensation *there*."

∗∗∗∗∗∗∗∗∗∗∗

Lissa drummed her fingers on the side table as she waited for Linda to arrive. Nervous about driving once again, she bit at her nails. "Why?" she questioned aloud but Linda had reassured her driving was part of getting back to normal.

Pulling the curtain back she scanned her driveway for Linda's car then sighed impatiently. "Where is she?" Lissa growled.

Lifting her head to the sound of a car, Lissa rose and limped to the doorway. She forced a smile, endeavoring to hide her frustration.

"So are you ready to see if you can drive now?"

Lissa turned her head sharply, surprised that Linda had mentioned the very thing she'd been wanting to do and assumed would not be allowed to.

"Yes," she snapped eagerly.

Linda stepped from the car, Lissa slid her body into the driver's seat. She had not driven since the attack, it felt odd behind the wheel.

"You know what to do." Linda grinned.

Turning the key, Lissa felt the engine rev. She slid the lever into reverse and lightly stepped on the accelerator, then moved her foot to the brake before moving the car into drive.

"Piece of cake. I don't even need my left foot."

"Well, just drive down to the south end of the island."

"Okay." Lissa drove silently, concentrating, vacillating between feeling good about her progress and self-doubt.

"I'm thirsty, let's stop at Godwin's and get a Pepsi." Lissa pulled into the parking lot of the grocery store and slid the car into park. She opened the door and quickly maneuvered her leg to the pavement.

Then everything fell out from beneath her. She had not adjusted to the weight, her balance was off. She felt the cup of the prosthesis dig into the sides of the stump and felt herself fall downward as she grasped the door handle. Holding tightly to it, she kept herself from hitting the hard pavement. Her knee twisted and she felt the pain as it radiated into her thigh and hip.

"Shit!" Lissa blurted loudly and turned to Linda rushing toward her. "No, I'll do this myself. I can pull myself back into the car."

"Are you hurt?"

"My knee hurts like hell. This damn contraption is worthless, it needs refitted, I need—" Lissa's face twisted in anger.

"Maybe it's too early to be—"

"Ya think?" Lissa snarled then caught her breath. "Sorry. I'm sorry Linda for being such a bitch."

"You have the right."

"No I don't. This is my problem, not yours and I need to learn to live with it and live with it I will. It's just going to take a little longer than I thought."

****

It was the pain that had made her wince, made her pull back, hesitate as she placed her foot on the pavement. The pain had caused the reaction. She would have to learn to control her pain, get used to it - at least for a while - and learn to react differently, more consciously.

As the doctor had explained, her wound was still healing, changing. It would take some time before the swelling went completely down. It would take some time to find the right cup to fit the remaining leg. It was like a pair of shoes, some gave you blisters, and others did not.

Her confidence diminishing to little or nothing, Lissa concentrated nervously on how she looked. She fidgeted with her hair, her clothing and looked in the visor mirror, winced at the tired image staring back at her.

The future seemed uncertain and full of disappointment. How could Rick want her now? There was no way she could compete with the svelte women who she knew were drawn to him.

She was convinced that his motivations were disingenuous, and that the attention he gave to her stemmed from pity and she hated that. Mistaking his displays of concern for pity, Lissa found herself pushing him away even farther.

This last thing, having to be driven to the physical therapists after feeling she'd progressed so much proved that it was useless.

"Quit feeling sorry for yourself." Linda jabbed her in the shoulder. "I know what's going on in your head. One little slip, one fall and you're ready to exile yourself to living the life of Quasimodo. *Po' wittle Wissa,*" she pursed her lips, pouting the words. "Snap out of it, po' widdle Wissa."

Rolling her eyes, Lissa blushed. "Sorry. I do that, you know, have these little pity parties when I fail at something."

"I've been married four times, how do you think I feel? And I did that to myself, it's not as if one of my husband's bit my leg off," she guffawed. "If anybody is a failure then it's me." Linda skimmed a sarcastic glance Lissa's way. "Now straighten up and fly right, as my father would say. Put on your big girl panties and grow a pair."

Lissa laughed, "Ugh, the image! Couldn't you come up with a better metaphor than that?"

Chapter 21

It was not such a long drive to Cary from Topsail Island but she dreaded it just the same after the failed attempt at driving. Though grateful for Linda's help, Lissa felt uncomfortable with the situation. She was tired of saying thank you and please and relying on others. It was beyond frustrating to have to depend on someone else for your very existence.

She sighed and glimpsed Linda's profile as she drove. It would be a tedious, if not tense, journey to Cary. Lissa had never liked Linda's driving.

Linda had lived in the South for over thirty years. Her original home had been Long Island. The once thick northern accent was now punctuated with endearments like sweetie, honey, sugar; her vowels had become longer leaving her to drawl words and phrases like *you guys*.

Linda, she had become one of *them* - a little more laid back, less judgmental, less convinced that the northern way was the only way to do things. Yes, she fit in just nicely. But the driving, well, Linda stayed in the right lane, carried on a conversation, fiddled with the radio, tailgated and drove over the speed limit. These things alone belied her city roots.

"Nervous?" Linda teased.

Lissa shrugged.

"I know you'd rather be driving, and I know my driving makes you nervous. But if *you* were driving, we wouldn't get there until sometime tomorrow," Linda tittered. "I've only had one accident and that was when some asshole slammed on brakes in front of me and that was seven years ago. It was not my fault."

Now, struggling to relax, Lissa wondered if she'd made the right decision to go all the way to Cary for physical therapy, certainly there were adequate PTs in Wilmington. And the drive would be shorter but she'd chosen a therapist in the middle of the state because Dr. Morrison had insisted that Southeast Therapy Center in Cary was the best there was.

Gripping the edge of the seat and pressing on an imaginary brake pedal did keep her mind off the impending doctor's appointment. Forcing herself to listen to Linda's banter, the earnest conversation about politics on Topsail, was interesting and informative. And right now Lissa didn't give a damn about it.

It had been years since she'd cared about the progress, the encroaching development. Lissa had lost interest in the local bullshit, resigned to the fact that once the council, DOT and whomever else was in power, made up their minds to do something there was nothing anyone could do.

Linda, however, was up on the latest. Voice inflection and volume finally caught Lissa's attention as she listened more, she found herself nodding and feeling the old stirrings of righteous indignation.

"It just makes no sense," Linda started vehemently. "Topsail is not an island, it is a big sandbar. So how in the hell can the state allow developers to build on a piece of land that is bound to shift and change by its very nature?"

"It's—" Lissa began.

"I'll tell you why. It's the same reason that people are coming here and destroying the wetlands. I thought it was against the law - that legislation had been passed to protect wetlands, but *no, those laws* don't mean a single thing if a company or individual has enough money. In fact, if you have enough money the laws don't mean a thing."

"It's not just the money, it's who you know and who has the power," Lissa added fervently.

"I'm getting tired of seeing - well, hell - the dunes are gone. If I see another bulldozer and —"

The scene imaged in her mind - the youthful version of chaining herself to a bulldozer decades ago. She found herself nodding, agreeing and recalling those feelings of distrust and anger.

Maybe, after her leg healed, she might look into some of the things going on around the island.

"We're here!" Linda shouted. "All in one piece, no dents, no tickets. Sorry if my driving scared you."

175

Lissa crinkled her nose. "No, it wasn't too bad. In fact, I enjoyed the conversation. I never realized, Linda, how passionately you felt about the island."

"I think I'm a day late and a dollar short, sweetie. The progress has metastasized." She raised an eyebrow and reached for Lissa's arm. "Come on now, let's get you inside."

The women settled themselves in the lobby. Linda instantly picked up a boating magazine. Lissa leaned back against the seat waiting, perusing the certificates and photos hanging on the walls. She felt the stiffness in her leg, the irritation of the prosthetic against her skin. She truly hoped this therapist could offer something new.

In the waiting room two other patients sat. One held an *Us* magazine in her hands and she seemed rapt in whatever it was she was reading. Another patient, a man, sat uncomfortably in the corner. He eyed Lissa, his gaze following to her amputated leg. For a moment, his eyes met hers then quickly glanced away. Had she seen disgust in them?

She'd become aware of the adjustment that would come with her new disability. It was almost like having to learn to walk all over again, at least a different way. But there were other adjustments that would have to be made, things she would have to get used to. The man and his reaction were proof of that.

Her leg or lack of one would be a topic of discussion and ridicule in some cases. It would definitely set her apart - make her different - but then she'd always felt a little different. Now, with a deformed limb the difference was visual. Now, it could be pointed at and need explanation. Now, she truly was different.

What was it, that sense of survival her father was always talking about? *Some people revel in their misfortunes others use them to make themselves stronger.* Right now it rang so true.

Regardless, Lissa accepted who she was and had grown to like that imperfect person. Now she liked her anonymity. And she liked the fact that she was moving ahead and was not going to let her disability be a liability. She was even getting used to the pity parties she gave herself now and then - an acknowledgment that they were slowly diminishing made her feel even better about herself.

Lissa was most certainly her own person, not many influenced her in her beliefs or decisions. Hers was a new awareness and she knew it would take time to adjust to this handicap.

She hated that word, handicap. She didn't feel that way. She wasn't in a wheelchair or on life support; certainly she was not like some she had seen.

Shrugging with the thought, Lissa was sure she could handle any negativity that came her way. *I can do this, I can do this.* She'd been telling herself that since the attack. Reinforcing the thought she said it again, whispering it this time, "I can do this, I can do this." Trembling, she endeavored to muster the courage to face the changes. There were changes and there would always be changes. Cary was another step in a direction that would eventually make her better.

Biting her lip, Lissa let her eyes peruse the walls, she studied again the certificates of the two physical therapists , this time more closely.

Dr. Phillip Sewel and Dr. M.S. Soucek. Were her eyes playing tricks on her - Soucek? She mouthed the name. *Not many of those around.*

Could it be? She hadn't met any people by that name, not since Murdoch. She smiled as the young face imaged in her head for only a moment before moving on to other framed items on the wall; the photos and prints.

There was a painting of a marlin breaking the water, twisting in the air, another of a sunrise, pink and aqua over the ocean, a photo of a lone surfer riding in the tube of a wave. *Maybe it is Doc*, she thought again.

She stood and limped toward another print, a quote beneath the photo read, *Either you decide to stay in the shallow end of the pool or you go out in the ocean* - Christopher Reeve.

She stepped to another. *I go to the ocean to calm down, to reconnect with the creator, to just be happy* - Nnedi Okorafor.

She turned to face another wall, another print with quote beaconed to her. *I have seafoam in my veins, I understand the language of the waves* - Jean Cocteau.

She shook her head thinking that if this was Doc's office, how ironic it all would be. She having been born and raised on the water, loving it so and opening that world to Murdoch, how it was he who dressed himself as lover of the sea, and she who was now forced to pull herself away from it.

Smirking , Lissa looked back to the certificate of Dr. M.S. Soucek. It was not a common name. Murdoch Sheradon Soucek. *It probably is him.* She felt herself beam, rushes of the past swept through her head along with images of the young teenagers who had spoken of their understanding, their love for and the spiritualism of the sea.

We lived in a bubble, she thought while nodding, *it was such a long time ago.* Her eyes narrowed as she smiled, *I hope he really has kept the connection with the ocean.*

While they had been together as teens she'd watched his curiosity and love of the ocean grow. She'd watched him enter the church and worship at its power. Back then he'd loved it as she did, it was what drew her even closer to him.

Lissa rubbed her leg, picturing the young man from the past. They'd parted so abruptly, it had hurt. She'd ached for years, had lost trust in love, in relationships. The break had affected her whole life leaving her to rush into a marriage that shouldn't have been and then doubting her heart, becoming afraid to step into other serious relationships.

Sometimes the echo of that pain seeped into her thoughts and though the years had veneered it, the knowledge of just how cruel love can be never left her. Still, the thought of the good times, the sweet love of their youth, warmed her.

Picturing Doc, his long hair pulled back in a ponytail, his tan and pink shoulders, sunburned skin peeling from them, she smiled. God, how she had loved him. She had ached for him. He had been the one who filled her with magic. It was something, she could have sworn was beyond words, that had manifested first with a touch, a look, a smell and the taste, all so enhanced by the world they created, fiercely intense and making more sense than anything else.

That young love had made her set the bar high - ruined things for her in some ways, always wanting that purity, the honesty, the bare bones exchange of feeling between two people. She had come to believe that those types of feelings only came with youth.

There were things she still did not share with Rick, places in her that she dare not open up about. Why should she? They were gone.

Lissa limped back to her seat, thoughts of Doc warming her as she pictured her and Doc playing on the beach, him grabbing her, carrying her to the water, tossing her into the waves - she'd sat on his shoulders trying to push him under.

Then there was the first time they'd made love, *their* first time. It should have been awkward. But it was so right, completing the flow of motion they had set between themselves.

Lissa closed her eyes, awash in a sea of delight.

"Calista Roseman."

The calling of her name startled her, she blushed, her eyes studied the floor as she rose.

"I'll help her." Linda reached for Lissa's arm.

"Thank you, that's fine. I'll take her from her." The aide smiled to Linda.

Her thoughts enveloped in the past, Lissa still tingled with disbelief and anticipation of who just might be her physical therapist.

"The doctor will be with you in a moment." The aide motioned to the table and helped Lissa as she seated herself. She smiled back as she left the room, leaving the door ajar.

It was only moments before he entered the room, his eyes scanning the chart in his hand. "Calista Jewel Roseman." He lifted his head to meet her eyes. A broad smile crossed his lips as he neared. "My God, it is you. You haven't changed a single bit, Lissa. "

He leaned in to hug her, pulling her close, holding her tightly.

She could smell him, the sense brought so much back. For an instant she felt the ache as she relaxed into arms that had once held her so passionately. It would have been natural for her to tilt her face upward to his, expecting his lips to cover hers.

Instantly she felt awkward as she looked into the face that had aged, she noticed the faded scar across his brow and cheekbone, still it was a nice face that had grown into one of maturity and confidence.

Holding her to arm's length, Murdoch studied Lissa for a moment.

"You look wonderful." Quiet for just an instant, his lips drew downward. "Been a very long time."

Lissa grabbed his hand and held it between hers. "You did become a doctor after all, so fitting, *Doc*. I'm so proud of you."

"Doctor of Physical Therapy - not much blood and guts here." His eyes twinkled, the smile returning as he stared into hers. The smile never relaxing, it was obvious he was happy to see her.

"I always wondered what happened to you. If you went off into the big corporate world like your father, because you said you did not want to go into medicine, and if you did all the traveling you talked about."

Doc nodded. "Did a little bit of that. I'll tell you about it sometime."

"Your father? How's he doing?"

Leaning against the table, Murdoch shrugged. "Dad always did his thing, you know, you remember. Things were less than good between us." He paused. "He passed a long time ago."

"Sorry." Lissa reached for his hand again. "And your mother - Lorelei, is that right? Lorelei?

"My mother. Ha, Mother is doing just fine."

His tone inferred that the subject was closed and he moved on, reread the chart. "Would you mind removing the prosthetic?" He said, avoiding eye contact.

Lissa depressed the release button and slid the orthotic from the stump.

Murdoch's hands gently held her leg and began removing the sleeve, then the sock. He examined the stump. "How long have you been wearing your prosthetic?"

"This is a new one, I got it only a couple of weeks ago. The other one was rubbing and pinching me - it just didn't fit."

"Still adapting." His eyes rose to meet hers, he grinned.

"Do you wear it every day?"

"Yes."

"For how long at a time?"

"A couple hours."

"Lean back, Lissa."

She leaned back onto her elbows.

Cradling her leg in his hands, Doc faced her. "I'm sure you've had this procedure before." Slowly he began rubbing the end where the scar from her incision had been. "I'm trying to break down any scar tissue that is building."

Lissa nodded and watched him, his brow knit into concentration.

It seemed surreal looking at the familiar face, the same eyes, nose, contours, she noticed the signs of aging and caught her breath. Seeing Murdoch after so many years - someone who had been such an integral part of her life - felt odd, and in this capacity, as a doctor, it felt even stranger.

She recalled the friendship, the playful banter between the then teens and it struck her how time had not erased the feeling of intimacy - she trusted him.

"I'm sorry about this." Doc shook his head as he massaged. "I know how much you loved surfing."

"To tell the truth, I haven't surfed very much in the last twenty years - only now and then. There just hasn't been the time."

"Life kind of does that, doesn't it?" Doc snickered. "What's that they say? 'Life happens while you're planning it.'"

Lissa nodded. "True, it's so ironic, I was planning on getting back into it. Guess I can kiss that dream good-by."

"Not necessarily, Lissa. Science has come up with all kinds of handy gadgets."

"Blades, like the Olympian?"

"That's one way to go, but there are other options. There are all kinds of orthotics designed for various activities. Some not so cumbersome as this one," he nodded. "There's one that offers a vacuum seal, much like this, easy on and off. I've heard it's very comfortable and adaptable. Why I have a couple of patients who have a whole quiver of prosthetics. One for running, skiing, dancing, walking - all kinds of activities." He smiled at her. "But we can discuss that later." Doc continued massaging the end of her leg, cradling it in his arms. "Do you like the orthotic you've been fitted with?"

"It's okay - well, not really. I still have some difficulty with balance, some movements are just not comfortable." She stammered, "I-I just don't know how to explain it, really, it's tough getting used to. I was hoping that here—" Lissa watched Doc, his face contorted in concentration. "I'm so ready to get going - to start living again."

"Tired of sitting around and feeling sorry for yourself, huh?"

"I've done, I *do*, a lot of that."

"It's normal. But you need to take things slowly."

Lissa nodded.

"There are all kinds of orthotics out there. You find the ones that fit you and your lifestyle. You just have to start slow and get used to things. It's going to take some time and then there will be adjustments until you find the right one or ones for you." Shifting closer on the table to Lissa, Doc raised his eyes to meet hers. "They can work miracles now."

"You're saying there is a possibility that I can surf, and run and jump, all without falling on my face?" She chuckled. "Will that ever happen again?" Lifting her eyes to meet his, Lissa felt them tear. Why were they doing that now? She'd cried only the once since the attack. She'd taken it all in stride and had become resigned about the whole incident as if it was just another thing she would have to accept about life - another

185

mountain to climb. She had considered herself an accomplished *mountain* climber but now she wasn't quite as sure.

Doc's gaze was on her leg as he massaged it, his response to her question was slow coming. His brow pinched and the muscles of his jawline tensed.

Waiting for an answer, Lissa felt her throat tighten and for a moment it felt as if she could not breathe.

"Relax Lissa - lay all the way back." Doc's hands guided her to lie back onto the table.

She felt the tears sliding from her eyes toward the sides of her face. *Shit,* she thought, *he's almost a stranger, why am I so bent out of shape now? I haven't seen him since I was a kid.*

Doc gently brushed Lissa's hair back from her face. Grabbing a tissue from a box he dabbed at the wetness streaming from her eyes. "Relax, take a deep breath." He stroked her hair again and watched as she calmed. "I am sorry, Lissa. Don't worry, I'll do everything I can to help you."

She searched his eyes, studied the face she'd once known intimately. Everything was flooding in at the same time - the pain from her leg, the acknowledgment that she'd never be the same and the hurt he caused her - it was all pain, an acknowledgement that life dealt dirty blows. Lissa wanted to disappear. *Why?* she thought to herself.

Hadn't she forgiven him? She'd moved on. Hadn't she? It was all so long ago, so why was she feeling these things. Why in the hell did it feel like yesterday?

Lissa felt foolish, trapped, she wanted to run but the orthotic was gone, she physically could not do what she wanted. She bit her trembling lips, recalling how her father had told her once that losing love was like experiencing a death. *You never got over it, you just lock it away somewhere.*

Now, a key had slipped into that little place where she kept pain. Everything was alive - the past, the loss of her limb.

"Why?" Lissa heard herself say the word.

His eyes meeting hers, Murdoch sighed. "There are no answers for that. And remember, as you told me so long ago, 'When we venture into the ocean we are in the shark's domain.'"

Her chest heaving, her pulse beating rapidly, Lissa shook her head. "I know, but why?" Her eyes held his.

Recognizing the Lissa he'd known, Doc leaned closer.

"Why. I know I hurt you back when we were kids. I'm sorry for the way things turned out back then. There were things."

An apology, it meant the world. It couldn't go back and erase the hurt she had felt, but it gave a sense of closure. *Funny how we hold on to things*, she thought. She had wanted closure almost as much as she had longed for reconciliation.

"It's okay." She whispered.

Their eyes holding, tears streaming from Lissa's, Doc brushed another strand of hair from her forehead. "We had a wonderful time then, didn't we?"

"You were young, I was young."

187

Catching his breath, Doc squared his shoulders, straightening his stance. "It was a long time ago. I know you've moved on. We had to, didn't we? I hope you're happy." Holding her hand he pulled Lissa upright and bent to retrieve the prosthesis.

She studied his profile as he helped her reattach the orthotic, his brow pinched in concentration. His face, now older, held the slight droop of encroaching jowls. The shadows beneath his eyes belied a stressful life or at least worry. He was still handsome though, still broad shouldered, just a few gray hairs accented his brown hair, now cut short. Gone were the sun streaked strands, gone was the innocence.

Lissa felt a trace of longing from long ago to touch him, to soothe him.

She closed her eyes for a moment, felling the butterflies, the exhilaration - time had erased the years between the present and the past. The moment was playing tricks on her, she thought, as Doc lifted his head to smile, his hazel eyes gazing into hers.

"Sometimes—" Doc began.

She felt so vulnerable and self-conscious as he spoke. This man who had once held her in his arms, kissed her and made the world open for her, was touching her again.

Lissa fought to hold her composure. "It doesn't matter."

"What doesn't matter?" Doc asked.

"Oh, I'm sorry. I didn't mean to interrupt. Go on, what were you going to say? Sometimes? You started - sometimes?

He chuckled. "Yeah, sometimes these things take a while, but I think I can help you Lissa."

"And the limp? Will I have a limp?"

His fingers touched her skin;. it felt more like a caress than procedure. "I wish I could do more, but—" He leaned into her closely, "It's the goal. And if you work hard, I'd say no limp and yes, with the right prosthesis and practice, no one will be able to tell you wear one and you'll be able to surf - and anything else you want to do."

"Really?" Lissa felt her heart beat quicken, she felt the young girl she'd once been, the one she'd forgotten about. The butterflies began, she moved her eyes to his hands still touching her leg.

And then she noticed the ring. Why had she not seen it before? She smiled. Yes, of course he was married. Why should she be so surprised?

Embarrassed somewhat by the illusion, the grand illusion that Doc had feelings for her still, she wanted to laugh. Most certainly the past was the past, they were all grown up now. The comprehension of that fell like a ton of bricks. *He must think I'm a fool,* she thought.

Twenty-five years had changed them both. There could be no living in the past. The reality was she was a handicapped person, he was her doctor - only her doctor, nothing else. He was married. There could be no more. Now they would be friends, that's all, just friends.

"Lissa," Murdock whispered, catching her attention. "I know you're going through a lot now. It's a different reality for you. There will be other milestones, too, acknowledgments about your disability and having to adjust to things. It's going to be difficult for you to wrap your head around the losing of your leg. But in time it will be second nature. I promise you that."

Her head lifted to his gaze. "It's so weird, all these feelings."

He nodded, "I know. Seeing you here today brings back lots of good memories. And then this tragedy with your leg, well, I understand, don't be nervous, don't be ashamed. I'm your doctor - and your friend. Relax, Gimpy," He teased,

"Gimp? You're calling me *gimp*?"

"Yeah?" Raising an eyebrow, he grinned.

"Okay, Scarface." She caught herself, instantly feeling ashamed for saying it.

Doc touched his fingers to the scar. "Hard not to notice that."

"Sorry,"

"It's okay, I've gotten used to it. And *you* need to get used to unkind and cruel reactions to your situation. They are going to happen."

"I've seen some of that already."

"Most people don't mean to be cruel, they're mostly curious, but it does set you apart. Actually, I think having a handicap adds another dimension to people. You find out quickly what is important and what is not, so don't let this little thing with your leg diminish you in anyway." Doc's eyes steeled. "There is so much more to you than this." He gently touched the soft tissue of her stump.

"What happened to you?" Lissa motioned toward her own eye.

"A long time ago I was in a car accident." He paused, his eyes turned from hers for a moment. "I'll tell you about it someday."

"Sorry."

"That's life, shit happens. At least we can joke about it."

"At least." Lissa winked. "Same old Doc, huh?"

"Same old Doc, just a little older. Not as full of myself."

"I never saw that side of you."

"Maybe just a little more confident, then."

Lissa nodded.

"In a way, you're fortunate that you happened to come to me. I can understand so much more than anyone else would. I know you and I really care."

The words were liberating and Lissa relaxed as Doc continued explaining what her capabilities could be.

"I would like to see you at least twice a week for the next couple of weeks and then we'll go from there."

Lissa rose from the table and smoothed her clothing.

"I'm happy I got to see you again." Doc's eyes twinkled as he held hers.

"Me, too. We did have a great thing back then."

"You really changed my life, Lissa - opened doors for me that would have never been opened. I should have thanked you for that. But I was a kid, my dad," He paused, "and my mother had me wrapped up in things and you know, life, things happen. Anyway, it's been wonderful seeing you." He tapped the chart in his hand. "We'll get things right for you, my old friend. Okay?"

"Old friend, yes, that's what we are."

It felt liberating, even cathartic, seeing Doc, it made her feel as if a new chapter in her life was beginning. The past, all the things that came with it seemed purposeful, as if the circle was completed and a sad part of her life had been rectified.

Her leg, her disability would be mended and by someone with whom she had a caring relationship. Was it trust? Whatever it was, it felt right. The day had brought more promise than she had ever expected.

Chapter 22

"How did things go at PT?" Asked Rick.

Lissa set her purse on the kitchen table, the question of whether or not to tell him about Murdoch, their affair when they were teenagers, slid through her mind.

"Oh, fine. I guess I've got lots of hard work ahead of me. Or so the therapist says." *It was so long ago, it doesn't matter anymore, why bother Rick with this?* Her eyes avoided his as he stepped toward her.

His arms reaching around her waist, Rick pulled Lissa close. "What do you say we take a nice bath," He kissed her passionately, "Put on the dog tonight - I love that peach colored dress - and we take in a movie and go to the Pilot House.

Lissa relaxed into his arms, pushing the thought of Murdoch away. She wanted to feel Rick, to believe in him again. He felt warm and comfortable as always. Lissa struggled to recapture the feelings she'd had for him before the attack. She pushed herself against him, waited for him to pull her into his body. *All the nonsense about Doc, I feel so silly now.* Lissa looked deeply into Rick's eyes. She wanted to love him.

"Why are you shaking?" Rick asked.

Pushing away Lissa shook her head. "I don't know." Again her eyes could not meet his.

"I know what you need." Rick stepped into the distance between them. "A nice long bath." His eyes sparkled wantonly.

Lissa smiled back and waited for him to gather her in his arms. She wrapped her arms around his neck and kissed it, moving slowly to his ear and cheek.

At first the thought of the pleasure of submerging into a warm tub of water filled her, then the image of disassembling her prosthetic cooled her thoughts. "I don't know."

"Look, I'm okay with it. Really." Rick kissed her cheek. "Just keep the sleeve on it to cover it up."

Again she felt the uneasiness from him. Again the idea of finding an excuse or feigning interest tugged at her. She inhaled deeply, "Umm, sounds wonderful." She moved her thoughts to the dress, it was long enough to cover her leg. Maybe it would be fun going out tonight. Rick did have her back; they'd worked out a stance, a way of leaning against him as she walked that made the limp barely noticeable.

"Doc says that he thinks he can help me get rid of the limp."

Rick reached for the lacy hem of her blouse and pulled it gently over her head, bent to kiss her throat, to caress her body as they moved toward the tub. "Good, whatever is good for you is good for me."

Resting against the commode, Lissa released the button and slid the orthotic from her stump. She could have sworn she saw him scowl once as she slid the sleeve and then the sock from her upper leg. It seemed as if she waited almost too long for him to steady her as she struggled to find her balance but maybe she was just imagining things.

"Come here, beautiful." Rick took Lissa's hand as he stepped naked into the bathtub and lifted her in after him.

Wrapping her fingers around the biceps of his arms, Lissa balanced herself. He felt like a stranger and as if she was going through the motions trying to keep him from recognizing the doubt.

At one time the feel and grace of his body excited her, now she struggled to mask her uneasiness. *Maybe,* she told herself as she leaned against him, tiptoeing to reach his lips. His kiss felt nice. *Maybe I can get it back.*

"Why are you trembling? Rick asked.

"I don't know." Lissa leaned against him as they slowly oozed into the warm water, sliding against one another. She liked that, the ritual the two of them had created - *maybe it's coming back. Maybe it's just my imagination.* Submitting to the physical pleasure of his touch, Lissa relinquished her apprehension to enjoy his body as they caressed and kissed their most intimate parts.

He washed her hair, she his, in between kisses. They took turns scrubbing each other with the loofah, lingering at places the other found erotic.

Then came Lissa's foot. Instantly the apprehension reappeared, she drew back.

"No, relax," Rick cooed, his eyes begged as he stroked her leg.

But now it felt so awkward. Hesitating, Lissa drew her leg back.

"You have to trust me. Don't push me away." Rick pressed his fingers into her instep and stroked upwards into the pads of her foot.

"No, not now." She pulled away as she leaned. "Maybe later."

"It's okay, Lissa, I'm okay with this. You have to trust me."

"Uh uh, not now."

****

Lissa lay next to Rick, his breath light as his chest rose and fell. His lips parted somewhat; the tiniest of smiles curling the corners.

He was a good man, a good lover - attentive, thoughtful. He loved her, she was sure of it. And Lissa loved him. She thought of that love, what kind it was, it's depth and how much she was holding back.

Doc's image appeared as she perused Rick's slumber. She bit her bottom lip and felt her heart ache, hoping she had not made a fool of herself at his office. *That must not be, it cannot be.*

Chapter 23

It was titillating to think of Doc as she rested at home with Rick. She played the game of convincing herself that they'd both grown into different more adult lives where they could cherish what had transpired between them.

She relished the love making with Rick as she dreamed of holding Doc closely, feeling him inside her.

Rebuking herself for doing so, Lissa found herself over compensating - waiting on Rick, agreeing with him on nearly everything, laughing too much, until the next time when they fell in bed together.

Lissa prided herself on the strides she had made while seeing the therapist in Cary, never mentioning his name, calling him the doc, or simply Doc.

Lissa felt the tear of her moral fiber - the mix of emotions running through her, one moment exuberant that she was now friends with the man who'd meant so much to her and the next moment longing for the kind of love they'd once shared, the trust and the feeling that they were of the same cut of cloth.

It will pass, the feelings will sort themselves out, she told herself. *After all, the sessions would be ending in a few weeks and I won't see him anymore after that.*

Why spend time dreaming of a man who couldn't be with her? And this man, Rick, wanted her now.

****

This would be the eighth visit to Cary and to Doc. Rick had never questioned her sessions there and Lissa never mentioned her old friend.

Linda seemed content as she drove, nodding her head to the country tune on the radio. She turned to Lissa.

"Okay, your daddy had a little talk with me about my driving. I know I have a lead foot, sorry. I'll try to keep to the speed limit."

Lissa shrugged. "I wish he wouldn't have said anything. I know you're safe, I'm just not used to other people—"

"I know, me either. I'm a nervous wreck when I'm not the one behind the wheel. John says it has something to do with my controlling nature."

"Ha, he tells me the same thing."

"So," Linda began, "Do you like the therapist who's working with you?"

She wanted to tell Linda everything - that the man working with her so intimately had once been her lover. And how now they were friends. She wanted a confidant that would understand, she parted her lips to speak.

"Is he young and sexy?" Linda teased.

Lissa caught the words before they spilled from her mouth. Linda was not the one to confide in. Eventually anything she said to her would end up in her father's ear. She shook her head. "No he's not too young but he's nice and seems to know how to help."

She turned her attention back to thoughts of Rick. They'd spent a wonderful weekend together and had taken the skiff to Lea Island. He'd packed a picnic lunch and they sat on the shore, did a little fishing and exploring the island. Rick helped her with her balance and she even took off on her own, alone with no one to depend on. It felt good. Even as she stooped to pick up a shell, she felt confident.

Now, the ride to Cary, Lissa thought of Doc again. Of course, the image of his face lingered in her mind. *We're friends now. The past was a nice thing. Some people don't even get to love like that.* It was nice to have a friend like him, one who knew you, knew what made you tick - a friend whom you could trust with something as important as your wellbeing.

"You've come a long way, Lissa. This physical therapist is working wonders, you seem so much more confident, like the old Lissa - only better," Linda chimed.

You have no idea. Lissa nodded her head and turned up the volume of the radio.

****

His face beaming as she walked into the room, Doc held his hand out to help Lissa to the table. "I hope you had a nice weekend." He unfastened the orthotic from her leg and began massaging.

"I went to Lea Island, it was nice. I even walked on the beach and picked up shells."

"Um, how's your balance, any discomfort, chafing?

"No."

"Have you been feeling any pain or numbness?"

"Coming along fine. Maybe there is a bit of discomfort at the stump."

"Still?"

She nodded. "Just a tiny bit. That's normal though, I'm getting better at it, just a little pain, some numbness. But I can handle it."

Doc shook his head and chuckled. "Now that sounds like the Lissa I used to know."

Adjusting the table to a sitting position, Doc instructed Lissa to relax as he reached for her leg and placed it on his lap. He sat close to her, facing her, his hands constantly massaging the

201

leg, then moving to the tender area where the cup of the orthotic would have rested. "How does this feel?"

"It feels good, I've been feeling some stress there but this feels good. Thank you."

He pulled her leg to his shoulder and pulled down just above the knee, stretching the hamstring. "It's important to keep the rest of your leg toned - you need to stretch and exercise it often."

It still amazed her somewhat, the tone in his voice, how professional he sounded. It was so unlike the young man she used to know. It left her with the profound feeling of what time does and how people develop and how her Doc, the boy she'd loved, had turned into such a knowledgeable and professional man.

Doc manipulated her leg and offered suggestions for ease of mobility and strength. "Do the exercises," he ordered jokingly.

"Yes sir."

He sat closely, facing her. Their hands often grazing one another's. His leg pressed against hers.

Doc teased, she teased. The atmosphere was light and cheerful. He was familiar, at ease, cajoling in his professional instruction.

Her confidence and abilities grew as he introduced expedient movements, encouraging her to try yoga and other stretching exercises.

Lissa felt as if she was progressing not only in knowledge but in attitude and acceptance; it was Doc who was making her feel that way.

Her esteem grew for him as the visits continued, she began seeing him as an extension of the boy she'd once loved - a man now. Sometimes, however, it was hard to distinguish between the two, especially when she and Doc recounted past events or fell into the easy banter they'd once shared. Lissa wondered if Doc was experiencing the same with her.

"I was thinking this weekend of back in the day when you were teaching me to surf, that was one of the best times of my life."

"Thank you, Doc. It was for me, too."

"I learned a lot that summer, not just about surfing, but about other things, too. You opened my eyes to many things - what was important, what wasn't. You know, it was because of you that I did not become a medical doctor."

"I did that?" Lissa shook her head. "I'm sorry."

"No don't be. If you remember, I really did not want to go into medicine. I was going because my parents were shoving me into it. What happened that summer, or at least a few months past it, was realizing that my father was living my life, my mother was guilting me into doing what she wanted."

"I figured as much."

Doc nodded. "After I left - you," he said apologetically. "I did go back to Davidson, or I was going to go back. Then my father surprised me with a flight to England to visit my sister. Man was I pissed. I told him I was going to UNCW. He seemed ready and willing to accept that and then—"

"What?"

"We had an accident. He was killed and well, and—" he touched the long scar on his face.

"Scarface."Lissa grinned.

"I've been told it makes me look distinguished. And then there was my eye."

"Doc, I'm so sorry."

"It's okay. I lost partial sight in it. " He sighed, and moved closer to her. "Now let's take a look at that leg and talk about *your* future." Smiling he eased himself next to Lissa on the table and slowly began messaging her leg. Lifting his eyes to hers, Doc spoke, "I tried getting in touch with you. You were married. I left things alone then."

Silence ensued for quite a while. Doc continued rubbing the leg, Lissa turning from him, realizing how he must have been torn. He had hurt, too. She could only imagine the pain he had having to choose between his parent's wishes and a young teenage surfer girl. "I hope you are happy now."

He nodded. "Beautiful wife, great kids. Who could ask for more?" He nodded toward a photo on his desk, two young adult children stood between Doc and a young woman.

"Is she the second wife?"

Murdock nodded.

"Younger? She doesn't look old enough to have children that - you dog," Lissa teased.

"We're all dogs," Doc teased back. "I refuse to make excuses, the first marriage was for my mother and I guess you can imagine how that went. The second go-round, I married for—"

"Love?"

"Yeah. She's a great woman."

"Um."

"Ava is a buyer for Marker Jewelers," he beamed.

"They're pretty big, you sound proud of her."

Doc nodded. "One of the largest in the country. She just got back from New York."

"Must be nice," Lissa teased.

"She got tickets to the Panther's game last winter and we went to Giants Stadium. She gets perks like that now and then."

Lissa nodded. Yes, he had gone on with his life and he seemed happy and settled. "How old are your children?

Without looking at her, Murdoch's hands manipulated her leg, he answered, "Barry is twenty. Beatrice is eighteen. They're both in college."

"And you're proud of them."

"I sure am. They're both smart and of course, like all kids their age, think they know everything."

"Did you have any children, Lissa?" This time when his eyes found hers they were not as curious or as full of the wonder as they had been initially.

"One, Abigail, Abby. She'll be twenty-four in a couple of weeks..."

"Whoa, you must have—"

"I know, I know, but you weren't there. Tom was." She turned away. "Sounds bad I know, and I'd like to say I wish I hadn't, but I've got Abby and she's my whole world. I'm very proud of my little girl."

The room was quiet as Doc manipulated her stump and leg. But Lissa felt relaxed and calm with him. It was like talking with a good friend, he was a good friend. She trusted Doc's judgement and did not feel in the slightest bit diminished in his view of her.

"I don't see a ring," he began.

"Nope. We gave it a go. Tried but it just wasn't working. It lasted around fourteen years, on and off. I think we were apart for most of those years than together."

"Sorry."

"My Abby is a great girl. Her father always provided well, even if he wasn't around much."

"Ever try it a second time?"

Lissa shook her head. "I don't think I was cut out for married life."

"Really?" Doc asked curiously.

"I don't like to fail at things."

"I know, I remember." He chuckled again. "Seeing anyone?"

"Uh huh, I've been seeing a man for several months now. He's a good man, a very good man - we've talked about getting married."

"I hope—"

"Rick." She said the name aloud. "His name is Rick."

"Rick," Murdoch repeated the name. "What does he do?"

"Fisherman."

"Oh."

Lissa caught the disapproving tone, hadn't there been a conversation once with Grayson Soucek about fishermen? She couldn't recall something from twenty-five years previous but she did remember his disdainful attitude toward the occupation of the locals. Had Doc adopted that attitude as well?

"Rick attended law school."

"He's a lawyer?"

"Was. He was a lawyer. Well, not quite. He never took the bar."

"That's too bad."

"Maybe, he said he just couldn't make himself do something that his heart wasn't in." Her eyes fell on Doc's. "Sound like anyone you know?"

"Man after my own heart, sounds like."

"He went back to Alaska and started working for his father again until he saved up enough for his own boat."

"He's from Alaska?"

"Yes, we went there a couple of months ago, before the attack - loved it. Went sledding, watched the whales, went fishing. It was a blast." Lissa's face lit up.

"I always wanted to go to Alaska."

"You should go, you'd like it."

"Ava can't stand the cold weather, if it's under seventy she's unhappy."

Lissa nodded.

"What brought him here?" Doc asked.

"Warmer weather." She grinned. "He was at Beaufort first and then came to Topsail a few years ago."

"And you've been on the island all these years?"

"Mostly. I went to UNCW, got my BS. During my marriage we lived in Detroit for a while. Lived in Florida for a few years." She laughed. "But I'm not nearly as worldly as you, Murdoch."

"A hotel in New York is not that different than a hotel in Paris. "

"Really. You can believe if I was in Paris I sure as hell wouldn't be in a hotel."

Doc smiled at her. "No, *you* wouldn't, you'd be stirring up something somewhere."

She smiled. "Oh, I'm not nearly as idealistic as I used to be."

"Too bad, it was one of the things that made you so attractive." Murdoch's eyes met hers, they held for a few moments. "I," he started. "I've been thinking."

"Oh no." Lissa teased.

"Yes, I have a proposition for you." He blurted the words.

"A proposition? Oh." She fought the urge to say, *How would your wife feel about that?* But that would have suggested some feeling that she still held out hope for a romance with him. Did she? The statement alone made her nervous about her true feelings.

"Yes." He moved in closer to her, touching her shoulder with his. "I still have Grammy's beach cottage at Topsail. And it's been so long since I came down to the island. We've been renting it out," he explained. "Ava has been prodding me to get back down there, to take her to the beach."

Lissa lowered her eyes. "I'm curious."

Doc sighed heavily. "Well, since I'm going to be going down to the beach, there's no sense in you driving all the way up here all the time. So, you can come up a couple more times and then we can meet at Topsail."

It was a surprise. And why would he want to meet her alone? What about Ava? Rick?

"The proposition is - in exchange for the physical therapy, I'd like to start taking surfing lessons again. I'll learn to surf, you'll get back on the board to build up your confidence and your strength."

"What?" She paused, took a heavy breath. "I don't know if I ever want to get back in the water again, let alone surf."

"Lissa, you loved it. Surfing was part of who you were and you told me, remember, that you were thinking of going out more, that's why you jumped in the water."

"No." Lissa shook her head. "I don't think I can." She grinned sheepishly. "Sharks, remember the sharks? One took my leg. I can't chance losing the other one, Doc."

"I remember the tenacious Lissa, the one who chained herself to a bulldozer, who didn't back down from anything, and, from what you've told me, the one who raised a kid on her own and runs a business. Lissa, you are selling yourself short. Do what you love, *let* yourself do what you love."

"But you know how to surf. I taught you twenty-some years ago."

"I haven't been on a board since then. And I've gotten a little out of shape." He patted his belly. "I've been cooped up inside a building for the last twenty years."

Lissa eyed him curiously. She thought of the fun the two of them had had and the bond that had been created. She longed for something like that, for the feeling - the playful feeling, a sense of youth that she'd forgotten about.

"They make prosthetics that will work. Get on the net, check out the surfers who have lost limbs, there are several and they go back in the water, they don't let it stop them."

"I don't know."

"You have no idea what science has come up with. I'll help you pick one out. You'll love it."

Her eyes catching his, Lissa felt the swell of joy inside, the feeling of hope returning to her. This man was helping her to believe in herself again. She wanted to trust him and believe in what he was telling her.

For a moment she glimpsed back into the past, recounting the trust she'd felt for him long ago. And what had become of that trust. He'd let her down, abandoned her. *But he told me he was sorry.* Lissa listened to the words in her head and then his words, so sincere, so healing.

What would Rick think of her getting together with an old lover? We're just friends. Lissa nodded reassuringly to herself and smiled up to Doc. "I think that is a great idea. And you really think I'll be able to surf again?" Her eyes begged, searching his for an answer to the question.

****

Swiping a finger across the screen of her phone, Lissa felt a twinge of guilt as *Rick Moran* flashed in bright yellow. She nervously answered, swallowing hard as she pushed the thoughts of Doc from her mind.

"Is that Rick?" Linda asked, her fingers fumbling with the volume knob of the radio.

Lissa nodded.

"Hey babe, how's my favorite person doing?" His voice was light and enthusiastic.

"Good, I'm fine. You sound like you're in a good mood. Have an outstanding catch today?"

"Hell yes! I had a damn fantastic catch."

"Grouper?" The playfulness was creeping into her own voice as she pictured Rick's smiling face.

"Nope. Better than a grouper."

"Tuna, a whole school?"

"Better than that."

"It must be something really big. I can't imagine—"

"Hell, honey. I was at the dock, just dropping off this party of four I took out to the Gulf Stream and you'll never guess who was in the slip next to me."

"Who?"

"You'll never guess, I never would have thought - the boat was an old trawler, must be thirty years old but in cherry condition."

"Who? Who was in the trawler next to you?" She asked impatiently.

"Ortum. You remember me telling you about my old college roommate, Ortum?"

"Sort of. He sounded a little wacko."

"Ha, a little? Ortum was always one beer short of a six-pack but damn if he wasn't a shrewd businessman."

"So, do I get to meet him?"

"That's why I called. I want you to come down to the boat and meet him. His boat is right next to mine - forty-three foot trawler, man it is fine. It looks brand new."

Lissa could tell Rick was ecstatic. In fact, she'd never heard him so excited. She'd heard the stories of the friendship, the wild rides, trips, experiences. She knew he and Ortum had been close.

"Honey, Ortum's a good guy, I know you'll like him. Forget all that stuff I told you about when we were in college. He's mellowed, well, somewhat. But he's offered me a great deal. I want you to hear it."

Her fingers over the speaker, Lissa turned to Linda. "Do you mind dropping me off at the marina? Rick wants me to meet him and an old friend."

"No problem."

Lissa lifted the phone to her face. "Okay, I'll be there in a few."

"I could hear Rick over the phone. Sounds exciting." Linda raised a brow. "So who is this *Ortum* fellow?"

"They've been friends forever. Rick worships the ground he walks on."

Linda nodded. "I've known men like that. Better be careful, if you don't watch it these long lost buddies will undo all the training you've done and you'll have to start all over again."

"I never had to train Rick, he's always been attentive."

"Even now?"

"Uh huh, even now."

"Then what's the problem?"

"What do you mean?"

"Lissa, I'm not stupid or blind. Since the attack you've drifted away from Rick. I see it, I sense it. What gives?"

Lissa shrugged, "I don't know, Linda. Honestly I don't know." *What was it?* She thought as she exited the car. *What is wrong with me?* She walked casually toward the Cloud Nine and the trawler at the end of one of the finger docks. She was proud of her progress, a limp, but a diminishing one. "Thank you Doc," she whispered under her breath. Smiling, she reassured herself that there was no need to share any information.

Chapter 24

She walked steadily, doing her best to conceal the limp. Her tight jeans hugged the curves of her body, boot cut, they flared just a bit to conceal the orthotic.

From the top of the dock, she noticed the two men seated, chatting, laughing. Rick looked different, more carefree than she'd seen him in months.

His unruly blond hair dancing in the breeze, he reached his fingers to his chin and scratched at the few days' growth of beard on his face.

Ooh, he looks good, I like the hair, the beard.

She felt her heart jump, an ache in her thighs and eagerness she was not so accustomed to.

Turning her way, Rick waved, smiling like a boy, like a boy who'd just been told he was getting a brand new car.

Lissa masked the titillating feeling best she could as she walked past Rick's forty-two foot boat and to the trawler. The scrawl on the transom read *Rose Tattoo*. Rising from his deck chair, the robust and tanned man studied her as she approached.

He was a burly sort with a broad barrel chest, emblazoned with the tattoo of a red rose. His legs were muscular as were his arms. And his hands were expansive, gnarled a bit by what she suspected to be hard work.

His dark blue eyes caught hers and held them as he reached to help her board the vessel.

"Yes ma'am," Ortum nodded. "This here is a woman. Now, not some thin reedy, pretentious female, but a real woman, Rick. You've done well my friend. I like a woman that looks like one."

Lissa laughed. This was a man who had no need or desire to be politically correct.

Still holding his eyes, Lissa steeled her own. "Had me pegged as soon as you saw me, didn't you? Or did Rick tell you how much I enjoy compliments?" She tilted her head to the side and snickered.

"Honey, I don't give a flying fig what the prevailing political climate is. I've learned all I need to know from experience, I call 'em like I see 'em," Ortum chuckled.

When he laughed it came from his belly, his lips exposing off-white perfect teeth. Lissa studied his face; she liked his nose - somewhat bumpy, though chiseled into fine lines that were strong yet delicate. His eyes sparkled even when he wasn't smiling. Lissa had the feeling that Ortum loved life; the feeling hung as a thick, almost palpable aura.

Handing a cool St. Pauli Girl to Lissa, Rick settled against a gunwale and watched the banter between his old friend and his new love. If she could keep up with Ortum, see through his bullshit and get to the real man, then she truly was the woman he believed her to be.

"Don't tell me you haven't told her about the time you and I went down to Florida?" Ortum guffawed.

Lissa sat waiting for the story, it would be another good one, full of bravado and adventure, she assumed.

Ortum turned his head to her, sipped from his beer and began, "We took a bus, a Trailways, from Alaska, damn that was a long ride." He turned to Rick. "How many days did that take us?"

"A week, I think or close to it."

"I think we stopped every twenty miles, seemed like it anyway, then we finally pulled into Largo, Key Largo. We left out of Largo on this fifty-two foot lobster boat - we were planning on raking in a good load of lobster and making a killing."

"Damn, those lobster traps are heavy," Rick interrupted. "They have cement on the bottom, you know." He nodded to Lissa.

"You telling the story or am I?"

Rick leaned his beer back and nodded to Ortum. "Go ahead."

"We were seventy-eight miles out from the Bahamas, making us over one-hundred-and-fifty from the U S mainland. And damn if that boat didn't catch on fire."

"The Ruby Ellen, that was her name."

"Yeah, the Ruby Ellen. She caught on fire. You should have seen your boyfriend, he was moving his ass I tell ya, trying to save those damn traps."

"There was at least fifty of them," Rick interjected.

"They were catching on fire, too. Rick was dancing around trying to save those damn things. I was trying to save the damn boat. And we were out in the middle of the ocean and it wasn't one of those calm days either. Let me tell you."

"I was ready to dive into the water," Rick sniggered.

The two men looked at one another, laughed, drank, laughed some more, breathed sighs and nodded.

"So what happened?" Lissa asked.

"We got the fire under control."

"We got back to port."

"Oh." Lissa looked from one man to another. *Hmm,* she thought, *they're not telling the rest of the story. Must have been a doozy.* "So that's it? The boat caught on fire and you almost jumped overboard?"

"You had to be there." Ortum tilted his head back, swigging the remainder of the beer in his bottle.

Rick was silent, watching his friend. The light in his eyes told Lissa that sure, there was more, but either it wasn't to be shared in mixed company or that it truly was one of those things that could not be comprehended without having been there.

She let the subject drop, nodding, acknowledging that she'd had times like that in her life as well.

"After that old Charon started going to AA." Ortum sniggered. "Became a better man."

"Who's Charon?" Lissa asked.

"He owned the boat," said Rick.

"You think he really owned it?" asked Ortum.

There was a pause, a few seconds of silence.

"So you've seen him around?" Rick interjected.

"Now and then." Ortum slid his eyes to Lissa. "Something about a man, or woman, that goes to AA. I admire people like that."

"Really?" Queried Lissa.

"Yeah, they know there's something wrong with them. They know they have a flaw and they're willing to try and fix it or amend it in some way. That's something to be proud of - recognizing your flaws. It's a shame there isn't a Pretentious Pricks anonymous or Arrogant Assholes anonymous or even a Self-Righteous Shitheads anonymous. You see, those kinds of folks go around their entire lives thinking there is nothing wrong with them. They get to spend their whole lives treating people like crap and they get away with it."

Lissa grinned, she liked Ortum. He made her laugh.

The three talked on into the evening, sipping beer, relating stories of when they were younger and of antics which they never would have dared now.

Rick pulled in the crab pots at the end of the dock, Lissa threw a few potatoes into a pot along with some celery and cobs of corn. Ortum lit the gas burner, stocked the cooler with beer and ice and lit the candles as the sun disappeared behind the pink sky.

The conversation never ceased as they prepared their meal nor during drinks afterward. They were in that heady place - all on the same page or nearby, discussing philosophy, literature, God, love, death. If one could have smelled the place they had created amongst themselves they would have captured the pungent aroma of faith, if one could have felt the place, they would have felt the chilling dampness left on one's skin after a light rain, and if one could have seen the place, they would have sworn they'd seen the inky cloud of octopi fluid as the trio exposed without care the raw nature of themselves. The evening was surreal, profound in the exposure of identities.

Lissa liked Ortum, his rawness, his earthiness. He was uncapturable, at least by her, meant only to be admired and held in awe. Like the Great Oz before the curtain was lifted, except Lissa hoped there would never be a curtain.

Once, Rick had shared with her a low moment in Ortum's life. "His daddy drowned when he was four years old, he grew up penniless, helping his mother with his brothers and sister. He kept himself submerged in sports all through school and excelled in all of them, got scholarships to college and got his MBA in marketing. He worked in New York for around two years and then quit - told me he wasn't selling himself for anybody - didn't want to play the game. He wants to live his life the way he wants.

"Ortum has been all around the world but on his own dime and he's lived on his own terms, that's for sure. I'm pretty sure he won a lawsuit a few years back when some jack-ass in a cigarette boat t-boned his ketch - a nice, really nice fifty-foot Westerly Centaur. At least, that's what I heard. But then he also swore to me one time that he saw angels ascend from the spray of a sperm whale blowhole."

Then, Lissa had remarked, "Nutty as a fruitcake sounds like to me."

But now, having met the man, she wasn't sure that he hadn't seen the angels and that perhaps he was one himself. Looking at Ortum , Lissa could have sworn she saw a slight aura hazing around his body, was she imagining it? Had she thrown back too many Gold Slagger shots?

Ortum took a breath, a deep one, a slight grin curling the edges of his lips—BBRRUP! He belched. He raised an eyebrow then smiled broadly. "Hell, damnation and shit, that was a mighty fine meal! And ma'am," he nodded to Lissa. "You are a good woman." He scowled at Rick. "Have you told her?"

Rick shook his head, "planning on it just as soon as everybody stops spreading the BS around."

The two men looked at one another, nodded, raised their brows, nodded again and then belly laughed in unison.

"What the hell are you two talking about? Tell me what? Rick, what is it you are supposed to tell me. I'd nearly forgotten about the phone call. You had me going then and now after all the yakety yak we've been doing, the deep shit we've been wading through, geez, I forgot all about it. Tell me." She turned to Ortum. "Must be pretty good. What have you two cooked up? Spill it, one of you say something." Lissa inched closer to Rick.

"You are going to love it." Rick slid his hand over hers and squeezed.

Ortum rose to move into the air conditioned cabin of the trawler. The couple followed dutifully behind him, settling themselves at the settee.

Ortum slid the glass doors shut, fumbled with the A/C dial setting and, towering over the couple, pursed his lips and grunted. "I'm offering my old friend an opportunity to move past this little gig he has going on here." He inhaled deeply then seated himself across from Rick and Lissa. "I've got a little resort down in Nicaragua, San Juan Del Sur, nice little town. Now, the resort isn't much, it's rustic, if you know what I mean and it is little, I'm not going to embellish. Things are still pretty cheap down there, bought it for a song. Rick can help me grow it; he can make a killing doing the same thing there as he does here, taking out the rich folk to go fishing." He nodded to Rick. "And the cost of living? Practically nickels and dimes."

"Tourists have dough but the ones who come here save all year to spend a few days. The ones that come to Nicaragua don't have to scrimp to come down, they have the money. Rick will make three times what he makes here working the same gig. And his cost of living is minimal - way cheaper even than living on Topsail.

"They haven't fucked it up like they have here in the states, Costa Rica, overbuilt, condos everywhere, everything sky high. Now is a good time to buy in Nicaragua - the prices are low.

"Elena, this little old lady down there, got to be in her late seventies, comes from Cuba. Came when Castro came into power. She bought a little bit of land and has a small restaurant with a bar and a marina out front. It's nothing fancy. But she likes me, says I'm honest and she's selling it to me."

For a moment Lissa felt the coldness of loss, she felt her face numb.

Rick squeezed her hand again. "What do you think? How would you like to live in Nicaragua?"

"For how long?"

Disappointment filled his eyes. Rick had expected enthusiasm. Lissa was always talking about how she wanted to travel. "What do you mean? We'd be moving there."

Lissa shook her head. "I don't know." She slipped her hand from Rick's. "My dad, the shop, there are things, my leg. It's a lot to think about. I can't just up and leave."

"The lady's right. It is a lot to think about. A new life, a new lifestyle. But the good thing about it, Lissa, is if you don't like it you can always come back. Topsail isn't going anywhere, neither is Nicaragua. This is just an opportunity to try something different, to see how other people in other parts of the world live. And believe me, life is much different there than it is here. You learn to appreciate things."

"When is all this supposed to take place?"

Leaning in, Ortum drummed his fingers on the table. "First, I want your boyfriend to come down for a few weeks, sail his boat down, try it out. I've got several big parties coming in. Then he can come back here for a week or so and then I'll need him back for a couple more. He can fly back then. But after that I'll need an answer. Basically, I need him to make a decision by the end of the summer."

Chapter 25

Now it didn't seem necessary to mention to Rick that Murdoch and she would be surfing together, that it was only therapy, that there was no past between she and her physical therapist. After hesitating to tell him, wondering if she should, and how she would go about doing it, it didn't matter.

Rick was ecstatic, already counting the money he would earn from the high dollar fishing expeditions. "It's going to take a lot of work."

"It's not work if it's something you love," Ortum explained.

Lissa felt her heart fall beneath her chest, already she missed him but part of her wondered if this wasn't fate stepping in and opening a door to something - someone else.

"It sounds like a good opportunity for you, dear." Lissa's eyes rested on Rick's. "I think you should do it."

She watched his lips droop into a frown and questioning arise on his face.

"But - you. I want you to come with me."

"I can't come now."

Ortum rested his elbows on the settee table. "We have some fine doctors there Lissa, top notch doctors. You'll have access to the best. There are the socialized hospitals there, you'll wait all day but the ex-pats go to the private ones and they're still cheaper than over here. They're just as good if not better."

Lissa bit at her finger, she could feel the pall descend on the threesome. Hesitation was settling in her bones as the feeling of change and loss fell on her. Still there was the sensation of looming possibilities with Doc. But they were friends now. Right?

Lissa shrugged, smiled and responded to the two men waiting for her response to the offer.

She feigned enthusiasm. "Damn, this is such a great opportunity for you Rick. I know how you've wanted to grow your business." Reaching for his hand, she squeezed it. "I don't want to hold you back."

"You're not."

"I feel like if you don't go it will be because of me and I don't want that."

"I'll do whatever you want me to."

"I want you to go and see if it's something you really like."

"Who in the hell wouldn't like it?" Ortum chortled. "Sorry, don't mean to butt in, this is something you two have to discuss."

"No. There is no discussion needed," Lissa retorted. "Rick wants to go. I can see it. He needs to go." She turned to search his eyes. "Go there and check out all the resources for me. And like Ortum says, we can go there and if we don't want to stay we can come back or maybe we'll make it our second home - a few months there, a few months here."

The evening ended on a high note, the men chattering on about the future, Lissa enthused about the adventure of it all. Still not sure though, that she would tear herself away from events brewing in her own life.

She attempted to erase the thoughts of Doc as she and Rick lay in bed facing one another, kissing each other softly as they entwined into a slow rhythmical dance of exploration and pleasure.

Rick gently wiped the beads of sweat from Lissa's brow. Their bodies slippery against one another after making love in in the V berth of his fishing boat. Unlike Ortum's boat, Cloud Nine had no air conditioning.

Rising from the berth, Rick opened the port and starboard portholes and a hatch to help circulated the cooling night breeze. He lay naked against the sheets as he nestled close to Lissa. "What do you think? You've been so quiet since we talked about going to Nicaragua, and I can sense it, you're not as enthused as you act." He cupped her face in his hands. "I want you with me. I love you." He kissed her softly at first, then deeper. "I want you with me forever."

"I can't leave now."

"I know. I guess I shouldn't expect you to. I know there is the shop and your father. You have to live your life. And I know the attack changed everything for you, your leg, having to get used to things. But Lissa, your father has Linda now, don't feel obligated and miss out on something that could change your life."

Pausing, Lissa turned away, a flood of images swept through her – sunsets, the curve of the island at the north end, dolphins playing, and the windswept oaks -- she turned back to him. "I love Topsail. There are still grains of sand on the shore that I walked on as a child."

Doc's image formed in Lissa's head as she turned from Rick, closed her eyes and fell into a deep sleep.

Chapter 26

Doc stood at the top of the beach access, a surfboard leaning against the railing. A woman, his wife, Lissa surmised, stood next to him. Her bright red shoulder length hair blew about in the wind, the skirt of her dress flirted with the breeze.

She must be uncomfortable in those heels, thought Lissa as she studied the woman from the distance.

Ava Soucek, her mouth drawn tightly into a line, quickly scanned the shore until her eyes found Lissa. Her mouth then pulled upward into a broad grin; she waved a hand high above her head.

Was she pretty? Lissa did her best to study the woman from the distance. She wasn't tall, not much taller than herself and she wasn't model-esque. Doc had mentioned a couple of times that his wife was pretty, and yes, yes she was, Lissa surmised, squinting to get a better look at her.

There would be a time, Lissa reassured herself, when she would get an even closer look, a chance to sum up Doc's other half.

But it was evident from Ava's stance that she was a woman sure of herself. She stood next to her man, straight and pressed against him with her arm in his; she held an air of defensiveness. But what woman wouldn't feel that way, when her husband was spending time with an old girlfriend?

Lissa wondered if Doc had mentioned their affair, their teenage romance. But whether he had or not, no woman in her right mind would let her husband romp in the ocean with a scantily clad female, even if she had only one leg, even if she was a patient. Lissa surely would not have.

Leaning against her husband, Ava cast a glance to Lissa. She ran a hand along his arm to around his neck, pulling him to kiss her lips. Her movements said, "He's mine." She waved to Lissa again and smiled.

How insecure she must be, thought Lissa. *I am no threat.*

Ava descended the stairs quickly, out of sight in only moments. Doc, the surfboard held tightly under his arm, descended the steps to the beach confidently, his eyes focused on Lissa, his lips forming a broad smile.

"Damn, this is going to be fun. I'm going to stink but it'll be fun."

"It will come back to you, it's like riding a bike." Lissa commented as she waded into the water.

"Riding a bike? Maybe the balance, that's the part I need practice with." He stepped closer to her. "And for old time's sake, I wanted to see you back on the water. You were so fantastic, so graceful. You know, you had me from the beginning."

My balance? I haven't surf in so long and now I have to try it without my leg, on a prosthetic. "You? You are worried about balance. Good grief, I don't even have a real leg, it's—"

"Just remember," he scolded, "and I assume you've been utilizing proprioception? You've been doing or should have been doing it all along. Come on Lissa, you can do this, the feeling is in the residual. The prosthetic will do what it's supposed to do."

She glanced back at him as she glided the board over a wave. He looked good, strong, though his pale skin disproved the existence of any outdoor activities. *What did he mean?* She thought. *Scolding me like a child.* Tenacity replaced doubt and she paddled harder. *And what did that mean? You had me from the beginning. What is he talking about?*

"I'm impressed. You've got a longboard and it's a Bing?" She asked sarcastically.

"I like having the best, makes me look good," Doc chuckled.

"The only thing that is going to make you look good is your performance, Dr. Soucek."

"Smarty pants," Murdock chuckled. "What's wrong with having nice things?"

"Nothing." She slid her eyes to his. "But the board is not going to make you a good surfer."

"Sure it will."

Now she remembered the attitude. She recalled how long ago he had appeared so sure of himself and how he even

231

boasted of the surf board he had purchased back then. *Some things don't change,* she chuckled to herself.

Sometimes she wasn't sure if he was joking or if he wasn't. She caught his eye as she continued to watch him.

Doc grinned, he winked, his eyes holding that same twinkle that they had held long ago. It had overwhelmed her then, left her in awe of the power his confidence conjured.

Thinking of it, recalling the days past, it seem so incongruent, his confidence in tasks and ability yet so insecure when it came to his parents. Perhaps that is where he found his peace, through sports and fancy cars. The realization brought the sense of time and how it binds, to the fore; she oozed into the familiarity.

Recognizing the old feelings, she could smell and taste what had once consumed her. Part of her wanted to reach out and push his arrogant ass from the board, the other half wanted to pull him in the water, splash and play with Doc like she had in her youth, to relive the happiness. The recollection of that carefree love swept over her like seawater itself.

"This is going to be good, Lissa. Surfing is going to strengthen your leg muscles. And that new prosthetic, you're going to love it." Murdoch relaxed on the surfboard. "I've learned that when someone is enjoying something, the healing is quicker." Letting his arms fall into the water, Doc paddled nearer to Lissa to float side by side with her. "No sharks today, I hope."

232

"Thanks, for mentioning that. Until now I wasn't even thinking about them."

"What happened to you was a fluke. The chances of it ever happening again are almost nil. You, Lissa, love the ocean too much to give it up."

Propping herself to sit upright on the board, Lissa swayed with the movement of the water. "Doesn't look like we're going to get much action today."

"Maybe that's a good thing. We'll do a little at a time, baby steps."

She blew a breath, closed her eyes and began, "To tell you the truth, I'm a little nervous, but it does feels good. I needed this."

Doc's smile faded, his eyes studying the water as he licked his lips. "Yeah, me, too."

"I was body surfing the day I was attacked. I hardly ever surfed. Maybe a few times a year, but I didn't have the time once I had Abby and started working for my father and going to UNCW. "

"Tell me you taught your daughter to surf. You were so good."

"The kids she hung out with did that. She's a fish, loves the water, but prefers diving."

"So you gave up the thing you loved most in the world, huh?"

Lissa shrugged. "We do what we have to do."

"How do you like working at the shop? Kind of keeps you tethered to here. I'm surprised, you always said you wanted to travel."

"Again," her eyes holding his, "You do what you have to do. I never had the time to travel. And yes, I like working at the shop. I'm the head guy now." She laughed.

"So you take care of the business end of the shop?"

"Yes."

"And you're doing repairs as well?"

"Yes, a few minor things, I do mostly sales and we have another mechanic that does the complicated stuff," Lissa tittered.

"And your father?"

"Daddy's in his sixties, he's worked all his life, raised me without any help, he deserves some free time to enjoy his life."

"What happened to all that righteous indignation about the development of the island?" Doc nodded back to the beach, Lissa's eyes perused the shoreline.

She shrugged, "I hate it, but what can I do. I have no power and no desire to get in the mud with politicians. That's a dirty world."

"Yes it is, but someone has to do it."

"It's been a long time since there had been natural dunes on the island. Hurricanes did not help, they had flattened a few but Mother Nature could have remedied that if developers had not torn down the remaining ones." She grinned sarcastically.

234

"A building and sand dunes cannot occupy the same space. Buildings destroy the integrity of them."

The words sounded genuine, but they lacked the enthusiasm Doc had expected. "Lost the fire, huh?"

Lissa shrugged again. "I just keep the fire in check, it's more of a controlled burn. I vote, but I'm out numbered and I'm tired of being angry over something that I can't control."

"Life's too short to be angry over things like that. I've learned my lesson."

His eyes looked apologetically to hers.

Could he be referring to when we were kids? She thought. And there it was again, that fluttering feeling in her stomach, the emptiness in her throat, the pull of sorrow - all carrying her back to her youth. Lissa turned her back to Doc, steeling herself, endeavoring to untangle herself from the tendrils of time. "Once the dunes were all over this island, even in its interior. Those were bulldozed."

"I remember that day very well."

"Which one?" She slid her eyes back to meet his.

"You were chained to a bulldozer. You wore a pink cap, your hair was longer. I thought you had to be some kind of woman to do what you were doing. It took guts. It took conviction."

"I didn't change anything." Her eyes drifted from his and she paddled farther out.

"Maybe you could have," he hollered. "Look at it now. It doesn't even look the same."

"Your father had a lot to do with that."

"Not everything."

"Maybe not everything but he started it."

"Somebody had to sell it to him, somebody sold him the land. He didn't steal it. How can you blame just him?"

Lissa sat up on the board, Doc drifted next to her; his breath quick.

"Damn, I'm out of shape."

"You are." Her eyes blazed into his.

"Look, my dad was a bastard, he didn't give a damn about much of anything except money. But it takes two, sweetheart. This land wasn't stolen and built upon. Somebody had to sell it. Somebody sold their precious land for money. They wanted it just as much as the developers."

"I don't think they would have sold it if they knew what was going to happen."

"Are you sure?"

"I don't know, and I guess that's what burns me up more than anything. I don't expect people who aren't from here to care or love or even understand. I really can't blame them for being money grubbing assholes. That's how they make a living."

"They're not all money grubbing assholes, but thanks." He scowled satirically.

"It's the people I grew up with, the people who worked side by side with my father that sold their souls for a few dollars."

"It's not a few dollars, Lissa. We're talking millions - billions."

"Screw money!"

Rising with the swell of a wave, Doc pulled himself to sit. "Screw money? Shit. How naive are you? You're a businesswoman. You have to make a living. You have to eat."

"I'm not a pig. I don't want the whole damn cake. I don't want to destroy something else so that I can have what I want."

"I'll give you that. You were never selfish, neither was your father."

"Yours was."

"And there's a whole lot of people on this island that are, too."

"And they do it all in the name of progress!" Lissa nearly shouted. "They reconcile their greed in the name of *progress.*" Her lips tightened, her chest rose as she breathed heavily. "Cancer progresses, not all progress is a good thing."

"I agree."

Lissa relaxed her shoulders as they moved with the water. It felt familiar, the arguing with Doc. It roused old feelings. "The north bridge - there was a time that when coming from Sneads Ferry onto the island - right in the middle of the bridge you looked out straight into the ocean, nothing blocking the view.

Then someone built a bunch of houses that no one lives in and the view disappeared."

Doc nodded.

"There are areas on the island where houses are built nearly to the road, there are buildings built so high you can't see the ocean, there are no dunes, there used to be dunes everywhere, not just in front of the water—"

Doc nodded as she ranted. "I know, I know. Poor planning, greed, all kinds of reasons for the way things look now. But to many who don't live here, it is still a quaint little beach town. They like it."

"They don't know what they've missed."

Doc's bare leg grazed hers as he caught her eyes. "I know. I often wonder how it would be if things had been different."

Already the fire had been ignited inside her and then his touch fueled it even more. Lissa felt the want in her throat, she told herself no and moved away quickly. Theirs was a friendship, that's all it could be. She smiled at him coyly though, teasing. "You never did understand - you *tourist*." She shot an accusing gaze to him.

"*You* don't understand. Change, she is a coming,"

"Humph." Lissa felt the weak rise of a wave, she paddled with the momentum it brought. She rose to a crouch, searching for balance. It was there, she moved her body to it find it. Rising to stand, and for just a moment it was like it had always been. Then she lost her footing and splashed into the water.

"At least you tried," Doc joked later as they sat on the shore.

"Wussy-man."

"Yep, I'm too chicken. I didn't even try."

"Next time."

"Next time for sure."

Chapter 27

Rick had been gone nearly a week. He'd called twice - the first time he must have been fairly close to the mainland and they talked for nearly an hour. He was obviously excited about the trip as he chattered on about the particulars of the arrangement between him and his buddy Ortum. He asked how she was doing, how the P T sessions in Cary were going along.

Lissa neglected to tell him about the change of venue, how she was no longer traveling to Cary and how Murdoch Soucek was now coming on weekends to his beach cottage and surfing with her. It seemed too late to mention all of that - too late to mention that her doctor was an old lover - and, Lissa reasoned, too late to mention things that really didn't matter. Doc was simply her doctor, an old friend. There could be no harm in that. Could there?

Rick's call ended with him professing his love, how lonely he was and how eager he was for her to join him.

There had been no calls the following two days, Lissa assumed that Rick was far out to sea where there was no access to phone towers.

Earlier, as she drove to Doc's cottage, the phone rang again. It was Rick. She saw the lighted letters on the screen but ignored them as she drove south into Topsail Beach. A few moments later, came the beep, beep indicating that a text had come in.

Lissa tapped the icon and read, *Hi sweet girl, miss you already. Took me three days to get over here - ocean calm as a lake. Pulling the boat up on the hard for a little hull maintenance. Luckily no engine trouble. Pulled into San Juan Del Sur, lots of other boats here, mostly sails. And so far the people are really nice. Not as tropical as Costa Rica, lots of dirt roads, beaches aren't covered with high rise condos and Speedo wearing tourists. Very low key. The sand is nearly black from the all the volcano activity here. Maybe that will keep the developers away. Small community of ex-pats that seem to be just my kind of folks. Sorry I missed you. Will call back later. Love you and miss you, Rick.*

The guilt fell over her like a shroud as Lissa read the words. She felt her stomach sink and her shoulders ache.

She knew she was being deceptive. Knowing in her heart that she longed for one man and not the other. It was so unfair, she hated the thought of hurting Rick. The man had been so good to her, she knew he loved her.

He was every girl's dream - totally unselfish. She'd had those before, where a man manipulated her time, sought changes in her, demanded understanding when he had none to give. Rick was just the opposite. So it made no sense that it was not Rick who was her first thought every morning or that it was

242

not Rick who she pictured in her mind's eyes with the smiles and responses to the things she wished she could say and do.

It was Doc. He's the one she saw in everything. He's the one she imagined conversations with, moments with, exchanges with.

No, it made no sense that a man who had hurt her so deeply was who she longed for so intensely.

Maybe in time, things would work themselves out. So far nothing had happened between her and Doc. Maybe this infatuation or left over teenage love would disappear and a true friendship emerge. Maybe things would change by the time Rick got back from Nicaragua.

Her mind still tangled in thought, Lissa pulled into the drive way of Rick's sound side cottage. His wife's car was parked on the side of the house.

Lissa felt uncomfortable as she watched Ava exit the front door.

She smiled. "I got in all the way to Godwin's store and remembered that I left my briefcase." Ava ran her fingers through her hair. She'd died the tips blue. They bounced just above her shoulders.

It's the trend now, Lissa reasoned.

"You two going to the beach today?" Ava questioned , her tone light and unassuming.

"Yeah, the therapy really helps a lot."

Ava nodded, "I think it's good for Murdoch too, he's been getting a little flabby." She winked at Lissa. "You should come over some time and have a drink with us."

"Thank you," Lissa responded cheerfully.

"You two have a good time surfing." Ava called back as she stepped toward her BMW. "Tell Ricky to be sure to be ready at six, we've dinner with the Bronsons at the Hilton."

Lissa nodded and watched as Ava backed onto the road and drove away.

"Are you ready?"

Lissa heard Doc's voice call from the front door.

"As ready as I'll ever be."

"I think you're doing great, Lissa."

She eyed him curiously.

"On the other hand, I'm scared shitless."

"Why?"

"I look like a fool."

"No you don't. You just look like someone who hasn't been on a board for a while," she teased. "I'm the one that should be scared shitless."

"Remember, what happened to you was a fluke. The likelihood of it happening again is a million to one. And the Lissa I knew was not afraid of odds like that. "

"I'm not sure I'm the same girl you remember, Doc."

He shook his head. "Don't sell yourself short. I've seen enough people with handicaps in my life. Most shrivel away from society, you don't."

"I'm not handicapped," Lissa growled.

"See, that's just what I'm saying. You don't succumb to tragedy, you deny it and move on. I always liked that about you. Your feistiness, your—"

"Feistiness? Hell, I've told you that I really didn't surf very often, I quit fighting the progress—"

" Lissa, you're not your average person - you're strong. And I don't think you even know it. You didn't even know it when we were kids."

There it was again, reference to their youth, when there were no games, when they were in love. *Would you stop it!* she wanted to shout. She wanted to move forward, not live in the past. "Doc, we're different people. And to tell the truth, we were different people then, too."

"No we're not. We have always wanted the same thing."

"Bullshit. How in the world can you even think that? You're a city boy, I'm a small town girl - earthy."

"I'm earthy," he blurted.

Lissa eyed him curiously, how could he even think he was like her, maybe he yearned for simpler things. She pressed her thoughts to recall when they were younger and how he loved his grandmother's house, this one, so much more than the monstrosity his father had built, the one Hurricane Fran had destroyed.

Maybe he did want things simpler, less pretentious. Maybe he was still fighting to find that part of himself.

"I know what you're thinking," Doc's grin spread across his face. "You think I'm a spoiled rich asshole who values things more than heart and soul."

Her face lifting curiously to his, Lissa pursed her lips and raised a brow. "Yep."

"That's not true. It may have been true at one time - to a certain extent, but it's not so much that way now." Doc slid the surfboard under his arm and stepped into a pair of worn canvas shoes. "You always had heart, you always knew how to express that heart. It was difficult for me, I never knew what I wanted, only what my parents wanted for me. I had to depend on them for my life, your father taught you to depend on yourself. I was headed in that direction when I met you. I was starting to believe in me. But," he shrugged, "it hasn't been until the last couple of years that I've come back to feeling that it's okay for me to want to live a certain kind of life."

"So you're going to sell your business and become a beach bum?"

Doc guffawed, "Not hardly. I've enjoyed my career. I'm good at it. Notice, I'm not a surgeon or physician. In that sense I got to be the kind of doctor I wanted to be, not the kind my parents wanted. And I'm very good at what I do. I've had a good life and now it's time for me to enjoy what I truly want." He looked sternly into her eyes. "I don't believe in coincidences."

Lissa gasped.

"No, I don't. I think I'm here to help you. Maybe I wasn't there in the past but the path led to you, to now."

Lissa was silent. She didn't know how to respond to him now. Gathering her board and beach paraphernalia, Lissa spoke, "Sounds like you've been giving things a lot of thought."

"Yeah, I have, especially in the last few months."

It was overwhelming, the innuendo. Was he saying she was changing his life or was it wishful thinking again? Lissa shook her head, shook away the futile thoughts, endeavoring to steer the conversation to a lighter tone. "Today you're going to do it - stand up. If I can do it you can, too."

"Right." He rolled his eyes.

"You'll get better." Lissa nodded.

"You did well last time - stood up."

"For two seconds."

"But you did, and you will get better every time you go out."

Lissa nodded. "This is very kind of you, Murdoch. You're obligated to no more than doing what you can at the Center."

Moving aside to allow Lissa to enter the beach access first, Doc answered, "Are you complaining?"

Lissa kicked off her flip flop as she reached the sand and strode rapidly toward the water, trying her best to keep up with Doc.

"Come on, move it." He laughed back to her and bent his head to study the swath of shells there.

"Screw you, Scarface," Lissa called back.

"Holy crap, look at this!" He bent, retrieved an item and held it in his hand, examining it.

"It's stunning." Lissa reached to take the shark's tooth from his fingers.

"Got to be from a great white."

"I don't know but it sure is big. It's the biggest one I've ever found."

Lissa placed it in his hand. "It's nice."

"Want it?"

"No. You found it. Maybe we can find another."

Slipping the tooth into the pocket of his swim trunks, Doc teased, "Maybe this will keep the sharks away."

Their laughter was loud and playful as they paddled to breach the oncoming swells.

"Today is going to be good," Lissa hollered to Doc.

"I know, it is already."

Chapter 28

"It's our big meal," Linda explained. "We try not to eat much after lunch, you know, John's and my metabolisms are practically nothing now that we're in our sixties." She giggled.

"You know, now that we're *old farts*." She slid a playful glance to Lissa as she placed a platter of fresh grilled grouper in the center of the dining room table. "You have got to try my onion pie." Linda sliced a wedge from the pan and placed it on Lissa's plate.

"Hmm, onion pie. This is a new one."

It smelled divine and looked absolutely scrumptious. Severing a small piece with her fork, Lissa popped it into her mouth. "Damn, that's good - doesn't sound like it would be but it sure is yummy."

Linda raised an eyebrow. "Sauté three cups onions, add two eggs, half a cup of almond milk, then pour into a cracker crust and top with the cheese of your choice - I like mild cheddar - then twenty minutes in the oven and voila, you have onion pie and not an ounce of sugar." She grinned, cat-like, settling her hands above her hips onto her waist. "Trying to cut back on my sugar, I've lost seven pounds."

Nodding, Lissa maneuvered a cut of grouper onto her plate. "Okay, I know you and Daddy asked me over here to talk about something." She gazed at her father. "What is it?"

John lifted his eyes, the look they held told Lissa that the ensuing conversation was not going to be a pleasant one. What was it he would be crawling her ass for now? She hadn't messed up at the boat shop, everything was in order there, no complaints from customers lately and no problems with the help.

The idea of him having knowledge of Doc slipped through her mind but how would he have known about that? She'd not even mentioned him to Linda. She'd not even said the name, Soucek. No, she thought, Linda couldn't have, wouldn't have.

"So, you're going surfing with your doctor?" The conversation began just as Lissa rested her fork on the plate. She looked up to her father's face, then over to Linda's.

"Don't look at me. Don't blame me, all I did was tell your daddy the name of the physical therapist you're seeing. He did the rest.'

Lissa scowled , her mouth pursed.

"Look, Sweetie. I picked up a card at the office, it had the two doctor's names on it. I asked the receptionist how to pronounce the name and she said he was your doctor. I didn't think anything of it and I didn't think anything of it when your father asked me about the appointment." She raised her hands in defense. "What's wrong with your daddy knowing what doctor you see? How was I to know he was an old boyfriend?"

"Old Sam was on the Sea View fishing pier and saw you surfing with some fellow. I didn't know you were surfing again. How can you with your leg?"

Lissa tapped on the prosthetic. "It's not easy but I'm doing it - and with Doc's help."

John's voice rose as he continued, "I hear the renters from little the house in Topsail Beach were gone and the Souceks, husband and *wife*, had moved back in." He leaned toward his daughter. "You're in your forties, you're a grown woman. I can't tell you right from wrong now if you don't know it already. But surfing with this fellow? We know what that led to the last time. And, Lissa, he's married."

"It's part of the physical therapy."

"Bullshit."

"It is!"

"He's married. Don't tell me his wife is okay with you two."

"I'd never let John do that," Linda remarked. "I'd never let him spend time with another woman, especially with the kind of history you two have."

"I'm a patient," Lissa defended.

"You're a beautiful woman," John countered.

"I'm a gimp."

Linda shook her head. "It doesn't matter. You're pretty, you're smart and you're way too nice to this asshole that dumped you when you were just a kid."

"There were reasons," she paused. "And he's my doctor." Lissa raised an eyebrow. "I know he's off limits and besides, I have Rick." Lissa closed her eyes against the allegations. "That thing with Doc was a long time ago. We're friends, just friends now."

"Does Rick know about your friend, the doctor? Does he know about all this?" John asked rhetorically as he pushed himself back from the table. "Where's he at? I haven't seen him around for a few days. Don't tell me you've—"

"Rick left for Nicaragua."

John caught his breath. "Run him off, he found out about this old lover of yours—"

"No Daddy. There's nothing between me and Doc, he's my doctor, my physical therapist. He's an old friend."

"*Doc*, he's been called Doc since he was a kid."

"Rick and I are still together, Daddy. He's going to Nicaragua to fish for a while with an old friend of his."

Lissa's father inhaled, bit down on the cigar he'd just placed between his lips. "I'm a man, Lissa. I know how these things go."

"Murdoch's married, Daddy." She blurted the words, repeating them, using them as a shield against any wrong doing she might do. "Rick and I are still together."

John shot her a knowing glance. He'd always been able to read her mind, to see past any roadblocks she threw his way. His responsive glare told her she wasn't fooling him. "Yeah? You get your ass in a sling this time, Gal, I can't bail you out. Got it?"

"That won't happen, Daddy."

"I know how these things go. I remember you not eating for months and the piece of shit you married on the rebound." He shook his head. "I'm just telling you, as if it will do any good. You always rode your heart like you did those waves."

An uncomfortable feeling settled in her mid-section as she settled her raised fork back on the plate. "I am not doing anything wrong," she snarled.

"Sorry honey, we didn't mean to get you so upset." Linda patted her hand.

"Where there's smoke, there's fire," John growled.

Linda pulled her chair closer to her husband. "Lissa is a grown woman and if she doesn't know right from wrong by now, well, don't you think she does? And this isn't any of our business. Remember, hotshot, I was a married woman when you met me and that sure as hell didn't stop you."

"That was different."

"How? You tell me how that was different."

"You were separated."

"Newly. I could have gone back. I would have gone back if you hadn't of taken that picture of me. You pulled it out of your pocket."

His face reddening, John nudged Linda. "Come on now, that's enough."

"Aw Geez, are we talking nudity? Nude pictures? I don't care to hear about that," Lissa teased.

John shook his head. "Hell no."

"Your father took a picture of me sitting in the dunes, I was wiped out, hadn't seen forty in a while, never had any kids, and the only man I'd ever been with was dumping me for some other woman who he'd gotten pregnant. Hell, I was sobbing and just a mess." Linda wrapped an arm around John. "You're daddy took that picture, I didn't even know it and the next time I came into the boat shop for some bait he showed it to me - said I was beautiful and that he would never make me hurt or cry like that."

"Daddy, I didn't know you were so romantic." Lissa winked at her father. "Why you're just a big old teddy bear, aren't you?"

He shrugged and looked into Linda's face. "I love you, always did. Even when you and that worthless husband of yours would come in together. I always wondered what in the hell you were doing with him."

"Waiting for you." Linda purred.

Turning to Lissa, John spoke, "I don't want you getting hurt. I know about love, I know what it does - changes your whole insides to where you can't see straight."

"Daddy, maybe you're right. Maybe I have some long lost feelings for Murdoch, but I know it can't work. We live different kinds of lives. His wife is gorgeous, she makes me look like Attila the Hun, and she has both legs."

"Does she know about you and lover boy surfing together?"

"Yes, and she's okay with it."

"Does she hang around while you two—"

"Ava is a busy woman, flies to New York and Europe all the time. You see, she's a worldly woman, beautiful, hobnobs with the elite - I can't compete with her. "

"Love isn't about what you do, it's who you are," Linda broke in. "The most attractive thing to a man is a woman who is in love with him."

"I'm not in love with him. Don't you two understand that? We're friends. The past is the past. I'm over all of that. So is Doc."

Her father lifted his eyes to hers, they told her he saw past her words. Lowering them he muttered, "If you say so."

"Look, if everyone wasn't cool with the situation, don't you think Ava would be crappy to me? She must be okay with him taking lessons with me. She walks with him to the dunes before lessons - waves to me. She met me at the parking lot once and we chatted about how good it was for him to be outside doing

255

something and how glad she was that I was surfing again. Hell, she even invited me over for drinks sometime. "

"Keep your friends close, your enemies closer," Linda snickered.

Chapter 29

Six-thirty, the sun was coming up and Lissa was on her back porch perusing the morning colors dancing across the water. Nemo was outside doing his business; she opened the screen door for him to come back in.

Lifting his lazy head to look at her, he wagged his furry tail and opened his mouth to pant a cheerful greeting.

Relaxing into the rocking chair Lissa held the coffee mug with both hands and glanced at her cell phone resting on the side table. She reached a hand to her side and patted her old dog. He groaned a languid acknowledgment and closed his eyes to sleep.

She'd had him since he was pup, actually he'd been Abby's dog, but now, old and slow, he was hers.

Lissa leaned her head back against the slats of the chair, closed her eyes and listened to the morning sounds of the marsh - the rustle of cattails in the breeze, the bird songs, the sound of her neighbor revving his truck as he readied to leave for work. She smiled and waited for the blackbirds to make their morning rush.

Every morning around this time the rush of thousands of small birds taking flight from the marsh to some other destination resonated across her back yard and beyond. It was a cloud of chirps and the flapping of wings that filled the sky. Somehow the sound reassured her that life was not only good but profound.

Sighing, she eased her thoughts to fully focus on what she had wakened to - Murdoch. Her thoughts swarmed around the man with whom she'd been surfing, nothing specific, just images of his smiles, laughter, his eyes and the way he held himself. She looked to the phone again and as if having willed it to do so, it buzzed - she had a text.

When is a good time? It read.

Lissa typed in the letters, *Anytime between 10 and 3. Whatever is good for you.* Her heart raced a bit before reminding herself that Murdoch Soucek *was* married, he had a lovely wife. There was no way he could be interested in her. But it didn't matter. He was in her head, her heart.

Sounds good, c u at 12. Doc responded.

They'd been meeting for four weeks, talking more than surfing, reminiscent of the religious/political discussions in their youth. Lissa looked forward to the sessions and from the looks on Doc's face, he must have, too. He was so adept at helping her with the prosthetic, the nuances of how it moved and how she moved with it. It was his language, and it rolled off his tongue with ease and knowledge, leaving her to feel confident and safe.

The last two meetings, they'd met in North Topsail, fewer people were there. Doc explained that he liked the solitude, that he didn't care for all the tourists gawking at him and his pale skin as he attempted to surf.

Maybe this time, since they were meeting around lunch, Doc would bring something to eat. He had the last time they'd met.

She'd been surprised when he'd opened a small basket of warm rolls and Havarti cheese. She supplied the bottled water; she always had water on hand, especially since the weather had begun to turn so warm. Meeting with him was fun. It had been decades since she'd enjoyed the water as she did with Doc.

Wrapped in thoughts of the coming lesson, Lissa grinned, letting her imagination wander to the last time they'd met and how he brushed against her leg, he was always doing that. But this last time he had not moved away.

The sensation of that touch and how they'd held each other's gaze pulsed in her belly.

The phone buzzed again, it was Rick. Lissa gasped, found her composure and answered. "Hello."

"Hi Sweetie. God I miss you."

"Miss you, too. How are things going down there?" She listened as he talked excitedly about Nicaragua, taking fishing parties out, swimming in the clear water. He was especially impressed by how kind the people were, the simplicity of it all and the easy going lifestyle. "I love it. You'd love it."

He'd gone horseback riding in the jungle a few days before. "There were huge iguanas in the trees, Lissa. It was so cool. We ate one for dinner that night." He laughed. "Tastes like chicken."

She laughed.

"I miss you," he added. "I hope you're thinking about this, about me. You do miss me, don't you?"

"Of course I do. I've just been busy with the shop and well, I've started surfing again, Rick."

"Surfing? How in the world are you doing that?"

"It's a new orthotic - I'm getting better with it, I'm balancing so much better. If I didn't know better I'd think I had both legs. You can hardly tell at all that I'm different."

"Babe, that sounds fantastic. I'm so happy for you."

"Thanks, I'm taking—"

Interrupted by the flash of Doc's name and number on her phone, Lissa battled as to which man she'd talk with. The first buzz, then the second. "I have to go Rick. Okay."

"Okay, babe. I love you."

"Hi. We still on for today?" She responded to Doc, her voice light and cheerful.

"Yes, around one would be good. Does that work for you?"

"Sounds good." Lissa checked the time on the phone quickly, seven-thirty. *Five hours,* she thought. "I'll be there."

"Or be square." It was a goofy statement, Doc thought, but he liked the sound of her voice.

"Or be square? Are we going to wear penny loafers and poodle skirts today?"

"Watched an old movie about the '50s last night."

"Uh huh," Lissa giggled.

"Guess it's still in my head."

Silence for a few seconds and Doc added. "Well, I just wanted to be sure. I know it's early, but I knew you'd be up enjoying the morning."

"I'll be there."

"Maybe I'll bring something to eat."

"Sounds good."

"Bye."

"Bye."

****

Think I'll do a little fishing before we meet, Lissa thought, eager to get to the beach where she'd be meeting Murdoch. Her heart raced as she gathered her surfboard, rod and reel, and tackle box. The thought of seeing him wrapped around her as she filled the car. It was all she wanted, to see him.

Behind the wheel as she drove, Lissa caught her breath. She pictured his lips smiling at her, him resting his arm against hers, him leaning so closely into her that if she had turned her face they would have touched. Married men weren't supposed to be like that. But Doc never faltered when he touched her or when she felt his eyes studying her, resting on her shoulders or watching as she talked , as she gave instructions, things he should have already known. She blushed at the thought of him watching her as she spoke. Lissa was keenly aware, that rather than he paying attention to her words, he was watching her, studying. She could only surmise that he must feel the same as she.

The imageries and feelings frightened her as questions of infidelity ran through her mind. Was there trouble at home, a growing distance between husband and wife?

Her hands on the wheel, Lissa surrendered to the images in her head - Ava, Ava and Doc. How could Ava know the man Lissa knew? She was occupied with other things. Lived in a world so unlike the world Doc wanted to live in, Lissa told herself, a world of travel and business and hurried people who had no idea what living was all about. And, she left him alone - *alone*. Lissa would never leave him alone to feel detached and distant, unwanted, unloved. Ava couldn't possibly know his heart like she did, nor understand him or reach the place that he needed to be.

Images of them together as teenagers settled in her and Lissa groaned an emphatic *no.* She could tell herself these things all she wanted, but it didn't make it true. "No!" She shouted aloud.

She flipped on the radio, a song played. "Thoughts of you, why do you hurt me like this?" The artist crooned.

The feel of Doc's presence, being near him, laughing with him enveloped her, swam through her body. There was no denying it now. She was in love with him, no use running from or using Rick to keep her mind from fanaticizing about someone that filled her so.

"Poor Rick, he deserves better." She felt the sting of tears as they welled in her eyes.

You don't stop loving somebody. You just put it away somewhere. Lock it away. Her father had told her long ago. But she'd found the damn key, *it* was there, the intensity and ache, longing that she'd carried as a teen. It was back, and had grown beyond her memory of it all. This she wasn't going to stop. She wanted that love, the feeling, that all-consuming, ethereal feeling that gave breath to life.

Chapter 30

"Catching anything?" Doc asked.

Turning sharply from thought and from the hypnotic movement of the waves, Lissa gasped. "Oh, you scared me!"

"Sorry. I didn't mean to. Catch anything?" He repeated.

"Not really, a few bites, but nothing." She turned lowering her eyes, afraid to meet his.

"It's getting too hot to catch much. You know the fish go deep when it gets hot."

She nodded.

"What's the matter?" Doc rested his hand on her shoulder.

"Nothing. I'm just engrossed in fishing."

"Hum, yeah sure. You're day dreaming about that boyfriend of yours. What's his name - Rick?"

Lissa reeled the line in, removed the bait and settled the rod in the holder.

"What's the latest word from him? Is he still raking in the dough down in Nicaragua?"

"He called yesterday. Yeah, he's been taking parties out."

"When's lover boy coming home?" Doc teased.

What was I thinking? He's teasing about Rick. I've just made something out of nothing. Damn! Lissa lifted her eyes to his. "In a few days, I've missed him. It will be good to see him again."

"Have you been thinking about going down there with him?"

What is that in his tone, in his eyes? Damn Lissa, she admonished herself, *he doesn't care. I've been imagining things. He's just asking.*

"I'd hate to see you go. We've been having such a good time. I haven't felt like this in years." Doc's eyes held hers, he reached to catch a strand of her hair and placed it behind her ear. "You're doing so well with this new peg." His eyes danced as he chuckled.

"Peg?" She shook her head. "First it's gimp and now it's *peg*. Man, you're cruel, Scarface." Crinkling her nose, Lissa teased. "You are so full of it."

"Oh, yeah, I brought you a gift." Doc pulled a rolled poster from a bag and unscrolled it, holding it up between his hands. "What do you think?"

Lissa perused the poster of the actors and athletes standing, some with a prosthesis, some without.

Jeffrey Rush dressed as Barbossa the pirate, his peg leg in full view, stood next to Colin Cook a surfer who lost a leg to a tiger shark attack. Actors portraying Captain Ahab, Long John Silver and Lieutenant Dan formed a line alongside Amy Purdy and Bethany Hamilton, other survivors of shark attacks.

"Geez, you really know how to make a girl feel attractive."

"Your picture needs to be up here - you'd be the prettiest one by far."

"You're full of it." Lissa bit her lip, her eyes found the shelled sandy shore.

"This Halloween you can go as a pirate."

"Okay, Scarface." She giggled. "Who was the notorious gangster that was called Scarface.?"

"Al Capone."

"I'll go as a scallywag pirate and you can be Capone. We'd make a pair," she tittered, searching his eyes. "You always make me laugh, Doc."

Stepping closer to her, Doc ran his fingers along her arm.

Lissa smiled nervously, glanced at his board and reeled in the fishing line. "Let's hit the waves, it looks like a good day today."

"I'm with you, chick."

It was a nervous day for Lissa, studying Doc. One minute he was laughing and joking, another he was reticent almost sad looking.

And then there was the flirting, or was it that? She just wasn't sure. She wondered if she should bend into him when he leaned so close into her. Should she not turn away when he held her gaze for so long -should she say anything? She certainly did not want to make a fool out of herself and she most certainly did not want to scare him away by confessing her love.

He grew quieter as the day wore on and she caught him staring off into the horizon several times.

"What's up Doc?" She teased. "You don't seem quite yourself today."

He shrugged. "Lot of things going on at the clinic, that's all."

"Can I help?"

He searched her eyes and paused. "No, I'll work it out. But thanks."

Splashing water toward him, Lissa chided, "Don't be a fuddy duddy, get on with it. You haven't caught a single wave today."

"Busy watching you. You've been doing great."

"I'm learning, getting the feel of this contraption."

Lissa relished the feeling of accomplishment, the periods of standing and maneuvering the waves grew longer and longer.

"I suck."

"As long as you don't do anything, you will suck."

"Okay, you win." Doc lifted with the next swell, waiting for the momentum.

"I hope you've put some sunscreen on that pearly white skin." Lissa joked.

"Yes, Mother." Doc paddled harder catching the wave, crouching as he maneuvered his feet along the board and finally stood. His body swaying easily as he flew through the water before wiping out.

"Damn, that was fantastic." He unwrapped a pita pocket of sprouts and turkey and bit into it eagerly. "Two decent ones."

"You've got stoke."

"Like hell I do." Lissa tipped the bottle water back and drank. "Is Ava in New York now?"

The question startled him. "No. She's home."

"Oh."

"She leaves tomorrow for London."

"Really? Are you going with her this time?"

"No."

"Ava will be busy—"

"The tower of London, Big Ben, the Tate Museum - there are so many things to see."

"I've seen them all - ten times."

"Take a train to Scotland or—"

"Lissa, I've done it."

"I would never tire of doing that - traveling, I want to see the world."

"Of all the places I've been this is the place I always gravitate to, this is what I call home."

"Why?"

"Everything I want is here." His arm was around her shoulder, pulling her into him. His lips were on hers. And it was heaven.

The stubble of his beard pricked her face, it felt good. His sour breath mixed with hers, it tasted good. Her skin melted into his as he caressed her face.

Kissing her, his lips sliding across hers, their tongues eased together.

"Not here," she said, pushing him from her.

"Come with me." Doc squeezed her hand and rose, bringing Lissa to her feet. "Follow me."

It's what she wanted, to feel him, touch him, be one with him. She wanted his eyes to drink her, lips to explore her, to ease the life she'd settled for. "Did you really love me?"

Sliding into the seat of his silver Alfa Romeo he lifted his eyes to her. "I never stopped."

Moving through Surf City, Doc sped up a few miles. Lissa followed behind, turned on the radio, turned it off. The sound of her heartbeat and the images in her mind were enough.

They parked in her driveway. Lissa led the way through her screened porch and into the bedroom. Nemo looked up at Doc, sniffed at his legs and rested his head back gently on his paws.

"Yep, that's my attack dog."

Doc chuckled, and reached for Lissa, pulling her into him. Lying her on the bed he bent to unfasten the orthotic. Hovering over her, kissing her face, her neck and breasts.

She moaned a breathy sigh; more sounds of pleasure grew from her throat, as Lissa imagined the sensation of Doc inside of her. She arched her body into his and tensed in rebellion as he lifted her to meet him.

Oh how she wanted to please him. How she wanted him to know her love. *What could make him feel pleasure? What could she give to the man who'd changed her life, been a part of it even when he was not there? He had been her whole world.*

The blood in her body ran tantalizingly hot as Lissa sought to arouse him in soft thrusts, returning his. Her lips searched longingly for zones where she could bring him to ecstasy. Their rhythm pounded in warm damp pools of satiated desire, the years of pain and loss melting away as if they had never existed.

****

"I never stopped thinking of you, Lissa."

"Why didn't you try to reach me? I called. I called Davidson. I went by your grandmother's. I wrote - I tried everything and you were nowhere."

"I'm sure my mother had any communications intercepted."

"And then there was the letter."

"What letter?"

"The one you sent to me."

"I never sent you a letter, Lissa."

She studied his face, shook her head and moaned. "It said that it was over, that you wanted me to quit trying to call and to leave your Grandmother alone."

"I never wrote you anything, Lissa. I swear."

"It was signed. It looked like your handwriting."

"Mother - Mother did that." He grinded his teeth. "I swear, that woman will haunt me forever."

"Wish there would have been email back then." Lissa grinned.

"Would have solved the problem, huh?"

She stared at him.

"After the wreck I didn't know what to do."

"You should have called."

He shook his head. "I don't know. I felt responsible for the wreck—"

"How's that?"

"Dad was pissed, and whenever he got pissed he'd reach for a cigarette. I pissed him off while we were driving."

"And he was reaching for a cigarette and—"

"Yeah. I know that was silly to think it was my fault. But at that time, that is where my head was. And then there was Mother."

"I guess she really gave it to you."

Doc nodded. "I worked through that, too. I stayed with my sister in Banbury for a few of months then I came back. I came back here. It was February - you were married."

"I'm so sorry. I missed you so much. I couldn't believe that you dumped me. You left me and never told me why. You just cut me off like I didn't exist. Tom, I'd known Tom from school. He didn't, I didn't, we were both drunk and I guess you can figure out the rest. Oh Doc, why didn't you talk to me, say something to me?" She shook her head.

"You had to get married?"

"Yes. I didn't know what to do. I was so screwed up. I went with him to hurt you and I married him to hurt you more. I was so screwed up and them I wanted to hurt my father because he was always right. I wanted to get over you, I wanted the hurt to go away." She kissed Doc gently. "It never did."

Spooning next to Lissa, Doc stroked her thick curls and wrapped an arm around her waist to pull her closer. "I love you."

Lissa turned to face him. "Me, too. I love you, too." She inhaled a breath, her eyes moving to the windows of her bedroom and the marsh reeds swaying outside. "It's been a great day." Her hands cupped his face.

Closing his eyes momentarily, Doc licked his lips. "I know." His mouth covering hers, he moaned. "I always loved you."

He was holding her, making all the bad stuff go away.

She was whole. "I loved you, too, I still do."

The buzz from his phone boomed into the silence, Doc's hands grasped it, a text lit the screen.

Doc nodded. "I'm sorry, but I have to go."

"Why?" She nodded. "Oh, I know - Ava."

"Sorry, Lissa. She wants me to stop at the store and pick up some chamomile tea."

"Um."

"Sorry. She always gets antsy when she knows she's flying out the next day. She says the tea calms her."

Lissa nodded. "I understand."

"We'll work this out, Peg."

"Peg?"

"Peg 'o' my heart." He patted his chest.

"Damn you're nuts."

His smile disappearing, Doc, leaned to kiss her gently. "I'm sorry."

Lissa watched as he rose from her bed and slid his swim trunks on.

"I'll call you."

She rose, pulled an oversized tee shirt over her head and walked with him toward the door.

"I don't want to put you through this."

She shrugged. "I understand. Nothing is easy."

Kissing her again, Doc sighed. "We should have never split. It messed up everything."

Lissa watched as he walked to his car, slid into the seat and pulled from the drive. She watched his car come to the end of her road, the taillights flickering and then as he drove out of sight.

Enfolding her arms around herself she warmed to the thought of his lips on hers, the feel of his body as they lie entwined. It was as if she was falling from space, caught in a realm of passion, satiated beyond explanation or description. The thought brought so much joy to her, easing any doubts, making her feel the way she had dreamed it would be, only more.

****

Sorry, but Ava has insisted that I join her in New York. My son is there vacationing with his girlfriend, so I thought it might be a worthy trip. I'll be back next week. I'll miss you. I love you. Doc

It was three A.M. the flicker of light from her phone had wakened her. Lissa sighed as she read the words.

Maybe it was not right. It wasn't a matter of could she be the other woman but why should she?

Chapter 31

What was it about the end of a love that made one feel so distant? One minute you're together, you're part of one another, and then the next you are strangers.

That's how she felt about Rick as she watched his car pull into her driveway. She loved him but was no longer in love.

Still, she didn't have to force the smile, Lissa was happy to see him. Grappling with all the ambiguity sapped her energy; the thoughts and feeling swirling inside her head had no boundaries and they kicked about like a pinball, from one emotion to another.

Her chest rising and falling Lissa, fearful that Rick would notice, she studied his long stride as he moved from the car door toward her. His face beamed. He'd grown a goatee, it looked fantastic. Could this be the man she'd watched drive away a few weeks ago?

Suddenly his lips were on hers, his arms encircling her, lifting her against him and into the air. His hands caressed her breasts, and he pulled her closer kissing her once again, this time deeper and more passionately.

He seemed different - not the same man with whom she'd been cultivating a relationship. He looked like the old Rick, only better. Lissa giggled to herself, perusing his long muscular body.

She *had* missed him. Smiling broadly, Lissa held the door opened as he entered. Her heart beat a mile a minute, her eyes held his for a moment more before focusing on his features. He looked so changed; he looked robust, eager, healthy and happy.

Scooping her up in his arms, Rick buried his bearded face in her neck, his lips caressing her skin and finding her mouth.

He felt different than Doc, too, more commanding. She felt the power of his body as she yielded to him.

It felt so raw, so basic, so familiar. Titillated by the newness she kissed him back, acquiescing to his pull, submitting to his caresses, returning them.

Rick carried Lissa to the bedroom, laid her gently on the bed and slowly tugged the tee shirt from his body. He was tanned everywhere, except for the portion shorts would have covered. His body was toned and strong.

Lissa closed her eyes, it wasn't right.

Hovering over her, he bent closer, his breath on her body, his hands caressing her.

She wanted to say his name, *Doc.* She dare not open her eyes to meet Rick's.

"You feel so good," he whispered pulling her body to his.

"Damn I missed you." Rick lay prone, his chest rising and falling, sweat beaded at his brow. He reached for her hand.

"Lissa, I've missed you so much. You have to come back with me."

Biting her lip, she closed her eyes. "I don't know Rick." She turned to him, suddenly feeling guilty for the pleasures she and he had shared.

"Don't say that. You don't know what I've been through. I've been horny as hell, for one thing." He laughed. "And then it's so damn nice down there. I think about you all the time, about us, being together." He kissed her nose. "Lissa, the people are great. There's no traffic to contend with, no local political bullshit either. The living is easy, babe. Say you'll come."

Lissa sat up, reached for a shirt and slipped it on. "It sounds great," her eyes perused his body, her thoughts moved to Doc, she felt ashamed. "I could really use a break from here but I need more time, Rick. There's so much I need to do. It's summer, the tourist season; I can't leave Daddy to work the shop alone."

"Hire someone else."

She shook her head. "No, he needs someone who can take over and do what I've been doing for the last decade or so. He needs someone who knows how to run a business, our business and it's just too busy to train someone for that now." Lissa fiddled with the orthotic nervously.

"Oh, you have a new one."

"Yes, it's easier."

Rick reached for her. "So unlike you, sweetie, not to want to travel. It could just be for a few days. I just want you to see it. This place is right up your alley."

"Not now. Let's not talk about it right now, okay?"

"Okay. We'll talk about it later." He turned to his side, reaching to caress Lissa's bare legs. "So, what have you been doing since I've been gone? I know we talk on the phone a lot. But I'm curious. You don't really go into things when I call."

"Tourist season, that's what's wrong," she tittered. "The busiest time of the year, hell on wheels and you know, Rick, if I don't make money now, it will be a tough winter."

"Tell me about it, I'm been doing the same thing for the last four years here, too." He leaned back on the pillow. "You're right. This is not the time of year to pressure you into coming to Nicaragua. You are busy, too busy. Sorry babe for pressuring you. But after September I expect you to board a plane and join me."

"I will."

"Just wondering, sometimes when I called you I didn't hear that tone in your voice, the one I was getting so used to. And I'm not sure if my mind is playing tricks on me or not but is everything okay? Has anything changed?"

"Changed? What could have possibly changed?"

"I don't know. There's something." He studied her face, searching her eyes. "Just a feeling. I noticed it a couple of times when I spoke to you on the phone. I thought - your hesitation,

280

things like that. I hoped it was just my imagination. You'd tell me if there was something else, someone else, wouldn't you? Tell me I'm not crazy, tell me, something."

Should she tell him about Doc, the married man, her physical therapist? She knew he'd hate her if she did.

"I'm nervous, out of sorts, just not myself since the attack, Rick. I can't seem to get it together." She reached a hand to stroke his shoulders, her fingers threading through his chest hair.

He nodded and pulled her to lie next to him again. "Yeah, I thought so. Ever since you lost your leg I felt like you were pushing me away."

Her eyes begged his. He *had* noticed after all.

"Don't ever think I think less of you or think you are less beautiful. Never think I don't love you and want you." He caught his breath for a moment, tears welling in his eyes. "I'm just not very good at displaying my feelings, Lissa. But you have to know I will always be there for you."

Lissa nodded. "I did, I did push you away. I was scared. I didn't want you to feel guilty, like you had to stay with me. And hell, Rick, how would you feel if one of your legs was gone? That you had to limp and put up with people staring at you, judging you and know that you could never measure up to their expectations?"

Holding her closely, Rick stroked her hair and wiped the tears from her eyes. "Sweetie, I wish you would have told me.

You should have let me know." He paused. "Don't get mad at me for suggesting this, but, have you talked to anyone about this - maybe a shrink?"

"So you think I'm nuts now?"

"No, maybe not a shrink, but a counselor or someone professional. I'm sure you're going through things I could never imagine."

"Maybe I should see someone, talk to someone about this." *Doc helped her, he was all she needed.* "I'll check into it."

"That's my girl." Kissing her lips lightly, Rick stroked the contours of her face. "You're beautiful, you know. I don't want you to slip away. I've been afraid that you might slip away from me."

She shook her head, closed her eyes and buried her face in his shoulder.

"The book you have on your shelf, the poetry book - I thumbed through it one time while you were in the hospital - there was a poem in there that made me think of us."

"Really?"

"Um hum. That's how I feel about you." He stroked her face. "I'm not the most demonstrative person in the world, Lissa. I know it. But you have to know you mean everything to me.

Lissa caught her breath.

"I've never been into poetry but that one summed it all up for me." He stroked her hair away from her face. "Where did you get the book?"

It had been years since she'd bothered to look at the book of poetry. She'd locked it away with all the other hurtful things in her life.

It had been wedged between several other books in her minimal library - Steinbeck, Cather, Nin, Hemingway, Helprin - the standards she'd drank in in her youth and held dear. The poetry book was from Murdoch. She was surprised that Rick hadn't noticed the inscription. Lissa held her breath, recalling the words, then she exhaled. *I tore that page out when I got mad at him.* Oh, how she wished she had that page now.

Chapter 32

Walking into Food Lion from the parking lot, she spied the Alto Romeo. It had to be his. She was surprised, Doc normally did his shopping either online or at one of the higher end grocery stores in Wilmington.

Rick reached for her hand. "I'm going to fix you the best steak you've ever had. There's this special rub I found out about in San Juan del Sur - very popular down there." Releasing her hand, he reached for the shopping cart. "I hope they have fresh mangos."

Lissa's eyes scanned the store quickly searching for Murdoch; he wasn't in a checkout lane or in the produce section where she and Rick now wandered.

Watching as he grasped a mango and turned it about in his hand, Lissa felt remorse for her behavior. He brought it to his nose to smell then returned it to select another.

"Ah, this one will do." He placed it in the cart and moved slowly toward the ginger display.

Keeping her head down, holding close to Rick, Lissa furtively turned her head to study the shoppers. Again, no sign of Doc.

Lissa watched as Rick's strong fingers felt the firmness of the ginger. She'd never realized that he was so interested in cooking. She liked the idea of it and leaned into him a bit as she raised her head to peruse the store once again for Doc.

Yet again, he was nowhere. *He's probably left by now,* she thought, threading her arm through Rick's.

"Steak, hope they have some nice tenderloins." Rick smiled and pushed the cart forward to the meat department. "I need some honey, honey," Rick chuckled. "Go down the aisle and pick up a small jar for me."

Lissa obeyed and stepped into aisle seven, her eyes scanning the sugars and sugar substitutes, the raw sugars to the selections of honey. Her eyes glued to the products, she walked past Murdock and Ava without realizing it. She heard a throat clear and turned.

There he stood, his hands curled around the hand of the shopping cart. His wife, Ava, stood beside him, her back turned as she perused the selections of teas. He smiled gently at Lissa, his gaze capturing hers.

Lissa felt the flutter throughout her body and the numbness of her face . The rise and fall of her anxious breath shocked her and she sought to calm herself.

"I guess, I'll settle for the Sleepy Time tea. I have to have something, or I won't sleep," Ava spoke as she reached for the box.

Lissa quickly grabbed a jar of honey and turned to walk back to Rick before Ava saw her.

"What is it?" Rick asked. "You're red as a beet."

Her hand touching her cheek, Lissa blurted a lie, "Some rude tourist is blocking the aisle - makes me so mad."

Rick took the honey from her hand and laughed. "Sweetie, it's only going to get worse - another reason to come live with me."

Smiling shyly to him, she spoke, "Maybe that's not such a bad idea."

"That's what I've been telling you. No more traffic problems, no more people parking in your yard - there are lots of benefits to moving to Nicaragua."

Her mind oblivious to his conversation, Lissa guided the cart toward the checkout lanes.

"Whoa, wait a minute, I still haven't selected the meat."

She stopped short, uncertain of what to do, confused, she took a breath. "Okay."

"What's up? You look upset over something?"

"No." she smiled trying to regain her composure. "I'm fine. I know I need to learn to not let the tourists get to me."

Rick reached an arm around her shoulder pulling Lissa to him he kissed her temple. "How's this one look to you?" He picked a package of steak and held it before her.

"Perfect - looks yummy."

They were there, Rick and Ava, two lanes over, checking the box of tea Ava had selected. Lissa watched Doc, standing staunching, his shoulders held back, his head lifted. She studied him, feeling her heart thumping, conflicted with the passion she felt for him, the shame she felt for wanting a married man and even more, the surge of emotions she held for both he and Rick.

He turned to scan the store, his eyes resting briefly on her - they softened into sadness. Turning to the cashier her reached into his back pocket for his wallet.

Lissa felt weak, felt the dryness in her throat. She could feel him across the distance and she wanted to reach out.

Thumbing through the bills, Doc turned his attention to his wife as she spoke.

Lissa watched as the couple exited through the sliding glass doors.

"Welcome to Food Lion," the cashier mumbled.

Lissa smiled as the young girl grinned and began sliding the groceries across the scanner.

Her eyes drew toward the spot where the couple walked, she watched them step into the Alfa Romeo. Her eyes followed the vehicle until it rested at the stop light, then sped up slowly to turn onto the highway.

****

"I'd like to say that I hate having to leave tomorrow." Rick sipped from the glass of wine. "You're the only reason I hate it, you know."

Lissa grinned and severed a piece of steak. "Thanks for making dinner - it really is very good."

"I'll miss you, wish you were coming with me."

"We've discussed that, sorry." She leaned back in the dining chair, "I'll miss you, too. The week has flown by."

"You're sure you won't come, nothing I can do to persuade you? Not even for a couple of days?" Rick rose, walked behind her and bent to caress Lissa's neck, his lips softy brushing against the nape.

"Um hum, let's wait until the end of the summer to make any decisions." She turned to face him, and ran her hand across his shoulder then down the length of his arm. *Beautiful,* she thought, *his body is so beautiful.* The physical-ness of him was so arousing - what woman wouldn't want him? She was sure that in Nicaragua there were sassy senoritas begging for his attention, she wondered if he'd taken advantage of the attention. Thinking of asking about it, she hesitated, reminding herself that she had been unfaithful. *I have no right.* Lissa lowered her eyes for a moment before rising to face him.

"I'll be back in a couple of weeks."

"I know." She turned to walk into the living room.

"Do you want me to come back?"

289

The question shocked her and she spun to face him. "What do you mean?"

"You're here but you're not here."

Lissa's eyes shifted away. "You're silly,"

"Will you miss me?"

"Of course, I'll miss you." She reached to his thigh, stroking it, moving in close to present herself to him.

"That's another thing. The sex has been fantastic. You've been devouring me"

"Is that a problem?" She ran her tongue across his lips.

"No. I can't complain about that. But after we do it, when we're not *engaged* your mind is somewhere else."

Again Lissa lowered her head, her fingers played with the fabric of his shirt. "This is a difficult decision for me Rick. Leaving my father, my home, it's just difficult, we've talked about it - can we *not* talk about it anymore?"

"Shame on you then, you misled me all these months," his voice chided. "You always talk about traveling and how mundane life here on Topsail has become for you, but now that the opportunity presents itself, well—"

"Guilty. I've done that. I guess when it comes right down to it, I just can't leave everything I've known my whole life." Turning from him, she gathered the plates and walked to the kitchen.

Her lips trembling, wishing there was a way to end all the ambivalence, to stop the lies. If only Rick would tell her he'd found someone else – something - anything to keep her from hurting him.

"When you come back—"she nodded and walked to the closet.

"What's up?" Rick moved to Lissa, towering over her, his eyes blazed emotion. Slowly his body guided her against the wall, he pressed his hands on either side of her. "What is it? Who is it?"

Lissa shook her head. "Nobody. I've told you, I'm confused."

"About me?" He inched closer to her, looking down into her eyes. "Don't push me away, Lissa. I know you've been doing that."

Catching her breath, Lissa's lips parted, "I'm sorry, I'm sorry I can't give you an answer now." Hesitating, she added, "I do love you, Rick. I'm sorry if I pushed you away, it's just that—"

His hand reached beneath her blouse, his fingers gently touching her skin, then moving to her waist and hips. He reached to pull up her skirt and finding the edges of her panties, Rick gently pulled them down. He pressed his lips on Lissa's, she could feel them smiling against her mouth.

"You do love me."

She nodded and, holding his face in her hands, Lissa kissed his brow.

"God, I love you so much. Please don't push me away." Lifting her into his arms, Rick carried Lissa to the bed, placing her diagonally, he lifted the damaged leg, found the button and released the prosthetic from the stump. "You see, I've been paying attention. I know how to do this." He removed the sleeve and socks and kissed the residual leg, the numb skin there, his lips moving along her thighs.

His arm behind her back, he lifted her to him, caressing her body, finding her face, he spoke against her lips -

> I long to know your lips again
> And taste the salt upon your skin
> And know your thoughts as you do mine
> And drink the sweet joy of us
> As we swim in our pelagic love.

The words were manna from heaven, the words were the ones recited by Doc decades ago. If only Rick had known that.

Tears streaming from her eyes, Lissa held his head in her hands, felt the softness of his kisses. She closed her eyes, Doc's image appeared, she felt *his* arms, *his* lips. She moved to *their* rhythm. The past seemed present and as if she belonged to Doc. Everything else belonged somewhere else.

Chapter 33

"Hi."

"Hi," she answered.

"I miss you."

"I miss you, too."

"Is he—"

"No, Rick left a couple of days ago."

"Why didn't you call me?"

"Nemo's been sick. I've been doggy sitting.'

"Sorry, anything I can do?"

"No, he's just old."

"You okay?"

"Yeah, I'm fine."

"I want to see you."

"Me, too." Lissa settled the phone on the kitchen table and reached for a bowl.

"What are you doing now?"

"Making a bowl of cereal."

"No eggs and bacon?" Doc teased.

"Bad for your heart."

"Lots of things are bad for your heart."

Silence lingered for a few seconds.

"You are." Doc whispered.

"Hmm."

"Where do you want to go today? It's kind of rainy outside, want to go to a movie?"

"Sounds good."

"Be there in a few to pick you up."

"Let me finish my breakfast," Lissa teased.

"Thirty minutes. That's all you get. I want to see you."

She gobbled the Rice Krispies, dragged a brush through her hair, pulled on a long stretch skirt and fancy tee. She liked her shape; the surfing was helping realize the contours of her body.

Stepping into a pair of sling back sandals, glanced in the mirror and nodded. "Okay." She picked up a tube of lipstick and dabbed her checks and mouth. "I guess, I'll have to do." She smiled, caught her own eyes, held her breath and imaged Doc drawing her closely.

He pulled into the driveway. Lissa stood at the door watching as he walked toward her. *Why hadn't she called Doc after Rick left?* She asked herself as he strode toward her. He was the one who always made her laugh, he made her happy - except when he had to leave for Ava.

"Your dog feeling any better?"

Lissa shook her head. "He's so old. I expect one day I'll wake up and he won't."

"Sorry, I know how you've always loved your dogs."

"Abby's dog." Lissa inhaled as she reached for Doc's hand. "He's Abby's." Lissa closed the door behind her and walked to the Jeep.

"So you think I'm bad for your heart?" Lissa cooed, reaching to squeeze his thigh.

He held the steering wheel with one hand, the elbow of his other resting against the open window of the Jeep. "Bad for my heart - yes."

Doc pushed a tab on the steering wheel, Van Morrison crooned a love song; his hand drifted to the glove compartment. "Open it up, look inside. There's something in it for you."

"In here?" Her fingers pressed down and the small door opened.

A gold colored box, embellished with a stark purple bow sat in the center.

"What is this?"

"Just a little something."

"You shouldn't, you know."

"Just open it."

Lissa's fingers wrapped around the gift; she pulled at the bow and pulled the top away.

Her eyes lighting, she slid a warm gaze to Doc. "Murdoch, you—"

"I love you. Put it on."

At the end of the platinum chain hung a shark's tooth.

"It the one I found on the beach a few weeks ago. I want you to have it."

"Kind of ironic, wouldn't you say?"

"All the damn shark got was part of your leg."

"And you have all of me."

"Something like that." He reached to hold her hand. "Why didn't you call me sooner? I've been going crazy wondering - it's all so weird. It's not right, it's not fair. I know. But I wonder about this guy—"

"Rick."

"Rick - I can't stand the idea of you with him."

"Now you know how I feel."

He nodded. "This whole thing sucks. I know you told me he was coming, but I thought for sure you'd call me after he left."

"I needed some time."

"Okay?"

"Uh huh, just thinking, wondering."

"About what? Us?"

"Uh huh - and Ava."

"Umm. I know, sorting things out is not easy."

"I know, too."

"Ava got back from Wilmington on Tuesday. She left Thursday for New York."

"She's gone a lot."

Doc nodded. "She's busy. She likes the job. You know, she didn't work for several years after we married and then she wanted to do something - said she was getting bored and wanted to go back into sales." He turned to Lissa. "She's very good at what she does and she loves it." Doc pulled the car to a stop and waited for the light to change. His eyes focused ahead.

Lissa fingered the tooth around her neck as she noticed him tighten the grip on the wheel, his jaw tense. "She's a pretty woman, Doc."

He nodded. "Yes she is."

She touched his arm. "We've gotten ourselves into a mess haven't we?"

He nodded.

"What are we going to do?"

"I don't know."

"You love her?"

His shoulders rose as he breathed a breath. "It's not that simple - I love her - I love you."

"It isn't simple. I've been thinking about things, about us and maybe—"

"It's been wonderful with you. I feel like everything is right when I'm with you."

"You mean, you'd give up the big city and trips abroad?"

"I've told you, it doesn't suit me."

"I remember. You preferred the Jeep to the Jag, your grandmother's cottage to your parent's monstrosity."

"You know, I don't think I spent more than a week in that place. Always liked Grammy's better." He brushed her arm with his as he rested it on the console. "And you told me Rick is from Alaska, right?"

"Yes, I told you that, remember I told you we visited there last spring. He introduced me to his family. It's beautiful there."

"You didn't tell me that part. Must be serious. When a man introduces you to his family, Lissa—"

"I know, that was before my accident - attack. I'm - that changed things for me Doc - and then you came back. Everything changed for me after the attack."

"Your relationship with Rick?"

"Uh huh."

"How?"

Lissa rolled her eyes. "Aren't you uncomfortable talking about our significant others while we—"

"I want to know - I want to know about you."

"I'm confused."

"You and me both, Lissa. We've started something. I want the best for you."

Lissa watched the corners of his lips turn as he drove ahead. She felt the twinge of jealousy, the feeling of inadequacy and was acutely aware that now, she was in love with a married man - with no promises for any kind of future.

"What's Rick like?" Murdoch asked, turning to Lissa. "He's a tall one, what, six-three, six-four?"

"Six-four-and-a-half."

"And he's a fisherman."

"Yes, I've told you this before."

"And he's in Nicaragua. How's that working out?"

"He wants me to move there - help him with the marina he and his friend are running."

Doc grasped the steering wheel tighter and inhaled. "I don't want to stand in the way of you and Rick. If you're in love with him—" Doc blurted.

"What?"

"I just want you to be happy, Lissa."

"How can I be in love with him and be with you?" Her eyes flashed angrily.

"I mean, if you think you have a future together."

"I don't understand you. How can you be with me and be willing to give me up?"

"I don't want to give you up." He pulled the car to the side of the road. "I don't know. I just don't know anymore. I've screwed so much up. I simply want the best for you. You deserve better than sneaking around."

"Ava?"

"That's it. It's hard letting go but I want to be with you, too, and that's not fair and not right."

"Do you want me to leave?"

"No. I don't want you to go and I'm not leaving you - something will work out."

What did he mean? Lissa thought. What would work it out? What would happen? Was he implying that she didn't need to give up Rick? What kind of future was there for them? Was he choosing Ava over her? Of course he was, he was living with her, married to her. The questions, the ambiguity did not stop. She sat silently, brooding thoughts raced through her head.

Doc reached for her hand, encircling his forefinger with hers. He held it firmly.

"No." She released herself from the hold. "I don't let people into my life," Lissa heard herself speak the words. Normally they were true. She hadn't let a man into her life - not wholly - since she'd been a teen. Not since Murdoch had broken her heart.

And Rick - they had been on their way. She'd been wanting to and was ready to. The trip to Alaska had brought them closer and she found herself relaxing into their relationship, feeling the glow and magic of love once again in her life. He was becoming comfortable, part of her - but the damn shark attack. It ruined everything, jumbled her life, screwed up any plans for normalcy. Since then, she had pushed Rick away.

But maybe, she thought. *In time I would have trusted him again. He was trying so hard. It was me pushing him away. It's my fault.*

"You don't let people into your life?" Doc repeated her words.

Lissa shook her head. "No Doc, I don't. You were the last person I allowed to see all of me, to trust with all of me. I'm not sure I can have that with Rick. And you're back - like you told me, I don't believe in coincidence either. Everything is for a reason; if I hadn't lost my leg, you would have never re-entered my life."

****

It was an awkward night and it had started out so well. The film, an action packed adventure, dragged as Lissa considered her place in Murdoch's life

She wondered how he could want to be with her - crippled, plain, podunk Lissa, who'd never been out of the south and whose life revolved around fishing boats and engines and very little else.

The guilt ate at Doc. He did love Ava, she was a good woman but there had been changes coming even before Lissa had walked back into his life. He'd felt the distance growing between them ever since she gone back to marketing and traveling. Her life was moving in a different direction. Where he felt as if he had found his place in the world, her life was just opening up for her.

Lissa just happened to enter his life again at a time when changes were occurring - when transition was in place in his life with Ava. But they had been through transitions before, they would survive this one, maybe, or maybe, like she insinuated, Fate had stepped in - Lissa had come back into his life for a reason or maybe he was standing in the way of Lissa's chance for a life with a new man, one without baggage.

Chapter 34

"Sorry about old Nemo."

"Thanks. He was old. Abby got him when she was eight, so he lived a long life."

"Spoiled rotten, I know that," Rick chuckled.

"Yes, I spoiled him."

His face covering the phone screen, Lissa managed a smile. She was glad that he was not in her presence and able to look in her eyes. He would have seen the doubt, felt the loss. She was doing her best to disguise her feelings.

Lissa watched as Rick propped the phone on a stand and rigged a line of tackle, his hands busily manipulating the lure and monofilament. His arms flexing as he plied the lure and line, tying a blood knot. Ordinarily Lissa would have been captivated by his lean, muscular frame but now her head was full of Doc, he was all she could think about.

Rick snickered, "You know, babe, I'm getting awfully lonely down here. I need someone to wrap my arms around at night. I think you could use some TLC, too. And now that poor old Nemo has gone to doggy heaven, well. Hey, Ortum give me that!"

"Hey, it's me. Lissa, you need to get your ass down here. I'm telling you the women are all over this man and if you wait much longer—"

"Don't pay any attention to him, Lissa."

She heard Ortum in the background.

"Oh hell yes, you listen to me. Get your ass here."

"Sorry babe, Ortum's had a few."

"Let me talk to her again, I'll convince—"

"Ah, come on now, Ortum. Give me a break - go on now."

Tittering to the banter between the two men, Lissa called out, "What's going on down there?"

"Babe, listen. Ortum's just being Ortum. You know, you've met him. He's full of shit."

"For sure."

"Listen to me, don't listen to him."

Lissa heard the muffled sounds between the two men. Her curiosity peaked and she wondered if Rick hadn't been as lonely as he depicted.

"Listen, I need you to come down. Just for a few days. How about it, babe?"

Any woman in her right mind would be gaga for Rick. Tall and muscular, handsome, he was Fabio, Hugh Jackman and Chris Hemsworth all rolled into one - and he could have been all hers. As far as she knew, he was still hers for the taking, if she wanted him. *Maybe I should go for a visit.* She thought of the prospect for a moment - the crystal waters, laid back living, sailing. She could surf there, too.

She pictured herself in a bikini, taking to the waves, limping slightly as she adjusted the orthotic, other women - with both legs.

"I'll think about it."

"I know what that means." Lissa pictured the scowl she knew Rick wore as he spoke. It tugged at her heart. She had never meant to hurt him.

Before the attack, when she was whole, other women eyed her as she held onto his arm. Jealousy oozed from their pores. Lissa always smiled back and inched closer to him, proud to be on his arm.

But now, how could she compare the two men? It was Doc's scarred face she longed to touch. His pale body she wanted against hers. How she longed to trace his features with her hands, to kiss them, behold them, to feel him next to her.

You see what you want to see, you see the heart. How many times had she heard that, read that? And it was so true. The man she loved was not perfect but he made her feel that way.

It made no sense to be so in love with someone who couldn't be with you when someone as beautiful as Rick wanted her.

And he was no slouch. Rick was intelligent, introspective, giving, attentive - all the things a woman longed for. So what was it? What was it that made her want Doc, made her cling to a past love? Had she embellished it over the years, making it into some sort of surreal magical experience?

"Hey babe?"

Rick's voice startled her.

"Nickle - I mean five centavos for your thoughts. You're staring off into space. Haven't you heard me?

"What?" Lissa studied the screen. "I'm sorry."

"You have your mind on something and I don't think it's me."

"Nemo - just thinking of poor old Nemo. I miss him."

"If you're thinking of getting another dog, don't. Not yet anyway. It's hard as hell to bring pets here and besides someone might eat it." He laughed. "No, just kidding. But now that Nemo isn't around this would be the perfect time to come. Later, we can pick out any dog you want."

"My leg, it's the prosthesis, it's been giving me some problems, too."

"I get the feeling that you're making excuses."

"Really Rick, I have been having some issues with the prosthesis. I think it's time to change, get a better fit."

"You know what to do, babe. Go see that PT of yours. You always seem to feel better after a session with him." He paused, the tone of his voice sobering. "You miss me, right?"

"Yes," she lied.

"You don't sound all that convincing."

"Rick," she started.

"That tone - tell me darling, what's going on. Am I loosing you?"

"I don't know."

She saw the disappointment in his face as he turned away. "I'm sorry."

"I should have never left you."

"No. This is such an opportunity for you, Rick. I couldn't let you pass this up."

"I can't lose you, Lissa - I don't want to."

"I just don't know—" the words stumbled from her lips.

"I'm taking the next flight out of here."

"No."

"I'll be there tomorrow evening. Don't you go anywhere. You need to talk to me. You can't leave me."

Chapter 35

His breath soft on her skin, Lissa opened her eyes to Doc's. His lips formed an easy smile, his fingers traced the outline of her mouth. "Do you have any idea how you make me feel?"

"Um hum, I do, just like me." She licked the fingers at her mouth.

"I wish I'd never listened to my father."

"Me, too."

"I wish I'd called you."

"Me, too." She pressed her lips to his neck. "I wish I'd been more patient."

"I know."

"Shoulda, coulda, woulda. Isn't that what they say?" Lissa sighed. "Youth is wasted on the young."

"I've heard that one before - so true." His hands cupped her breasts as he bent to kiss them.

"Things could have been so different."

"I know." She reached her partial leg across his hips.

"What are you going to tell him?"

"I don't think I ever really loved him, Doc. I mean, I was moving that way. He made me happy and I felt wanted and attractive, like I hadn't felt in years, if I hadn't lost my leg."

"You would be with him, in love with him."

"I wouldn't have found you again."

"Life plays such funny games with us, doesn't it?"

Lissa nodded. "It doesn't seem very funny now."

"No." He closed his eyes, his hands outlining her hips and buttocks. "It's not."

"What should I do?"

Drawing his face to hers, Doc guided his fingers over her brows and eyes. "I always loved your eyes, and your smile. Damn, you had - you *have* the brightest smile, lights up your whole beautiful face."

"Answer me. What should I do?"

"Dump him. I'm jealous. I can't stand the idea of another man holding you, wanting you. It makes me seethe, it crawls into me and makes me sick." His eyes blazed into hers.

"Doc - what about Ava? You can't expect me—"

"I don't. I don't expect you to wait for me. I just want you to be patient."

"Will you leave her?"

"I want to, there are things, money, Ava is not the kindest person in the world. She is rather possessive and jealous as hell over you."

"What? She's always so nice."

"She's not stupid. She's always seen you as a threat. But she's thrown herself into this job - she loves it and at times I think she wants it more than she wants *us*."

"An *us*?"

"Before you came back into my life, there were things. I knew she was bored or unhappy about something. I was the one that talked her into leaving her job in the first place."

"Everyone needs something to make them feel fulfilled," Lissa spoke.

"Before - you and I - we were going through this little thing. Getting acclimated to her new life and all the traveling. At first it was exciting, for me. And then things cooled. I saw Ava moving in a direction, a different one. I'd been trying to hold on, telling myself that it was me. That I was the one that needed to adapt, to make our marriage work."

"And maybe you could have if I hadn't walked into your office."

"Something like that. I think about it all the time."

"Maybe she'll leave on her own."

"Oh, you might be right, I don't know. But one thing is for sure, she'll take half of everything I've worked for."

"You don't think she deserves it?"

Doc snickered, "That's another problem. I've worked hard, my first wife got a big chunk of what I've worked for but she's the mother of my children."

"You and Ava didn't want children?"

"She never did. And she's grown accustomed to a certain lifestyle. There *will* be a fight."

"It'll get ugly, huh?"

"Maybe - more than likely."

"Sorry."

"Just give it time." Doc closed his eyes. "I don't expect for you to wait for me forever, Lissa and I don't want to diminish you or degrade you by having you be the other woman."

"That's how I feel."

"I'm sorry. I don't like hurting you."

"Then don't.

He turned to the sound of his cell phone vibrating and reached for it, "She's at the airport now, I'm late." Rolling from the bed, Doc turned away, padding to the bathroom.

Lissa heard the water running and the scrape of the shower curtain as he pulled it open and shut. *He's washing me away.* She felt her throat tighten and the cold chill of loss run through her body.

****

My world is a jumble of ifs and maybes and I don't know where I fit in. Watching you dress for a woman whom you call wife, knowing you will be caressing her, encouraging her - being the other half, makes me feel small, makes me feel like I did so long ago, like I can't matter as much as something or someone else.

I know you love me, Murdoch. And I love you. Fate stepped in and separated us once. It came back and brought us together. Now, I know that it is up to you and I to determine our futures.

The pain of losing you again is too much and I cannot relinquish myself to being the other woman when I was your everything at one time.

I need time to figure things out. I need to think with my head rather than my heart this time. Please understand where I'm coming from. Regardless, you know I will always love and treasure our time together.

Forever, Lissa

She parked two blocks south of the Soucek beach cottage and walked; Doc's Jeep was parked in the drive alongside Ava's Camry.

She tried the door handle it was locked then she reached beneath the tire well and retrieved the key case. Setting the letter on the driver's seat, Lissa closed her eyes, "Good-bye, Doc."

Three days later Lissa received a text. *I know I love you and always will. I don't know what to do either. I wish it was easier, I struggle with what is right and wrong and I don't know anymore.*

Today we are on our way to London. I'm staying this time for a while to clear my head. Keep me in your thoughts. My love, Doc

Chapter 36

"Is there someone else?" Rick pushed the kitchen chair to the side and settled himself there, looking forsakenly up at Lissa.

"No. Not really." She hesitated. "There was a man—from my past—I saw him a few times. He's gone now."

"Do you love him?"

"I did - at one time."

"Did you sleep with him?"

"No," she lied.

"I knew it. I could feel it. You've been pushing me away ever since you lost your leg and it wasn't just that. I could feel it, someone else."

Lissa wiped the tears away. "I'm so sorry. You've been so good to me. You don't deserve to be treated so badly."

"You lied."

"I didn't want to hurt you."

"You've hurt me now."

Lissa moved to Rick, she grasped his fingers. "I'm willing to try again. *I'll* try again if you want me."

His face red with anger and pain, Rick clenched his teeth. "How could you? I've stuck with you after the attack - I've been here for you."

"You went to Nicaragua."

"You told me to. I begged you to come with me. It's such an opportunity for me, and Lissa, for you, too."

"It is a good opportunity."

"And the reason you wouldn't come wasn't because of your leg, it was because of this other man - right?"

Lissa nodded.

"You don't love me anymore?"

"At one time I know we could have made it. I *was* falling in love with you. We were getting so close and then the trip to Alaska, I knew we could have made it. And then that damn shark."

"Don't blame the shark. If you loved me it wouldn't matter. I was there for you, I helped you get out of bed, take a shower, get dressed, I was there."

"You don't understand."

"Who is he?"

"My physical therapist."

Rick shook his head slowly. "Your doctor?"

"Uh huh."

"Ah shit. No wonder. Lissa, he's your doctor. You're going to fall for him. With something as traumatic as what happened to you, it's normal. This thing you feel for him - it's not real. You just think you're in love with this dude who is helping you. Patients fall for their doctors all the time."

"No."

316

His anger dissipating, Rick spread his hands on the table. "I see now." He shrugged. "I understand. Now that you've got yourself together you don't need him anymore and well, here I am. I still want you." He reached his hand to hers. "Come back with me. You'll forget about him." His brow furrowed.

"When is the last time you were with him?"

Lissa lowered her eyes then lifted them to lie to Rick once more, "A couple of weeks ago."

"You haven't talked with him?"

"No. He's married."

"Damn, Lissa. You've made a fool of yourself. Married men stay married, especially if money is involved and if he's a physical therapist, he's got some."

The words rang deep and painful with their truth. She had made a fool of herself. Doc was a married man who had more to lose than she did. Maybe it was the right thing do, to let him go. Maybe it was best for everyone.

"Let it go. Let him go, because believe me, Lissa, if he's not with you, he's *not* with you. Come back with me."

"Are you sure?"

"Yes." Rick rose from the table, took Lissa's hand and pulled her to her feet. "You see, everything is going to be just fine. We'll go to Nicaragua and we'll get to know one another again." His hands cupping her face, Rick bent to kiss Lissa.

****

Sammy would fill in for her at the business. He was a whiz at motors. Young and with a few diesel courses under his belt, he understood how to work on the newer models.

Lissa placed the keys in his hand. "Call me if you have any problems."

"That's what your dad said. He's kind of pissed at you for going."

"I know, he'll get over it."

Chuckling, Sammy walked through the door of the shop and called back, "See ya in a - how long you gonna be gone?"

"I don't know. I may never come back."

Chapter 37

The first leg of the flight took them to Costa Rica, a lush and beautiful country dotted with little towns surrounding polished and high dollar resorts. Lissa sighed and followed Rick to catch a taxi then board a bus to San Juan Del Sur.

"In a few hours we'll be there. San Juan Del Sur is very different than this. The people are very friendly and there's a fairly good sized community of ex-pats that will make you feel more at home."

The ride was long and bumpy. The bus was crowed and Lissa felt somewhat uncomfortable jostled about as the bus curved, rose and dipped on the narrow roads. Most riders were locals, except for she and Rick and a couple others, they chatted loudly and openly with one another. Rick joined in, turning around in his seat to participate in light conversation.

"San Juan Del Sur is a lovely place," the tall woman sitting next to her native boyfriend chimed. "Lots of ex-pats live there. It's quiet, we make our own fun. Every evening the community gets together, Jose here," she nudged the man sitting next to her, "plays a nice guitar. Sometimes his brother, or anyone else who plays an instrument, joins in. And we cook and talk and have a really nice time."

Lissa listened intently.

The man next to the woman smiled gently as he spoke slowly in his thick native accent, "You'll like it here."

Lissa gestured an acknowledgment and resumed looking from her window at the countryside's dense and sumptuous vegetation.

The bus passed an ox drawn cart carrying a family; they waved, rocking to the motion of their cart moving along the narrow paved road. They passed a couple more pedestrians and another mule drawn wagon. Lissa wondered how the people there felt about all the tourists coming to *their* homeland. Certainly things were changing there, Rick and Ortum were part of that change, bringing in more tourists.

Lissa thought of how the influx of out of towners to Topsail Island had ruined what had once been a very low key, quiet fishing town, how now there were hardly any commercial fishermen left at all with party boat owners and other factions destroying the fishing industry by imposing restriction so that no one could make a living at it at all.

I guess we're supposed to get our seafood from farms and third world countries where there are no regulations on pesticides, she smirked, feeling the rise of righteous indignation in her bones. The run-off from golf courses and asphalt roads that had been built was killing the shell fishing industry. *People don't think about things like that - how one man's pleasure is another man's destruction.*

She studied the roadside and the greenery, the simplicity of the lifestyle there. *This will change, too, in time. I guess the one with the most toys does win after all.*

Every few miles the bus would pass by a small village of tiny block houses, some with windows, some without. Chickens, pigs and goats milled about the homes together with scantily clad children playing in the dirt. They waved as the bus drove by.

"Lots of poor people down here," Lissa murmured lowly to Rick.

"Umm, you're going to see lots of that. Nicaragua is a poor country, but the people are nice, they're hard working, poor doesn't make you dishonest or bad." His eyes studied the countryside, too. "I learned a lot about good and bad when I was studying to be a lawyer." He raised his brows. "There, in *lawyer land,* the discrepancy is disguised beyond all recognition."

Past the houses, in between them were miles and miles of thick greenery. She spied a few iguanas hanging in the trees, they looked prehistoric.

"That's a Motmot." Rick pointed to a brightly colored bird perched in a Madrono tree, its long light blue tail and brilliantly colored feathers contrasted sharply with the tree's reddish bark and lush green leaves.

Lissa's eyes scoured the vegetation for birds and other animals she'd never seen before; howler monkeys chattered loudly among the branches dotted with green parrots and other colorful birds.

"Wow!" Lissa's face lit up. "A toucan, I've never seen one before."

"You'll see lots of things here you've never seen before."

Lissa squeezed Rick's hand, it was all so exciting and at once she was glad she had decided to come with Rick.

Maybe all the new sights and sounds would open her world so much that it would swallow the memories of Doc. His face imaged in her mind once again, she turned to Rick;, he smiled at her and wrapped an arm around her shoulder.

"You are going to love it here; it's so peaceful - so beautiful."

The bus rolled on, nearing the bay of San Juan Del Sur, already the scenery was changing. Most houses were stucco with tin roofs, they had windows, albeit with bars. But the city was clean for the most part and the citizens, as they walked about, were clothed.

"You don't see many sights like that in the US," Rick pointed toward the cliffs.

Lissa's eyes scoured the mountains overlooking the bay and city and fell upon a high cliff where stood the Christ of Mercy statue. It was as if the outstretched arm of Jesus was welcoming her personally.

"Oh my gosh, this is beautiful."

"Told you so."

The ride continued for another few minutes until the bus finally pulled into the depot of the small town. "Glad you came?" Rick asked.

Lissa nodded, her eyes brightened as she flashed a broad smile. "Absolutely lovely."

Rick guided Lissa from the bus to the small café there, pulled a chair from a table and adjusted the umbrella. "Ortum or Sal should be here any minute to pick us up."

Her eyes drinking in the new and foreign scenery, Lissa was astounded by the surroundings. "I hope this stays like this for a long time."

Rick nodded, "There is good and bad in everything."

Lissa's eyes met his, she nodded an acknowledgment. "Yes."

"Cerveza, por favor." Rick smiled to the waiter. "Dos."

"Stay away from the water here, unless it's bottled. Anything in a bottle is good, just don't drink the water."

"I know, I've heard - Montezuma's revenge."

"Right."

"Hey gorgeous!" Ortum called out from across the road. "I was hoping he wouldn't come back empty handed."

Lissa rose and met Ortum as he stepped toward her, his big arms pulling her into a bear hug. "You look like a beauty queen."

"You're full of it," she teased. It was nice to see him again. His honest and open face eased any concerns she'd anticipated.

She had liked him from the beginning, he was real, there was no pretense about him.

Ortum reached his hand to clasp Rick's in a firm handshake. Lissa saw him wink at his friend.

"We have a charter tomorrow morning," He nodded to Rick. "It would be a good chance for your lady, first mate, to get a good look at what she'll be doing."

Lissa slid her eyes upward to meet Ortum's sparkling gaze.

"I mean, that's what you'll be doing, I assume," His eyes twinkled confidently. "That why you're here, right? To work."

"Sounds like fun," Lissa smirked.

He patted her on the back, "Right, you can do it. I have no doubt about it, heh, heh."

Lissa turned to Rick. "What have you gotten me into?"

He shrugged. "Don't worry, He's full of shit, you know that."

Ortum laughed loudly. "We do have a charter tomorrow but Sal and I are taking them out. There's hardly a day that goes by that we don't have a charter."

"And who is Sal?"

"The guy that usually goes out on charters. He's good."

"All joking aside, I wouldn't mind helping out sometimes."

"No, I want you to relax, enjoy yourself here. But if you feel up to it, you can come along just for the ride so I can show you the place - the cliffs, the ocean - it's so clear." His eyes widened with enthusiasm. "The fishing here is phenomenal."

Ortum grabbed the bags from the storage locker beneath the bus. "Best way to relax. I'll have Rosa make a lunch for you guys."

"Sounds nice." Already she felt relaxed and welcomed. *I'm going to enjoy this,* she thought as she sipped from her beer. "I guess I'll have to brush up on my Spanish."

"Si," Ortum laughed. "You have to see what I've prepared for you, took my old study, where I never studied, and had Rosa doll it up for you. You've got your own room with plenty of space, lots of closet space for *spare parts*." He motioned to her prosthetic. "I understand you like a little privacy when it comes to that, can't blame you."

"No problem, guys. I'm fine. You don't need to work so hard at making me fit in. I will in due time." She grinned. "Just tell me one thing, since you've made another room for me."

"Yes?" Rick started.

"Aren't I sleeping with you?"

He bent to brush her lips with his own. "Yes, you're sleeping with me. I just wanted you to have your own place for your own stuff."

Lissa felt the vibration of her phone against her body, she reached into her pants pocket, Doc's name and number flashed on the screen. She hit the cancel tab.

Chapter 38

"Hola." A tall full-figured woman extended her hand to Lissa. "Mi nombre es Rosa." Her full lips spoke slowly as she lifted a strand of long black hair atop her head. Her dark eyes twinkled. "Welcome."

Lissa looked from Ortum to Rosa. *Yes,* she thought, *this is what it would take to tame this man.*

"Ha," Ortum laughed. "I know what's on your mind. But Rosa is one of the most tender and loving souls I've ever met." He leaned to kiss her cheek. "And man can she cook, you should taste her rondon."

Rosa rattled off several sentences in Spanish, Ortum nodded and took Lissa's and Rick's bags into another extension of the house.

"Hable mucho, always —" Rosa's hand mimicked speaking. "Yakkity, yakkity, yakkity." She laughed and crooked her finger for Lissa to follow her.

"I hope you like your room. But first I want you to see *this* room." She opened the glass doors to the solarium.

"My gosh, Rosa, this is beautiful - wonderful." Lissa's eyes perused the thick vegetation. Tiny parakeets flitted about, a green parrot screeched and relocated to another branch, a macaw, perched on a higher branch, stretched it wings and called out, "Shut the damn door!"

"Let me guess, Ortum taught that one to talk."

Rosa nodded. "They are nervous to see a new face but in time they will not be so busy when you come in."

A small pond a few feet away from where the women stood gurgled melodically.

"These are Koi," Rosa grinned.

"We have Koi in America." Reaching into her memory for the high school Spanish she taken, Lissa spoke, "Mucho bonito."

"You rest today, the bus ride is a long one and I'm sure you are tired. Manana ir de compras."

Lissa's head cocked to the side. "No comprende."

"Tomorrow we go shopping." Rosa's eyes lit up.

"I thought Rick and I would—"

"You can do that anytime. We let the men go fishing manana, get all dirty and smelly and we buy pretty dresses," she tittered, standing up and twirling about. "They like pretty women - poor little bambinos." She giggled again.

****

The women strolled along the narrow street lined with kiosks. Brightly colored dresses, blouses and serapes hung loosely swaying in the light breeze. Another kiosk displayed leather goods, shoes and purses, others pottery and jewelry.

Lissa slowed as she approached a pottery booth. She reached for the long thin jar with detailed carvings. It was lovely. Picking it up she asked the man behind the kiosk, "Cuanto cuesta?"

"Five hundred Cordoba," he spoke slowly.

Lissa reached inside her purse.

"No, no. Let me talk with him." Rosa moved slightly in front of Lissa and began. Spanish rattled from her lips while her hands gestured softly in the air.

Lissa caught a few of the words - Americana, senora, mentira. She knew that word, it meant *lie*.

"Doscincuenta y cinco," he spoke briskly.

Rosa turned to her, "He says two hundred fifty-five."

"I'll take it."

"It is still too much, demasiado. But he will go no lower."

"I'll take it," she repeated as she pulled the bills from her purse.

He wrapped it in paper and handed the item to her. Placing it in the tote she carried, Lissa smiled to herself as she and Rosa continued browsing the market.

"Do you ever go out on the boat with Ortum?" Lissa asked.

"He takes me for sunsets sometimes. When he wants hacer el amor. It is beautiful then, he likes grande perrito." Rosa giggled.

"Sounds like he worships you."

"As it should be." Rosa's lips parted to show her white teeth. "He is a good man. He treats me well."

"And you love him?"

"Si." Her brow furrowed. "Demasiado."

"Too much, why is that?"

"It is never a good thing to let a man know you love him much, he is like bambino with candy, they cry if they don't get it all the time, they get spoiled."

Always the games, Lissa thought. *People play games everywhere.*

Once again Lissa slowed her pace as the women approached a kiosk. A black velvet covered table with varying lengths of gold and silver chains lay displayed. From each chain dangled a semi-precious stone. Lissa fingered a jade pendant.

"Very pretty," the old woman standing to the side said.

Nodding, Lissa picked the necklace up.

"Four hundred pesos." The old woman stepped nearer Lissa.

"Oh no," she shook her head. "I'm just looking." She placed it back on the table and let her eyes drift along the length of necklaces.

"This one." Picking up the long silver chain, the woman grinned.

Lissa's eyes focused on the sharks tooth pendant dangling from the chain. Immediately her hand reached for her neck where her necklace had always been.

Instantly she remembered that she'd left the pendant at Topsail in her jewel box. The echo of Doc ran through her and she turned away.

Chapter 39

Rick's hand reached for Lissa's, he held it loosely as they walked along the shore.

She kicked her bare foot in the dark sand. "It's sort of like Caspersen Beach in Florida the sand is dark."

"Volcanic ash, I'll have to take you to Masaya, it's about an hour from here."

"It's a volcano? I'd love to see one."

Rick nodded, "There are several." He squeezed her hand tighter. "Are you sure you are up to - I mean, there's a lot of climbing."

Lissa tensed. "It's no problem, Rick. You worry too much."

He glanced at her leg, she'd worn shorts, the prosthesis was obvious. He lifted his eyes to hers.

"Quit looking at me like that."

"Sorry."

"You look at me like you pity me. I can't stand it."

"But—" he began.

Walking toward them along the shore, a couple nodded a greeting. Both the man and woman stared for several seconds at Lissa's leg. Rick lowered his eyes as the couple passed.

"You'll always see the leg, won't you?"

"What do you mean? I can't help but notice it, Lissa. If you don't wear something to cover it up, it's noticeable."

"That's not what I mean."

Rick searched her eyes for an explanation. "I love you. Regardless of whether or not you are whole person or not - you do have a disability."

Lissa tensed at the acknowledgment, maybe in time he would get used to her disability, she would always be disabled to him. "I know," Lissa offered compliantly.

"Come on now, cheer up." He picked up from the earlier conversation. "There are several volcanos on the Caribbean side but it is different, it is not as developed as here, more poor people. This side, the Pacific, is a little more touristy, we have more ex-pats living here.

"I've seen that, lots of Americans and Europeans."

"That's who I take fishing, the ex-pats and the tourists."

"You know it won't be long before it's all condos and—"

"Like Costa Rica, it's become overrun - the cost of living there is just as high as the states."

Her eyes begged the unspoken question. Her thoughts encouraging her to accept Rick - she should be happy that at least someone loved her.

"Yes, I know we are doing the same thing," he paused, "well, not quite - I like the little stucco house we live in and I have no desire to build a huge home or a huge marina."

"It's nice living simply."

"Life is never simple and you can't fight progress."

"You sound like my father."

"Your father is right."

You can guide progress, Lissa thought. It didn't have to be all concrete and condos.

She loosened her hand from Rick's; he strolled leisurely beside her as she played a scene from her past: walking with Doc, arguing with him, running along the shore until they splashed into the water. Lissa turned to Rick, her lips curled into a sly grin and she pushed against the sand to break into a run.

"Whoa, no running! That's the last thing I need is for you to fall and get hurt." He pulled her back to him, into his side as they continued to stroll.

****

"This side is more hospitable." Ortum leaned against a bulkhead, "Caribbean side is built up more - has more crime. This is the best place to be."

Rick watched a pole dip ever so slightly. "Just checking it out," he chuckled. "You watch, I'll bet we've got a marlin looking at that ballyhoo."

"Catch and release, I hope," Lissa said.

"Wouldn't have it any other way, babe." Rick watched the pole dip again and then came the strike, the zing: zzzzzzzzzzzzzzzzzz. He grabbed it from the holder and reeled - just enough - then let the fish have its lead; the line zigged and zagged across the water.

After several minutes of the fight, the fish broke water, whipping its body in the air then plunged once again into the azure waters.

Lissa watched another pole bend, she could feel the excitement building in her bones as she maneuvered her way to the transom.

"Be careful," Rick called.

"Looks like another marlin," Ortum called from the flying bridge. "Looks a little bigger than yours."

Lissa had caught a few marlin, small ones; she anxiously anticipated capturing this one and the fight it would take to reel it in. She reached for the pole.

"Ortum, take this one, I'll get the other."

Quickly the men maneuvered into position, Ortum sliding Lissa an apologetic glance as he took the pole from Rick.

Rick slid past Lissa to the transom pole and began reeling and resting; playing the dance between fish and fisherman.

"Oh, You want it, babe?"

"Well—"

"Sorry, but do you think you should be doing this. Let's give it some time before—" he burst into laughter as he watched the marlin twist into the air as it broke from the blue waters.

"Maybe next time." She said weakly, watching him as he reeled and waited, reeled and relaxed as the fish tired.

"About one-fifty, I'd say." Ortum held the line taut as he raised his marlin from the water. "Damn nice fish." He clasped the leader. "Yep," he nodded and fixed a tool to the line and released the fish back into the water.

"This has got to be a monster marlin," Rick concentrated as he fought the fish, tugging then resting, then finally bringing the fish alongside the boat. He struggled to hold the leader and fish above water.

"Two hundred - easy."

Lissa moved toward the bow, observing the men, their world was lit up with excitement and pride, the testosterone was thick as they boasted of the fight, the thrill of almost losing it, battling with nature itself.

Oh, she envied them - she had wanted it. Is this how it was going to be? So far she felt ostracized, relegated to being an observer only, considered unable to participate.

It's going to drive me crazy if I can't get out and do things. She wondered about surfing. That was her first passion, anyway.

"Time we headed in," called Rick.

Lissa smiled back at him and opened the lid to the well - three snappers, two mahi and an amber jack lay on their sides across the crushed ice. "I think we have plenty for dinner, at least for a couple of days."

"Sam says he's getting an iguana, wants you to taste it."

"Yuck! I'm not eating iguana."

"Tastes like chicken," Ortum teased.

"I don't care. There is no way I'm eating that."

****

"It does taste like chicken, a thigh - dark meat - it's good." Lissa licked a fingertip. "It's very pretty here, and you are right, the people are very polite and nice - accommodating." She placed her hand over Rick's and toyed with his fingers. "I think I'll check out the surf tomorrow and give it a go."

"Are you sure?"

"The girl is a surfer, she's been doing it for years." Ortum winked at Lissa, "Check out the surf shop near the marina and they'll set you up."

"Set me up?"

"Yes, every day a truck, we call it a shuttle, takes people out to the different beaches around here for surfing. Go do your thing, girl."

"No surfing right here?" She questioned.

"Maderas, Popaya, Las Penitas - there all good beaches."

"I'll go with you," Rick said.

"Hey bud, I don't think Lissa needs babysitting. And besides, you have a full day tomorrow. The Matterson's booked last week for a full day."

"I'll be okay by myself," Lissa answered.

"Yes, she will," Ortum reprimanded Rick. "A big group of ex-pats are there every day. She'll be fine."

Rick glanced at the apparatus attached to Lissa's leg. "If you think it's okay." He lifted a forkful of casada to his mouth.

"I think I've had enough rice and beans to last me a lifetime," Lissa sneered. "And plantains." She moved the starchy food away from the meat and fruit on her plate and speared a bit of papaya.

****

The next morning Lissa and Rick rose early. She reached for the prosthetic resting on the chair near the bed. Rick wiped his eyes and stumbled from bed, moving to her side. Pulling the chair to face her, he endeavored to help her adjust the artificial leg.

"I don't like the idea of you going out alone and surfing is kind of dangerous. Don't you think?"

"I won't be alone. Like Ortum said, there will be lots of others there."

"But what if you have a problem?"

"Rick, I'm a grown woman. I can take care of myself."

He lifted his eyes to meet hers, they glared something he had not seen before.

"Are you sure you're not embarrassed of me for having this?" She tapped the prosthesis.

"No, it's not that. I just feel like I have to take care of you."

"You are. But you can't worry about me all the time and you can't protect me forever. If I can't do things I love then what's the point?"

"Sorry, I was surprised that you started surfing again."

"Doc helped me."

"Doc?"

She realized it too late. Why did she have to bring up his name now?

"The guy you were seeing, the physical therapist?"

"Yes. It was just innocent; we used to surf together as kids."

"Oh, you didn't tell me that part."

"We knew each other when we were teenagers."

"And you're just telling me this now."

"It's nothing. We're over. He's with his wife in England."

"And how do you know that."

Lissa paused, shook her head, "I spoke with him a few days ago."

"So you're still communicating?" He stared angrily at her.

"Geez Rick, it's over. You need to let it go if you want us to work."

"How can I let it go it you're still talking with him?"

"He texted me, I did not respond."

His lips drawn tightly, Rick shifted his eyes away from Lissa. "I can't help it. Every time I think of you and him together—"

"I'm with you." She reached to touch his face, her eyes filling with tears. "I guess it's going to take time for us, for you to get used to this," Lissa tapped her leg again.

"No, that doesn't bother me," Rick blurted.

"I've seen the look in your eyes. Don't deny it."

"It's just going to take some time, Lissa, for me to get used to the things you need. It's an adjustment for me, too."

"I'll try. We'll try. Okay?" He smoothed her hair with his hands, "I'm sorry for over reacting."

"I'm sorry, I'll be more patient."

"Okay." He smiled broadly, "I *want* you to go surfing - you should go, okay? I want you to have fun and I won't worry. I promise."

"Sure?" Lissa asked coyly.

"I promise. And then Thursday you and I will go to Managua. You'll love it there."

"What's in Managua?"

"The circus."

Chapter 40

They walked hand in hand through the colorfully lit streets of Managua. It was festive with music and dancers. Rick pulled out a chair from a street side table and motioned for Lissa to sit. She moved her hands to scoot the skirt beneath her as he slid into the chair.

Checking the straps of her bra to make sure they were tucked away from the low neckline of the frilly white blouse Rick had bought her, Lissa leaned into him as he stretched to kiss her. "Pretty cool, huh?"

The atmosphere was thick with laughter and the haze of smoke and food aromas. Jugglers passed by, tossing plates and balls into the air. Miraculously, no one dropped anything.

Three men, of varying heights and dressed in bright yellow blousy pants, red and purple frilled shirts, loped by on stilts.

Lissa was thoroughly enjoying the entertainment and relaxed to let her eyes peruse the parade of performers.

"It's like Mardi Gras."

"I've never been to Mardi Gras."

"You'll love it!" He shouted over the noise.

Musicians strumming guitars, blaring trumpets to the beat of the drummers' syncopated tempo rang out loudly. Lissa moved her shoulders to the rhythm, her head swayed and she rose to dance, her hip moving around and back, her steps light as she felt the music enter her body.

Reaching a hand to Rick, she pulled him from his chair and smiling pushed her body against his, stilling moving, gyrating.

Wrapping an arm around her waist, he let the music fill him too as he took her hand in his, the other pressing gently against her back to guide Lissa as they danced. They moved along the edge of the crowd; others were dancing as well adding to the party-like atmosphere.

Maybe her worries about Rick were unfounded. Maybe he was just finding his way, too. In time he would become accustomed to the new *part* of her. Maybe in time he would no longer see the leg, see the handicap. She no longer considered having to use the prosthesis a handicap.

While surfing Maderas Beach she had been fine. In fact, she'd even forgotten that she wore an artificial leg as she rode the curl. One young man had even commented on her veracity, exclaiming how surprised he was to find she had a prosthetic leg.

The term did not bother her. It even reminded Lissa of Doc and how at ease, how natural his interaction with her was. He had never *seen* the leg. And he had striven to help Lissa be blind to it as well. She was glad they had met again, certainly it was fate that brought them together because without him she would have never accepted herself so readily.

Doc stood like a prophesy, a true friend and she would never forget him even if she had to let him go.

Gazing into Rick's eyes, she saw the hope and promise of what could be with him. Her head tilted back a bit in laughter as he held closely as they danced.

Then she went down, the apparatus digging into her leg as she felt the ground, the stones scrape across her skin.

Lissa heard the moan wretch from her throat and watched as Rick stood above her, scowling as a small group of people accumulated around the couple.

She looked up to him apologetically; he immediately stooped to gather her in his arms and set her on a nearby chair. "Damn gadget," he touched the leg, his eyes shifted disapprovingly at her. "You're just not going to be able to do things, Lissa. I can't take this, you need—"

She recognized the look on his face, in his eyes, the one she'd first seen at the hospital. "I need to go back to the hotel room. Will you help me? Please." Lissa said, her voice trembling, then calm and finally demanding.

Chapter 41

The little tree her father and Linda had brought stood dry and limp in the corner of her living room. Perusing the lights and garland, Lissa drew her knees to her chest and pulled an afghan over her body. There was a slight draft in her little block home. She snuggled against it to keep warm as her hands wrapped around a warm cup of cocoa. Snuggling her right foot into a plush bedroom slipper Lissa let the tears fall freely.

All the pumpkin pie, leftover turkey and gift giving had done nothing to remedy the sense of loss and pain of love she held for both Doc and Rick. "Time to move on, it's a new year." She reminded herself, squaring her shoulders and wiping her face dry.

Picking up the remote control, Lissa pressed the on tab for the television. It was a rerun of *Love Actually*. She flipped through more channels, recognizing familiar Christmas movies, *It's a Wonderful Life, Christmas in Connecticut, Miracle on 34th Street*—all wonderful films with happy endings but wasn't that the way it was supposed to end -boy and girl fall into one another's arms and live happily ever after?

Her eyes drifted to the envelope on the coffee table. Inside was a letter from Rick apologizing for his behavior; she'd read it several times before and did not know how to respond or if she even wanted to.

She understood though, Rick had reacted as most people would have, it was normal.

Lissa thought of the days before the shark attack and the time she and Rick had spent together, the trip to Alaska and meeting his family. Damn, he was such a good man, and he loved her. Back then it would have been true, it was so nice, everything was going along smoothly.

If only I hadn't lost my leg, if only I hadn't of jumped in the water, Lissa drew her shoulders in tightly and shook her head. "I was falling in love with him before that, and it would have been good, *we* would have been good."

She closed her eyes to the feeling, striving to recall what they had shared and if it had been real. "Why did I push him away?" she asked herself. "I was such an idiot." The image of Rick swam through her thoughts. "But maybe he wasn't sure either. Maybe he just couldn't handle it, wanted to, but felt guilty." She recalled the look in his eyes, the condemnation, the repulsion. "Damn, it's just not fair."

"Before that he really loved me, he said he did." *People who love you are supposed to love all of you.* The thought burned in her head. It was all so damn confusing and all Lissa could do was move away from what didn't feel right and after Rick's display he hadn't felt right. She needed to be alone.

Reaching for the envelope, she withdrew the letter.

I've been trying, I've tried so hard not to let it bother me. I know it's not your fault, you can't help what happened to you. I was a fool, please forgive me. I didn't mean to insult you that night. Don't forget what we had. I promise I'll try harder, I won't pressure you. Please forgive me.

Settling the letter back on the table, Lissa lay her head on the armrest of the couch, she muted the movie and watching the characters mouth words of affection, she picked the letter back up.

Answer my calls. Talk to me. She placed the letter on the table again and began flipping through the television channels.

"Nothing," She turned the set off and rising from the couch, walked to the bookcase, her fingers underlining the titles of the books there.

Resting on the book of poetry Murdoch had given her so long ago she pulled it from the others and thumbed the pages to where the poem he had read aloud to her was.

"In the broad and silky morn," she began. "Crap," Rick had recited the poem to her, too.

She closed the book. "I am a fool. I live in the past. I won't forgive. I won't let go. What is wrong with me?"

Her cell phone buzzed, bright letters blazed on the screen, it was Doc, *I hope the new year brings new beginnings for you. I love you just like you are.*

She had not seen him since August. He tried to call and had left messages wishing her well. She wondered if she should text

349

back. *He's married,* she thought as she pressed her phone to off.

Maybe he belongs back in the little box I created when I was young. "Maybe we were just not meant to be." She moved back to the couch and pulled her knees close again. Turned on the television and watched the actors speaking, pulling one another close and embracing, leaning in to kiss.

She felt her chest heave and the sobs mounting. She pictured the last scene, their scene, Doc answering the phone, talking with Ava - his back to her - and him getting out of bed to shower, this was the scene she could not repeat and if Doc was in her life that is what would be.

She had to put him back in the box.

Fingering the letter from Rick again, Lissa examined the envelope, it was somewhat worn from having lain on the table for so long. The postmark was nearly a month old. She wondered if he would still welcome her and she wondered too if she would feel right in his arms and if she would settle for what he had to offer her now.

Lissa scoffed at her doubts, "Always wondering. Shit or get off the pot." She chided herself as she noticed a strand of Christmas lights blink off.

"I need to water that poor little tree," she muttered as she eyed the pine. Her eyes scanned the floor and the needles scattered about.

"Okay, little tree," Lissa stood and padded to the kitchen sink. Her hand resting on the faucet, she filled a tumbler with water. The reflection of car lights moved across the walls and then she heard the crunch of tires against cement as the car pulled into her drive way.

She caught the slamming of a car door and wondering who could be visiting her at this time of night, glanced at her own reflection in the window, her hair was pushed to one side where she had been lying, her pajama top had a soup stain on the lapel.

"If you have the gall to visit unannounced this time of night then you deserve a mess." She ran her hand across her head to smooth out the unruly waves and pulled her robe tightly, tying the cloth belt.

The bell rang, she opened the door.

"Hi."

"Hi." She stood looking at him, his bare arms crossed against his chest.

"Hi. Please, may I come in. It's kind of cold out here."

Lissa nodded and stepped aside. "Why did you come?"

"I couldn't stand it any longer. I can't live without you - I tried. I didn't know what to do."

Her lips trembling, her body numb, Lissa stood still, her heart beating against her chest.

"I missed you, too. Are you back for good? "

Doc nodded, "For good, forever." He stepped closer to her. "I really tried, I know it must have hurt you. I remembered how I'd left you before, I couldn't help that. But now - I made the wrong choice then. I let my pride dictate what I did. And then I realized that I have only one life and I want it with you."

"Ava?"

"She took it better than I thought, but I've known or suspected for some time that we have been drifting. It wouldn't work, not with me knowing, not with, without you." Doc moved his arms to her waist and pulled Lissa into him. "You're my world. I could spend eternity doing nothing but listening to the ocean as long as you are by my side."

Reaching her arms to circle his neck, Lissa pressed her lips to his, he pulled her closer returning the kiss.

"You look beautiful." He tussled her hair.

"Low standards, huh?"

"Don't ever say that again. You are the most dynamic woman I've ever met."

"Thank you."

"Now, let's go for a swim."

"What? Are you nuts? The water is fifty degrees out there."

"At least walk with me."

Lissa reached for her hat and scarf; she bent to gather her shoes.

Doc watched as Lissa maneuvered the prosthetic into the shoe.

"Damn that turns me on." He chortled as he moved slowly toward her. Pushing gently against her body, Doc lowered himself beside her on the couch.

Her lips pressed against his as she drew a finger across his scared face.

Made in the USA
Columbia, SC
07 December 2021

50424858R00212